SLOW BURN

SLOW BURN

A NOVEL

JULIE GARWOOD

DOUBLEDAY LARGE PRINT
HOME LIBRARY EDITION
RANDOM HOUSE

Copyright © 2005 by Julie Garwood

All rights reserved.
Published in the United States of America by
Random House Large Print in association with
Ballantine Books, New York.
Distributed by Random House, Inc., New York.

ISBN 0-375-43525-5

This Large Print edition published in accord
with the standards of the N.A.V.H.

SLOW BURN

Chapter One

THE CRUSTY OLD MAN WAS GOING TO CAUSE AN uproar, and he was only sorry he wouldn't be around to watch it.

He was about to pull the rug out from under his useless relatives, and oh, were they going to take a tumble. But it was high time someone in this miserable family righted a terrible wrong, high time indeed.

While he waited for the equipment to be set up, he cleared the clutter from his desk. His gnarled fingers stroked the smooth wood with as much tenderness and care as he had once given his mistresses when he touched them. The desk was old and scarred and as worn out as he was. He had made his fortune in this very room. With his phone glued to his ear, he had worked one lucrative deal after another. How many companies had he purchased in the past thirty years? How many more had he destroyed?

He stopped himself from daydreaming about his many victories. Now wasn't the time. He crossed the room to the bar and poured himself a glass of water from the crystal decanter one of his business associates had given him years ago. After he took a sip, he carried the glass to the desk and placed it on a coaster near the corner. He looked around the paneled library and decided it was too dark for the cameras, so he rushed to turn on all the table lights.

"Are you ready?" he asked, impatience brimming in his tone. Pulling the chair out, he sat down, smoothed his hair, and adjusted his suit jacket so the collar wouldn't stand up. He tugged on his tie as if that would loosen the tightness in his throat. "I'm going to prepare my thoughts now," he said, his voice raspy from years of barking orders and smoking his cherished Cuban cigars.

He wanted a cigar now. There weren't any in the house, though. He'd given up the habit ten years ago, but every once in a while when he was nervous he would get a sudden longing for one.

At the moment he was not only nervous but also a little fearful, which was an odd, almost unfamiliar, feeling for him. He was desperate to do the right thing before he died, which would be soon now, very soon. He owed at least that much to the MacKenna name.

The old-fashioned video camera with a VHS tape was positioned on a tripod facing the old man. The digital camera was being held up directly behind the video camera, and the eye was also focused on him.

He looked beyond the cameras. "I know you think digital is enough, and you're probably right, but I still like the old way with the videotape. I don't trust those discs, and so the videotape will be my backup. You nod," he instructed, "when everything's turned on, and I'll begin."

He picked up his glass, took a drink, and put it down. The pills those aggravating doctors forced on him made his mouth dry.

A few seconds later, all was ready, and he began.

"My name is Compton Thomas MacKenna. This is not my last will and testament because I've already taken care of all that. I changed my will some time ago. The original is in my safe deposit box; a copy is in my file at the law firm I have employed for the past twenty years, and there is also another copy, which I assure you will rear its ugly head if for any reason the original and the attorney's copy are misplaced or destroyed.

"I didn't tell any of you about the new will or about the changes I made because I didn't want to spend my last months being harassed, but now that the doctors have assured me the end is approaching and there is nothing more they can do,

I want . . . no, I need," he corrected, "to explain why I have done what I've done . . . though I'm not sure any of you will understand or care.

"I'm going to start my explanation with a brief history of the MacKenna family. My parents were born, raised, and buried in the Highlands of Scotland. My father owned quite a bit of land . . . quite a bit," he repeated. He paused to clear his throat and take another drink of water before continuing. "When he died, the land came to my older brother, Robert Duncan the second, and to me equally. Robert and I traveled to the United States to complete our education, and both of us decided to stay. Years later Robert sold me his share of the land. With his inheritance, that made him a very wealthy man, and it made me the sole heir to the property called Glen MacKenna.

"I never married. I had neither the time nor the inclination. Robert married a woman I didn't approve of, but unlike my brother, I didn't threaten or carry on because he chose someone I didn't like. Her name was Caroline . . . a social climber. She obviously married Robert for his money. She certainly never loved him. She did do her duty though and gave him two sons, Robert Duncan the third and Conal Thomas.

"And now to the heart of this history lesson. When my nephew Conal chose to marry a woman without social standing, his father disowned him. Robert had chosen someone else—a woman from an influential family—and he was outraged that his wishes were being ignored. Conal's wife, Leah, was no better than a street beggar, but Conal didn't seem to care about the money he would lose." He let out a huff of disgust and said, "All Robert had left was his firstborn, a real 'yes' man who did whatever he was told to do.

"Over the years I lost track of Conal," he continued. "Too busy," he added as an excuse. "All I knew was that he'd moved to Silver Springs just outside of Charleston. But then I got word that he'd been killed in a car accident. I knew my brother wouldn't go to the funeral . . . but I went. Not so much from a sense of obligation, I admit. I guess I was curious to see how Conal made out. I didn't tell Leah or anyone I was there. Kept my distance. The church was packed with mourners. I even went to the cemetery and saw Leah with her three little girls, the youngest no more than a baby." He stopped as though envisioning the scene. Not wanting to betray any hint of emotion that might cross his faded eyes, he looked away from the camera for a second. He straightened in his chair and resumed. "I saw what I went there to see. The MacKenna line would continue through Conal's children . . . though it was a pity there weren't any boys.

"As for my brother's other son . . . Robert the third . . . he indulged him . . . taught him to be useless. He didn't allow him to have ambition, and in return my brother lived long enough to watch his firstborn drink himself into an early grave.

"The sin of excess has been passed down to the next generation. I have watched Robert's grandsons squander their inheritance and, even worse, defile the MacKenna name. Bryce, the oldest, is following in his father's footsteps. He married a good woman, Vanessa, but she couldn't save him from his vices. Like his father, he's a drunk. He has sold all of his stocks and cashed in his bonds and has gone through every dollar. He spent a good deal on alcohol and women, and only God knows what he did with the rest.

"And then there's Roger. He's been the most elusive—disappearing for weeks at a time—but it didn't take my sources long to track him down and find out what he's been up to. It appears Roger has turned to gambling for his amusement. According to the reports, last year alone he lost over four hundred thousand. Four hundred thousand." The old man shook his head and continued as though the words left a foul taste. "What's worse, he's been dealing with mobsters like Johnny Jackman. Just having the MacKenna name associated with a thug like Jackman makes my stomach turn.

"Ewan, the youngest, can't or won't control his temper. If it were not for his high-priced and very clever attorneys, he would be in prison now. Two years ago he nearly beat a man to death.

"I am disgusted with all of them. They are useless men who have contributed nothing to this world." The old man pulled a handkerchief from his pocket and dabbed at his brow.

"When those worthless doctors told me I would be here for only a few more months, I decided to take stock." He turned and opened the side drawer and withdrew a thick black folder. He opened it in the center of the desk and stacked his hands on top of it. "I've had an investigator do some checking for me. I wanted to know how Conal's children turned out. I must admit I had low expectations. I assumed, after Conal's death, Leah and her girls would have been living hand to mouth. I also assumed none of them would have gone beyond high school . . . if that. I was wrong on both counts. There was enough of a settlement from the insurance company after Conal's accident that Leah could stay in their house with the children. She took a secretarial position at a girls' private school. The pay was meager—I don't suppose Leah was capable of much more—but there was a trade-off. All three of her daughters attended the private lower school and upper school, their tuition waived." He nodded approval and said, "Conal evidently had taught her the value of a proper education."

He glanced over the report in the folder. "It seems that all three of them are hard workers. Not a slacker among them," he added with emphasis.

"The oldest, Kiera, received a full scholarship to a good university and graduated with honors. She received another scholarship to medical school and is doing exceptionally well. The middle girl, Kate, is the entrepreneur in the family. She too received a full scholarship to one of the finest universities in the east and also graduated with honors. She started a business while she was still in school, and today her company is growing and on its way to being very successful." He looked back at the camera. "It appears she is most like me."

"Isabel, the youngest, is certainly intelligent as well, but her true talent is her voice. I understand she is quite gifted." He tapped the report with his index finger. "Isabel plans to study music and history at the university, and it is her desire to one day go to Scotland to meet her distant relatives." He nodded. "This news pleases me considerably.

"And now to the changes in my will." The corners of his mouth lifted slightly in an almost imperceptible, devious smile. It faded as he continued. "Bryce and Roger and Ewan will each receive one hundred thousand dollars in cash immediately. It is my hope that the money will be spent on rehabilitation, but I doubt that will happen. Vanessa will also receive one hundred thousand, and she will get this house. She deserves at least that much for having put up with Bryce these past years. She has brought respect to the

MacKenna name through her work with charities and the art community, so I don't see any sense in punishing her for her choice of husbands.

"Now to the other MacKennas. I've signed over all my treasury bonds to Kiera. The maturity dates are outlined in the will. Isabel, a history buff like me, will receive Glen MacKenna. There are stipulations that go along with it, of course, and she will be apprised of these in due time."

His breathing became labored and he stopped to take another drink of water, emptying the glass before he finished speaking.

"Finally, to the bulk of my estate, which has been converted into liquid assets totaling eighty million dollars. This is the accumulation of my life's work and it will be passed on to my blood relations, but I'll be damned if I'll just hand it over to my depraved nephews, and so I offer it first to Kate MacKenna. She is the most driven of the whole lot and, like me, knows the value of money. If she chooses this legacy, it's all hers.

"I trust that she will not squander it."

Chapter Two

KATE MACKENNA'S WONDERBRA SAVED HER life.

Five minutes after she'd put the thing on, she wanted to take it off. She never should have let her sister Kiera talk her into wearing it. Yes, it did make her look voluptuous and sexy, but was that the message she wanted to send tonight? She was a businesswoman, for Pete's sake, not a porn star. Besides, without the push-'em-up-and-out bra she was already sufficiently endowed.

And why was Kiera so hell-bent on "sexing her up"—as she so eloquently put it? Was Kate's social life that much of a dud? Apparently her sisters thought so.

Of the three sisters Kiera was the oldest and the bossiest. She had vowed she'd get Kate to wear the little, black, way-too-snug cocktail dress, or die trying. Isabel, the youngest, had sided with Kiera, but then she always did, and Kate had finally given in and put on the silk dress just to get them to stop nagging her. When the two of them ganged up on her, they were a force to be reckoned with—a loud, unrelenting force.

Kate stood in front of the mirror in the foyer tugging on the bra in an attempt to get it to stop digging into her ribs, but her efforts were useless. She checked the time and decided if she hurried she could change, but when she turned to go back up to her room, Kiera walked down the stairs.

"You look great," Kiera said after giving her sister the once-over.

"You look tired." Kate was stating the obvious. There were dark circles under Kiera's eyes. She'd just gotten out of the shower, and her blond hair was dripping on her shoulders. Kate didn't think she'd even bothered to towel it dry. Her sister wasn't wearing an ounce of makeup, but she still looked beautiful. She was a natural beauty, like their mother had been.

"I'm a medical student. I'm supposed to look sleep-deprived. It's a requirement. I'd get tossed out if I looked rested."

Despite their pestering, Kate was happy to be with her two sisters again, even if it was for only a couple of weeks. They had had little time together after their mother died. Kate had returned to Boston to finish her graduate degree, and Kiera had gone back to medical school at Duke while Isabel remained at home with their aunt Nora.

Kate was now home permanently, but Kiera, after two weeks off, would be returning to Duke again, and Isabel would be heading to her first year of college. The changes were inevitable, Kate presumed. Life should move forward.

"While you're home you ought to take a day and go to the beach . . . you know, relax. Take Isabel with you," Kate urged.

Kiera laughed. "Nice try. You're not going to unload her on me, even if it's just for a day. I'd spend the entire time fighting off the boys chasing after her. No, thank you. It's bad enough right here with the phone calls. There's some guy named Reece in particular. He seems to think he's Isabel's boyfriend. Isabel said she worked at a couple of concerts with him, and they went out a few times, but it was nothing serious. She stopped seeing him when he wanted to be more than friends. Now he's calling here nonstop wanting to talk to her, and because Isabel refuses to take his calls, he's becoming more and more belligerent. I love Isabel dearly, but sometimes I think she can make life just a little too complicated. So, thanks for the suggestion about the beach, but no thanks."

Kate tugged on her bra again.

"Oh, **that's** lovely," Kiera said.

"This contraption is killing me. I can't breathe."

"You look gorgeous, and isn't that more important than breathing?" she teased. "Suck it up. It's for a good cause."

"What's the cause?"

"You. You're my cause these days. Isabel's, too. We're determined to lighten you up. You're way too serious for your own good. I personally think you suffer from the middle child syndrome. You know, you're filled with insecurities and phobias, and you have this need to constantly prove yourself."

Kate decided to ignore her. She put her small clutch bag down on the table and went to the closet.

"You're textbook material," Kiera continued.

"That's nice."

"You're not listening to me, are you?"

Kate was saved from responding when the phone rang. While Kiera hurried into the den to answer it, she opened the closet door and began to search for her raincoat. The television was blaring away in the kitchen, and she could hear the obscenely cheerful weatherman gleefully remind his audience that Charleston was still in the throes of a heat wave unlike anything the city had seen in thirty years. If the temperature remained in the high nineties for just two more days, a new record would be set. The possibility made the weatherman sound giddy with excitement.

The humidity was the real killer, though. The

air was heavy, stagnant, and as thick as glue. The steam curling up from the sidewalks and streets mingled with the pollution hanging like a hazy specter over the airless city. One strong gust of wind would help clear the sky, but neither wind nor rain was predicted anytime soon. Unless one was acclimated, taking a deep breath required concentration. The muggy air drained the young and the old, and left everyone lethargic. Swatting a mosquito away required more energy than most people were willing to exert.

Yet as horribly hot as it was, the party Kate had promised to attend was still being held outside on the grounds of a privately owned art gallery. The event had been planned weeks ago, and the white tent had been erected before the weather turned so oppressive. Only one wing of the newly constructed gallery was completed, and Kate knew it wasn't large enough to accommodate the expected crowd.

There was no getting out of it. The owner, Carl Bertolli, was a friend of Kate's. She knew it would hurt his feelings if she didn't show up. Because of the traffic, the drive from Silver Springs, where she lived, to the other side of Charleston would take over an hour, but she didn't plan on staying long. She would help with any last-minute details and then, when the party was in full swing, she'd bolt. Carl would be too busy to notice her departure.

A controversial artist from Houston was showing her work, and there had already been protests and threatening phone calls. Carl couldn't have been happier. He believed that any publicity, good or bad, was good for his gallery's business. The artist, a woman who was calling herself Cinnamon, had quite a following—though, for the life of her, Kate couldn't understand why. As an artist Cinnamon was mediocre at best. She was, however, excellent at drawing attention to herself. She was constantly in the news and would do anything to get noticed. Currently she was against anything organized. When she wasn't throwing paint on her canvases, she was halfheartedly trying to overthrow the government. Cinnamon believed in free love, free expression, and a free ride through life. Her paintings weren't free, however. They were outrageously expensive.

Kiera came back into the hall saying, "That was Reece calling again. He's beginning to give me the creeps." She stopped when she saw Kate. "We're not supposed to get rain tonight. How come you're all buttoned up in your raincoat? It's like a hundred and twenty outside."

"One can't be too cautious. I wouldn't want the dress to get wet."

Kiera laughed. "I know what you're doing. You don't want Aunt Nora to see you in that dress. Admit it, Katie. You're afraid of her."

"I'm not afraid of her. I'm just trying to avoid a long lecture."

"The dress isn't indecent."

"She'll think it is," Kate said as she slipped the coat over her shoulders.

"It's going to be odd not having her here to boss us around. I'm going to miss her."

"Me too," Kate whispered.

Nora was moving back to St. Louis. She had come to Silver Springs when her sister had taken ill, and she had stayed on to keep the household running until Isabel graduated from high school. Now that Kate was back and Isabel was going away to college, Nora was ready to go home. She missed being close to her daughter and her grand-children.

Nora had been a godsend and had taken good care of all of them, especially when they needed her most. However, she was set in her ways, and in the sisters' opinions, she was obsessed with sex. Kiera called her a born-again virgin. After their mother had died, she had appointed herself the girls' moral guardian. According to Nora, every man was out for "you know what," and it was her job to see that they didn't get it from her girls.

Kate peeked around the corner. Fortunately, Nora wasn't in the kitchen, so Kate turned the television off, removed her raincoat and draped it over a chair. She grabbed her keys and hurried for the garage. If luck stayed on her side, she'd be out of the house before Nora returned. She really wasn't afraid of her aunt, but when Nora got wound up, her lectures could go on and on and on. Some lasted as long as an hour.

Kiera followed Kate through the kitchen. "You be careful tonight. There are a lot of crazies out there who don't care for Cinnamon's views on government or religion. Doesn't she preach anarchy?"

"This month I think she does. I don't keep track of what she says and what she does, and I'm not worried about tonight. Security will be tight."

"Then Carl must be worried."

"No, it's all for show. I don't think Cinnamon believes any of the nonsense she spouts. She's just a publicity hound, that's all."

"The groups she's offended don't know it's all for show, and some of those groups are real radicals."

"Stop worrying. I'll be fine." Kate opened the door and stepped into the garage. The heat took her breath away.

"Why do you have to leave so early? The invitation said eight to midnight."

"Carl's assistant called and left a message for me to be there by six."

She got into the car, which felt like an oven, and pushed the remote control to open the garage door.

Kiera called out, "Are there going to be Kate MacKenna gift baskets?"

"Of course. Carl insisted. I think I've become one of his projects. He told me he wants to be able to say he knew me when," she called back. "Now shut the door. You're letting all the air-conditioning out."

"You're already becoming a household name. Pretty sweet, isn't it?"

Kiera evidently didn't require an answer, for she'd shut the door after making the comment.

Life **was** pretty sweet right now. Kate had plenty of time to think as she inched along the highway in the heavy traffic. Though she wasn't a household name yet, she was definitely headed in that direction. It was funny how a little hobby could end up becoming a satisfying career.

While she had been busy trying to figure out what she wanted to be, her company was born. She had been a senior in high school and scrounging for ways to make money so that she could buy her family and friends birthday gifts. She had also been taking a chemistry class. She'd gone into the teacher's office, and there was a lighted candle on the desk. Kate had always been sensitive to various scents, and the musky odor from the candle was offensive to her. The horrible smell had given her an idea to make her own candles. But she wouldn't do the same old same old. She would do something unique. How hard could it be?

She started out using the kitchen as her lab. By the end of the winter break, she'd made her first batch of scented candles. They were a disaster. She'd mixed several spices and herbs and made the kitchen smell like a sewer.

Her mother banished her to the basement. She didn't give up her experiments, though. Every spare minute she had that summer she worked on her project. She scoured libraries and labs, and by the end of her freshman year at college, she had come up with the most wonderful basil- and grapefruit-scented candles.

Kate's intention was to give them away, but her college roommate and best friend, Jordan Buchanan, saw great potential. Jordan took ten candles, priced them, and sold them all in one evening. She talked Kate into using her full name on all of her products. Then she helped her design a logo and some unusual boxes.

The clean and fresh scents along with the octagonal glass containers Kate found made the candles irresistible and an instant hit. Orders started pouring in. Kate, with two part-time employees, tried to make and stock as much she could during summer break, but her enterprise outgrew the basement, and so she moved to a rental space across town. It was located in a horrible area and for that reason was dirt cheap.

By the time she graduated from college, orders were coming from all parts of the country. Kate realized her weakness was in management and decided to return to school in Boston to complete her master's. To keep the company running while she was away, she made her mother a partner so that she could sign checks and make deposits. Because Kate poured her profits back into the company, money was tight. She lived with Jordan in her apartment in Boston and often spent her weekends with Jordan's large family out on Nathan's Bay.

It was a struggle, but Kate managed to make the business grow in her absence. Then, when her mother became so ill, Kate's ambition was put on hold so that she could return home to be with her. A long, sad year had passed since her mother's death, but in that year Kate had completed her graduate degree and formulated plans for expansion.

Now that she was back in Silver Springs, she was ready to take her company to the next level. She had branched into body lotions and three signature perfumes named after her sisters and her mother. The space she rented was becoming too cramped, so she was negotiating a new lease in a warehouse that was much larger and also closer to home. She was also thinking about hiring more employees. Anton's, a chain of upscale department stores, was eager to carry her products, and soon she was going to sign an exclusive and extremely lucrative contract.

And any and all money worries would evaporate.

She smiled thinking about that. The first thing she was going to buy when she had a little extra money was a car with a proper air conditioner. She kept adjusting the vents, but that didn't help. The air coming out was lukewarm.

She felt wilted by the time she reached Carl's outrageously pretentious estate. He'd inherited Liongate from his father and was building his gallery on the property. Two massive lion faces adorned the electronic iron gates.

A security guard checked her name off his list and let her through. Carl's two-story house was at the top of a winding drive, but the gallery that would showcase Cinnamon's work was halfway up the hill on the south side. A massive white tent sat adjacent to the white stone structure.

Another security guard showed her where to park. Carl was obviously expecting quite a crowd if the number of security men and waiters rushing back and forth from the annex to the white tent were any indication.

Kate cut across the well-manicured lawn, her heels sinking into the irrigated sod. She'd almost reached the stone path when her cell phone rang.

"Hello, Kate darling. Where are you?" Carl's melodious voice wafted through the receiver.

"I'm right here on your lawn, Carl."

"Ah, that's wonderful."

"Where are you?"

"I'm in my closet trying to choose between the white linen suit and the pinstripe blazer with the cream-colored pants. Either way, I know I'm going to absolutely melt, but I have to look dashing for all the critics who are going to be here tonight, don't I?"

"I'm sure you'll look very handsome."

"I just wanted to let you know that I won't be down for a while. I have to hurry and dress and then go pick up Cinnamon at her hotel. The limo's waiting for me. I have a favor to ask. Would you check on the tent setup for me? I won't have time to get there before guests arrive, and I want to be sure everything's perfect. With your impeccable taste, I know you'll see that it's glorious."

"I'd be happy to," Kate answered, smiling at her friend's flair for the dramatic.

"You're a sweetheart. I owe you," Carl said as he hung up.

Kate found the entrance and went inside the tent. There were air conditioners operating full blast around the perimeter, but they weren't doing much good with all the waiters coming and going. Huge buffet tables stood in a line at one end. They were topped with colorful flower arrangements in crystal bowls and gleaming silver servers. Small tables with white linens and white folding chairs were scattered around the rest of the space. Everything seemed to be going smoothly.

She spotted her gift baskets on a table at the back. The white tablecloth reached the ground, and her logo hung suspended in front. She hurried over to straighten it and to place the baskets in a semicircle. When she was finished, she stepped back to admire how lovely it looked.

She circled the table and reached for the chair but changed her mind. The Wonderbra was driving her nuts. The undergarment felt like a suffocating vise around her rib cage. She was in agony and was trying not to rip the thing off as she hurried into the art gallery to find a powder room so she could remove it and toss it in the trash.

Unfortunately, the ladies' room was blocked off and so was the men's room. There were servants cleaning both. Kate would have ignored the closed signs and gone in, but there were security guards stationed by the doors, and she was sure they wouldn't let her through.

Now what? Kate looked around for a vacant room with a door she could shut. There weren't any. She headed back to the tent feeling absolutely miserable, but her mood improved when she noticed two large baskets of flowers had been placed on the ground just beneath her logo to showcase it. She must remember to thank Carl for being so thoughtful.

The heat was stifling. She picked up a program and began to fan her face. With less than two hours before the crowd would arrive, waiters were hurrying to set up more portable air conditioners. Kate stepped to the back of the tent to get out of their way.

As she lifted a flap of the canvas to get a breath of fresh air, she spotted a cluster of trees circled by a skirt of dense shrubs a few yards away. Bingo. She knew exactly what she was going to do. The bushes would give her privacy, and it would take just a few seconds to unhook the strapless bra and pull it off. She looked in all directions to make sure no one was watching or going to follow her and headed for the trees.

A minute later she had accomplished the feat.

"Finally," she sighed with relief. Now she could breathe.

It was her last thought before the explosion.

Chapter Three

THE POLICE FOUND HER CURLED UP ON HER SIDE at the base of a hundred-year-old walnut tree. They found her bra dangling from an uprooted magnolia fifteen feet away. No one could quite figure out how the force of the explosion had extracted the lacy black lingerie but left her dress intact. Aside from being covered in leaves and dirt, the dress was still in one piece.

The blast had taken a huge chunk out of the side of the hill and left a hole the size of a small crater where the tent had been. The resulting fire scorched everything in its path as it poured like lava down the hill. The magnificent and regal walnut tree was split in half straight down the middle. One hefty branch snapped and landed in an arch above Kate, covering her completely. The branch acted as a barrier against the shards of glass, metal, canvas, and wood hurling through the air like bullets from an automatic weapon.

Houses shuddered as far as half a mile away, or so some of the residents swore. Others thought the trembling they felt was an earthquake and ran to stand in doorways for protection.

It was a miracle no one was killed or seriously injured. Had any of the staff or guests been inside the tent at the time of the explosion, the paramedics would have been hard-pressed to identify them.

Kate certainly should have been killed, and if it weren't for that ill-fitting bra, she surely would have been standing in the center of the blast. It was yet another miracle that all of her body parts were where they belonged. One of the metal tent poles had rocketed like a guided missile and sliced straight through the tree trunk resting just above Kate. The tip stopped one inch away from her heart.

Nate Hallinger, a detective newly assigned to the Charleston division, was the first to see her. He was making his way up the hill, trying to stay clear of the crime scene team walking the grid, when he heard a cell phone ringing close by. The musical ring reminded him of the Harry Potter movie he'd taken his nephews to see. The ringing stopped by the time he reached the uprooted walnut tree. He thought the phone was on the ground somewhere, and when he bent down on one knee to push a branch out of his way, he spotted a pair of shapely legs.

He shouted to the paramedics as he tried to get closer to the woman to see if she was dead or alive. Part of the trunk began to teeter, and if it shifted at all she would be crushed. He backed away when he heard her groan.

"Holy mother, George. Will you look at this?" one of the paramedics remarked.

"Look at what?" his partner said with a distinct Bronx accent. He was shimmying on his belly to get to the victim.

"The pole, man. Look at the pole. It stopped just short of her chest. Is she lucky to be alive or what?"

"Assuming she's all in one piece, then yes, I'll agree, Riley. She is lucky."

George was fifteen years older than his partner. He was training Riley, and though he liked working with him, the younger man's nonstop chatter occasionally got on his nerves. Riley loved to gossip—which George didn't approve of—but sometimes he did pass along interesting information.

Riley carefully lifted one of the broken branches and scooted toward the woman. "Did you hear?" he whispered. "The cops think that artist was the target, and the bomb went off too soon. I heard one of the firemen say it was overkill, but I'm not sure what that means, and I didn't dare ask 'cause then they'd know I was eavesdropping."

The two men couldn't reach her, so they called for help. It took four strong firemen to lift the splintered trunk out of the way. The heavy branches were removed a minute later, and the paramedics moved in. They both marveled that there were no broken bones. They braced her as a precaution and gently transferred her onto a stretcher.

Kate was slow to come around. She struggled to open her eyes. Through the blurry haze, she could just make out three men looming over her.

She felt like she was in a hammock and the wind was pushing her every which way. She closed her eyes again and fought nausea as she was being carried down the hill. She smelled something burning in the air.

Nate walked by her side.

"Is she going to be okay?" he asked

"Should be," Riley said.

"That's for the doctors to decide," George said.

"Can she talk?"

"Who are you?" George asked.

"Detective Nate Hallinger. Can she talk?" he repeated.

"She's got a bump the size of a baseball on the back of her head," Riley replied.

The other paramedic was nodding, but his attention, Nate noticed, was centered on his patient.

"She's probably got a concussion," he said.

"Uh-huh," Nate said. "But can she talk?" he asked, thinking that maybe the third time might be the charm with these guys. "Has she said anything?"

"No, she's still out cold," Riley said.

The fog in Kate's head was beginning to clear, and she was almost sorry about that. She felt like someone had stuck a hatchet in the back of her skull—and she tried to reach up and find out if there really was something there.

"Yes, she can talk," she whispered, her voice shaky. "She can walk, too."

Nate flashed a smile. The woman was a smartass. He liked that. "Can you tell me your name?"

She didn't dare nod. Any movement at all increased her headache. Aspirin, she thought. An aspirin would take care of it.

"Kate MacKenna," she said. "What happened?"

"An explosion."

She frowned. "I don't remember an explosion. Was anyone hurt?"

"You were," Riley said.

"I'm okay. Please put me down."

The request was ignored. She asked once again if anyone was hurt, and George answered, "Just some scratches and bruises."

"May I have an aspirin?"

"You've got a hell of a headache, don't you?" George remarked. "We can't give you anything yet. When we get you to the hospital—"

"I don't need to go to the hospital."

"Someone sure was looking out for you." Riley offered the comment.

Confused, she squinted up at him. "I'm sorry?"

"You didn't get blown up," he said. "If you had been inside the tent, you'd be a goner."

They reached the bottom of the hill and stopped to wait for an officer to open the back of the ambulance.

"I'm riding with her to the hospital," Nate said.

"I guess that's all right. Her vitals are good."

Nate whistled to get his partner's attention, pointed to the ambulance, and climbed inside.

"I don't need a ride to the hospital. I'm all right now," she said. "My car's here . . . somewhere."

"You shouldn't be driving anywhere," George said.

"My driver's license is in my car, and my purse and . . ." She realized how unimportant that information was and stopped talking.

"Think you could answer a couple of questions?" Nate asked.

She liked his voice. It was smooth . . . and not too loud. "Of course."

"Tell me what happened?"

She sighed. "I don't know what happened."

Why couldn't she remember? What was wrong with her? Maybe when the headache went away it would all come back to her.

"Did you see anyone unusual . . . you know, someone who didn't belong?"

She closed her eyes. "I don't . . . I'm sorry. Maybe I'll remember later."

She knew she was frustrating him.

"And no one got hurt?" she repeated.

He assured her. "The caterers and the staff were inside the building preparing trays and trying to keep cool. The owner was in a limo on his way to pick up the artist."

"Thank God," she whispered.

"If it had happened later, there would have been a massacre," George said.

The detective was sitting across from her, his arms on his knees, his hands clasped together, his gaze intent as he leaned forward and asked, "Try to think, Kate. You didn't notice anything out of the ordinary?"

The urgency in his voice cut through her haze. "You don't think this was an accident, do you?"

"We're not ruling out any possibility."

"Couldn't it have been one of the air conditioners?" she asked. "There were wires everywhere. Maybe one was overloaded . . ." She stopped when he shook his head. "It isn't possible that one of those blew up?" she asked.

"A hundred air conditioners couldn't have done that kind of damage. The explosive took out a good chunk of that hill."

Riley bent over Kate and once again checked her blood pressure. He smiled as he loosened the cuff.

"How's she doing?" Nate asked.

"Her numbers are still good."

"My head's feeling better," she said. It was a lie, but she wanted to go home.

"You still need to be checked out at the hospital," George said.

Hallinger closed his notepad and took a long look at her. Not many victims, he thought, were as gorgeous as this. He realized he was staring and quickly looked away. "That old tree saved your life. If you hadn't been standing behind it, you wouldn't have survived. What were you doing all the way over there? You were quite a distance from the annex and the tent."

She turned her head and winced. She really wanted an aspirin. "I went for a walk," she said. It wasn't a lie; she had gone for a walk. She just didn't think she needed to explain why.

"In this heat? I would think you would have wanted to go inside the annex, or walk on up to the house, or maybe even stay inside the tent near one of those air conditioners."

"You would think," she agreed. "But I didn't. I went for a walk. The heat doesn't really bother me." Okay, that was a lie, but it was a little one and she could live with that.

"Were you alone when you went for your walk?"

"Yes, I was."

"Hmmm." He looked skeptical.

"Detective, if someone had been with me, wouldn't he or she have been knocked unconscious, too?"

"If he or she had stayed around."

Before she could respond he asked, "How long were you out there?"

"Out where?"

"Behind the trees."

"I don't know. Not long."

"Really." The skepticism had moved to his voice.

"Is there a problem?" she asked.

"The crime scene unit found something about twenty feet away from you."

"What'd they find?" she asked and only then realized where he was headed. Oh my, the bump on her head had made her dense.

"An article of clothing," he said. "An undergarment, which was why I was wondering who was with you."

She could feel her face burning. "No one was with me. You're asking me about a black bra, right? And you're wondering if it belonged to me?" Before he could answer she plunged ahead.

"It did belong to me. The lady's room was blocked off, and I needed a little privacy. I saw the trees and I headed there."

"Why?"

"Why what?"

"Why did you want to take it off?"

He was being extremely intrusive, she thought, and she could have told him so, but she decided to be honest instead. "It was killing me."

"I'm sorry?"

Everyone inside the ambulance was suddenly interested in the topic. Riley and George were waiting for her to explain.

"The wire . . ."

"Yes?"

Good Lord. "A woman would understand."

"But a man wouldn't?"

He wasn't letting it go. She wondered if he was deliberately trying to embarrass her.

"You try wearing one of those things for an hour, and trust me, you'll take it off, too."

He laughed. "No, thanks. I guess I'll just have to take your word for it."

"Are you going to write that down in your notepad?"

He had a nice smile.

"Are you married?" he asked. "Is there a husband I should contact?"

"No, I'm not married. I live with my sisters." She tried to sit up and only then realized she was strapped down. "I've got to call them. They'll be worried."

"When we get to the hospital, I'll call them for you." He sat back on the bench and glanced out the back window. "We're almost there."

"I don't need to go to the hospital. My headache's almost gone."

"Uh-huh."

From the way he drawled out the response she knew he didn't believe her.

"You don't live in Charleston proper," he said.

"No," she answered. She knew he already had her address, phone number, and probably every other detail about her life. One phone call to an associate manning a computer would have told him everything he wanted to know.

"We live in Silver Springs, but it's a quick drive to the city. Are you new to this area?"

"Yes," he answered. "It's pretty laid back here." He smiled as he added, ". . . Usually. I'll bet this is the most excitement you'll have all year."

Chapter Four

IF ONLY.

Kiera and Isabel rushed through the emergency room doors. Kiera looked relieved when she saw Kate and smiled. Isabel looked scared.

The ER physician checked Kate and sent her downstairs for a scan. The techs were backed up, and she had to wait two hours before they finished with her. Then she was back upstairs and assigned a room.

Kiera was pacing in the hallway. Isabel was sitting on the edge of the bed watching television. The footage of the aftermath of the explosion was all over the news.

The second Isabel spotted Kate she jumped up, anxiously waited until she was in bed, and threw herself into her arms.

"You're okay, right? You gave us quite a scare, but you're okay, aren't you?"

"Yes, I'm fine."

Kiera grabbed the controls and adjusted the bed so that Kate could sit up.

"You're not seeing three of me, are you?" Isabel asked. She was fluffing the pillow behind Kate's head and causing her sister a good deal of pain.

"If she were seeing three of you, she'd be screaming now. One Isabel is enough." Kiera laughed.

"Not funny," Isabel said, but she too was smiling.

Kiera picked up Kate's chart from the metal slot at the foot of the hospital bed and began to read the doctor's notes.

"Should you be looking at that?" Isabel asked.

Kiera shrugged. "If they don't want you to read it, they shouldn't leave it. They're keeping you overnight for observation."

"I know," Kate said. "I want to go home."

"You should stay . . . as a precaution," she added. "Aunt Nora was still at her meeting, but we've left a message for her. No doubt she'll want to bring a cot in here so she can keep watch all night."

"Did she crack her head?" Isabel wondered, peering over Kiera's shoulder at the chart.

"I don't think so. Her skull is like granite."

Isabel took hold of Kate's hand. "You scared me . . . I mean us. You scared us. I don't know what we would do without you. It was lonely while you were in Boston. When Kiera was home, her nose was always in a medical book."

"She's going to be fine, Isabel. Stop stressing."

Isabel walked to the window and sat on the ledge. "Okay, I won't stress. So tell me . . . who was the man with the ambulance guys? He was really cute."

"Men don't like being called cute," a male voice responded.

None of them had noticed that Nate was standing in the doorway.

He was taken aback when all three sisters turned toward him. Damn, there wasn't a homely one among them. Isabel's face turned bright pink almost instantly.

"Please come in," Kate said. She introduced him to her sisters and waited for him to tell her why he was there.

"I forgot to give you my card," he said. "If you need anything or remember anything, no matter how insignificant you might think it is, I want you to call me."

"Yes, I will."

He hesitated but couldn't think of anything else to ask or say that would keep him in the room. "How's your head?"

"Better."

He nodded. "Okay then."

He was turning to leave when Isabel called, "May I ask you something, detective?" She took a step toward him and smiled.

Kate and Kiera shared a look. Isabel was turning on the charm, her never-fail charm. She brushed her hair back and took another step.

"Sure," he said. "What do you want to know?"

"Are the police going to put that painter, Cinnamon, in protective custody?"

He leaned against the door frame. "Why would you ask . . ."

She tilted her head toward the television. "She's on the news, and she's demanding police protection, which is really ironic when you think about it. She's always trashed the police until now. One of the reporters on the news quoted some of the horrible things she's said in the past. I think she said that you were all on the take or something like that. I don't know why she hasn't been sued."

She took a deep breath and then said, "Cinnamon says that it was a bomb and it was meant to kill her. She says people are trying to silence her because of her political views . . . and oh, her art, too."

"She thinks people are trying to kill her because of her paintings? Is she that bad?" Kiera asked. She laughed and shook her head.

Isabel frowned. "It's not funny. There were a couple of paintings on the wall behind her, and she kept pointing to them while she was being interviewed. I think maybe she was doing a little advertising."

"Has anyone determined what caused the explosion?" Kiera asked.

Nate turned to her. "We're not sure what kind yet, but it was definitely a bomb. We have a team working on it."

He looked at Kate again. "If you remember anything . . ." he said as he headed for the door.

Kate nodded.

Isabel waited until she was certain he was out of earshot and then said, "Isn't he adorable?"

"Yes, he's definitely adorable," Kiera agreed. "But he's too old for you. He's got to be in his thirties. And . . ."

Isabel folded her arms across her waist. "And what?"

"And he's interested in Kate."

Kate hadn't been paying much attention to the conversation until she heard her name. "As a witness," she corrected. "He's interested in me as a witness. That's all."

"He is not too old for me," Isabel said. "I wonder if he's single or married. I didn't see a ring on his finger."

"Let it go," Kiera said, her exasperation obvious. "He's not interested in you."

Isabel ignored her sister. "You should have asked him, Kate."

"I was unconscious, for heaven's sake." She gingerly lay back against the pillow. Her head was throbbing, but the conversation, as ludicrous as it was, did distract her. "When should I have asked him? In the ambulance?"

"No, of course not. I was just saying . . ."

"Yes?"

"You let another opportunity pass by."

"You've got to be kidding." She would have laughed if her head hadn't hurt so much.

"I'm most certainly not kidding. I swear I don't remember the last serious relationship you were in. In fact, I don't think you've ever been in a—"

"Kate darling!" Carl called from the doorway.

He waited until all eyes were on him and then rushed into the room with a flurry. Carl so did love to make a grand entrance, no matter what the occasion.

Isabel was thrilled to see him again. She'd only met him once, when he'd stopped by the house to pick up Kate for some sort of important benefit, but he'd made a lasting impression. Carl was so flamboyant, so bigger than life. She told Kate she was sure he must own at least one cape to wear in the winter to all those social events.

He clasped Kate's hand in both of his and leaned down to kiss her forehead.

"My poor, poor darling. This is a nightmare, a complete nightmare. It's amazing no one was seriously injured or killed in the explosion, and I tell you, if I were not wearing this white suit, I would get down on my knees to thank God."

Kiera coughed to cover her laughter. Kate tugged her hand away and said, "You remember my sisters, Kiera and Isabel."

"Yes, of course I do." He flashed a smile and said, "I do hope you don't blame me for what happened. I never should have allowed that crazy artist to show her work. I was warned, but I didn't believe anyone would take the woman seriously." He turned back to Kate and added, "And so I guess the blame **should** rest on my shoulders."

He wanted to be consoled. Kate was having none of it. "Carl, the police will sort it all out. You couldn't have known someone would go to such extremes."

"It's good of you to say so. Do you know the gallery was untouched? Not a stone was jarred loose. Isn't that astonishing? Of course I have a hole the size of a swimming pool in the lawn that I'm going to have to do something about, but when I think how much worse it could have been . . ." He paused, gave an elaborate shrug, and patted her hand again. "I shall let you rest now that I know you forgive me. If you need anything, anything at all . . ."

"I'll be sure to call you."

He gave her another dazzling smile, bowed to Isabel and Kiera, and left the room.

Kiera and Isabel stared at the empty doorway. The energy in the room seemed to have been sucked out with his departure.

"Carl's an interesting fellow," Kiera remarked. "A bit dramatic, but interesting."

"Aunt Nora was taken with him," Isabel said. "She told me he reminded her of a young George Hamilton. When I asked her who George Hamilton was, she got real mad at me and said she wasn't that old. I have no idea what she meant. Hey, Kate, what about Carl?"

"What about him?"

"Pay attention. We were discussing your love life—"

"No, we weren't. You were."

Isabel ignored the interruption. "And since you don't seem inclined to do anything about it on your own, I feel I should help."

Kiera burst into laughter. "And you think Kate and Carl would be a good match?"

Kate grimaced as she tried to keep from laughing, too. "Not only is Carl not my type, he's engaged. His fiancée is much more suited to his idiosyncrasies than I could ever be."

Isabel blushed. "Okay, maybe not. But, Kate, you need someone more laid back to balance your uptightness."

"There's no such word," Kiera said.

"Please, have mercy on me," Kate said. "Take Isabel home."

"Okay, we're out of here. Call me in the morning and let me know when I can pick you up."

Isabel wasn't the least offended that Kate wanted to get rid of her. She headed for the door then stopped. "Don't you ever scare me like that again. Promise me, Kate."

Kate responded to the fear in her voice. "I promise."

Isabel nodded. "Okay." She sighed as she added, "Now that you're home for good, things will be back to normal."

Chapter Five

KIERA DROVE KATE HOME FROM THE HOSPITAL
the next afternoon. They pulled into the driveway
just as a messenger from a CPA firm was about to
knock on their front door. While Kiera signed for
the delivery, the messenger dropped a fat package
into Kate's arms.

"Guess what we're going to be doing tonight,"
Kate said as she opened the door and headed to
the kitchen. She took a knife to the envelope and
emptied the contents on the table.

Isabel followed her sisters into the kitchen.
"What's all that?" she asked. She disappeared behind the refrigerator door as she searched for
something to munch on.

Kiera answered her. "Bills. I had Todd Simmons, the CPA, send over all of the accounts
Mom handled."

Isabel shut the refrigerator and walked over to

the table. She had a celery stick in her hand. "So why are they giving us the bills now?"

"When Mom became so gravely ill, she set it up that Mr. Simmons would take over the bills for one year after she was gone. I told her I could handle it, but she insisted it would be too difficult for me to manage from Boston. And you know how persuasive Mom could be."

"Is there enough money left to pay all of these bills?" Isabel asked, waving her celery stick at the pile of envelopes.

"I guess we're about to find out," Kiera said. "Mom was so secretive about her budget. Whenever I asked her how the money situation was, she always said the same thing, 'We're doing just fine.'"

"That's what she always said to me, too," Kate added. "It was so aggravating."

Isabel took exception to her sisters daring to criticize their mother. "She was being thoughtful. She didn't want any of us to worry. Kiera, she wanted you to focus on medicine, and Kate, she wanted you to finish your master's. Neither one of you needed any money because you both had scholarships and grants. Nora and I were dependent on Mom though, and she wanted to make it easy for us. That's why she did what she did. I'm sure of it."

"I wonder how much is left in the trust," Kiera said, ignoring Isabel's impassioned defense of their mother's financial decisions. "And do we know how much is still to come from Mom's pension?"

Kate shook her head. "I don't even know how much her monthly checks were. She refused to discuss it. Somewhere in these statements we'll get the answers."

"I'm not worried," Isabel said. "Even if we had to use up the money, Kate will figure out something."

"Why me?"

"Because Kiera has to do her last year of medical school, and she'll never get to come home then, and I'm going off to college in a week, so that leaves you. Besides, you and Kiera got all the brains in the family. You know what? I used to think I was stupid because I wasn't in advanced classes or got perfect scores on tests, but Mom told me that I was normal. Yes, normal," she insisted, pointing the celery at Kate. "You two are the weird ones. I don't want to hurt your feelings, but you're both kind of . . . nerds."

Kate laughed. "Mom never called us weird or nerds."

Isabel frowned. "She didn't call you normal either. Kate, what are you doing?"

"What does it look like? I'm opening the bills. I want to get started."

"Don't do that now. All of this can wait until after dinner," Kiera said. "You look worn out. Go rest for a little while. These bills aren't going any-where."

Kate didn't argue. She still had a lingering headache, and she wanted to take a shower and change out of the pair of slacks and silk blouse Kiera had brought to the hospital for her, so she headed to her room.

After her shower, she slipped into a pair of shorts and an old T-shirt, and fell asleep curled up on the bed.

She awoke to the sound of her sisters and aunt maneuvering around the kitchen, the aroma of baked chicken and apple dumplings wafting up the stairs.

The kitchen was directly beneath her bedroom, and she could hear their chatter.

"Kiera, you and Isabel are going to have to do cleanup tonight. I'm running late," her aunt said.

"What is it tonight, Aunt Nora?" Isabel asked.

"My support group, Miss Nosy."

Ever since the sisters could remember, Aunt Nora had been a regular at a support group. For years she attended one in St. Louis, and as soon as she moved to Silver Springs, she joined one at the local church. None of the girls knew what Nora was supporting all those years, but they knew better than to ask. They'd heard her right-to-privacy speech too many times to keep count.

She wouldn't allow them any privacy, though.

She wanted to know where they were every minute.

"And where will you be off to tonight, young lady?" Kate heard Nora ask Isabel.

"It's my night to sing at Golden Meadows," Isabel answered.

"The men and women at that nursing home are surely going to miss you while you're away at school."

"I think I'll miss them more," Isabel said. "They've been so sweet."

"You wake me when you get home," Nora ordered.

Isabel argued. "I'm a grown-up, and I don't think I need to—"

Nora interrupted her. "I promised your mother I would watch out for you, and that's what I'm doing. You're grown up when you go off to college."

Kate heard the back door open. "I forgot to tell you," Nora said. "The movers have changed the date on me. They'll be here on Friday. I expect some help packing my boxes."

"Of course we'll help you," Kiera promised.

"Does that mean you'll be leaving on Friday?" Isabel asked.

"Yes, it does," she answered. "But don't think you're getting rid of me for good because I'll be coming to see you as often as I used to visit my daughter. I'll just be living there instead of here. Now enough of this talk. You're making me late. Where's my pocketbook?"

"On your arm," Isabel said.

Kate heard the door close. She got out of bed, splashed water on her face, and went downstairs.

After dinner Isabel rushed off, and Kiera left to pick up some things at the supermarket, so Kate decided to get a start on the papers the accountant had sent over.

She began with a large envelope from Summit Bank and Trust. Kate didn't know her mother had done any business with Summit. The household account she had set up was with a local Silver Springs bank. Kate thought perhaps the papers had something to do with the pension. There were several invoices, copies of a loan application, and a letter on top of the stack from Mr. Edward Wallace, senior loan officer.

She read the letter and looked at the loan papers. "No," she whispered. "This has to be wrong." She read the letter again. She couldn't accept what she was reading, wouldn't accept it.

Yet she knew it was true, for there it was, her mother's distinctive signature.

"Oh, God," she whispered. "Mother, what did you do? What did you do?"

There was no pension, no trust, no insurance money, no savings. Her mother had taken out a three-year loan with a balloon payment of almost three hundred thousand dollars due in just four weeks' time.

She had put up everything she owned as collateral, and every asset would go to the bank if the payment wasn't made.

One of those assets was Kate's company. Another was her name.

Chapter Six

KATE WAS FRANTIC. SHE HELD THE LETTER from the banker and copies of the loan papers her mother had signed as she paced around the kitchen. She'd read and reread the documents at least five times now, and still she couldn't believe what her mother had done.

If the papers were in order—and of course they were; there was no reason to believe they weren't—then her mother had signed everything away. Everything.

"My God, Mother, what were you thinking?"

Apparently she hadn't been thinking at all, Kate decided. Had her mother realized what she was doing? Had she considered the ramifications?

Kate understood now why her mother would never discuss finances. She hadn't wanted any of them to know the truth.

Kate alternated between anger and sadness as she tried to clear her head and come up with a plan to salvage the future. She paced to the kitchen window and looked for Kiera's car to return. She would give the news to her sister the minute she walked in. Maybe the two of them could make some sense of this.

By the time several minutes had passed with no sign of Kiera, Kate had changed her mind. Although it would be nice to dump some of the worry in her sister's lap, it wouldn't change anything. What was done was done. Besides, Kiera had only a few days to rest before her next grueling round of medical school, and she wouldn't get a break for another eighteen months. This news would just pile more stress on her and keep her up all night. There would be plenty of time in the morning to talk to her about this . . . if Kate decided to tell her at all.

And Isabel? If she did tell Kiera, should she tell Isabel? That thought led to another. What about college? Where was Kate going to come up with the tuition money?

There had to be a solution. Kate sat down at the table, picked up her pen and paper, and ran the numbers once again.

The doorbell interrupted her. When she looked through the narrow window beside the front door, she saw a good-looking man shifting from foot to foot.

She opened the door and said, "Yes?"

He took a step toward her, and she instinctively

stepped back to get away from the smell of stale beer. He reeked of it. His eyes were bloodshot.

"Is Isabel here?"

"No, she isn't," Kate answered.

"Where is she?" he belligerently demanded.

"Who are you?"

"Reece. My name's Reece Crowell. Now where is she?"

The man standing in front of her was in his midtwenties. He wore khaki pants and a button-down shirt with the cuffs rolled up to his elbows. His dark hair was slicked back from a rather angular face, but he was handsome in a soap opera way. Kate had never met him and was surprised that Isabel had dated someone so much older. They were definitely going to discuss this later.

Reece took another step closer. Kate hadn't opened the door wide enough for him to step inside . . . unless he walked through her. From his angry expression she thought he might just do that.

"I know she's here," he muttered. "I want to see her."

"She is not home," Kate said. She kept her voice firm. "And Isabel has said she doesn't want to see you again."

"We're getting married."

The guy was definitely out of it. "No, you're not. Isabel is going to college, and you're going to leave her alone."

His hands balled into fists. "It's your fault. Isabel wouldn't do this to me. It's you. She said you wanted her to go to college. She's throwing away her career because of you and your bitchy sister."

She wasn't going to argue with him. "Isabel has moved on, and you need to do the same."

He tried to push past her, shouting Isabel's name. She stood her ground and used her hip to brace the door.

"If you don't leave now, I'm calling the police," Kate warned.

"You don't get it, do you? She's mine. We're going to Europe next week, and we'll be married before we come back. I've put too much time into her singing career to let you mess it up for me."

He came at her again, and this time she shoved with her whole body. She slammed the door and bolted it.

Kate leaned back against the door as Reece pounded on it and shouted obscenities. He stopped for a second, as if waiting to see if the door would suddenly open to him, and then he resumed the pounding and the screaming. Kate stood on the other side terrified that he was going to break the door down.

Suddenly the pounding stopped, and at the top of his lungs Reece bellowed, "This isn't over, bitch!" Then it was eerily quiet. Kate waited a second before she peered through the side window.

Reece was staggering across the lawn. He turned at the sidewalk and kept walking.

Kate's heart was racing. She rushed to the phone to call the police, and then she stopped. What could she tell them? Aside from being drunk and obnoxious, Reece hadn't threatened them with violence or done any damage. Maybe when he was sober he'd come to his senses.

But his parting words, "This isn't over," echoed in her head.

Chapter Seven

THE PHONE CALL CAME IN THE MIDDLE OF THE night.

Kate was awake. She hadn't slept at all. After Kiera and Isabel had returned home, she had told them about the incident with Reece. When she had seen the worry and fear on their faces, she simply couldn't tell them about their financial problems as well. They had had enough anxiety for one night. She wasn't about to burden them with more.

She had pored over the records multiple times hoping against hope that she might find a solution before she had to reveal the problem to her sisters. The ringing jarred her from her thoughts and she quickly snatched the receiver so it wouldn't wake the rest of the household. No one ever called with good news at two in the morning. She feared it might be Reece on the other end of the line as she answered.

"Did I wake you?" Jordan asked.

Kate let out a quick breath in relief. "No, I'm wide awake. What's going on?"

"Why don't you answer your e-mail? I've been sitting here in front of my computer since nine o'clock."

"I'm sorry. I was going through bills." Kate could hear the anxiety in Jordan's voice and knew something was wrong. It had to be something awful, too, or she wouldn't have called in the middle of the night. Good news could always wait until morning.

Kate knew better than to come right out and demand to know what the problem was. She and Jordan had been best friends for a very long time, and Kate understood how her mind worked. When pressured, Jordan closed up.

"What's going on there?" Jordan asked.

"Not much. Just the usual stuff."

"What usual stuff? Kate, I need to talk about mundane things for a minute. Okay?"

Oh, Lord, the news was bad all right. Kate felt a knot form in her stomach. "Okay," she said. "I've been going through bills, and guess what I found? Never mind, don't guess. Before she died, Mom signed away the house, the car, and all other assets, including my company and my name. She took out a loan the size of Nebraska and only paid the interest for the last three years. The balloon payment is due in thirty days. Oh, and last night, I almost got blown up."

"I miss talking to you."

"You didn't hear a word I said, did you?"

"I'm sorry? What did you say?"

The question wasn't a joke. Jordan sounded a million miles away. The knot twisted in Kate's stomach.

"I was saying it's hot here, hot and humid. What's going on with you?"

"I found a lump."

Four little words and everything changed in that instant. The worry about the house and bills and tuition was forgotten, and all that mattered was her friend.

"Where? Where is it?" She tried to keep the urgency out of her voice.

"Left breast."

"Have you seen a specialist yet? Have you had any tests?"

"Yes and yes," she answered. "Surgery's scheduled for Friday morning. The surgeon wanted to do the biopsy tomorrow, but I wouldn't let him. You need time to get here . . . right?" She sounded like a little girl now, a scared little girl.

"Yes, that's right. I can be there tomorrow."

"I'll book you on a flight. I'll e-mail you times and flight numbers, and I'll pick you up at the airport."

Kate knew Jordan was focusing on the details as a way of staying in control. It was the same thing she would have done. Control was one way to combat fear.

"I'll be waiting at baggage pickup."

"Yes, okay." Kate was so shaken she couldn't think of what questions to ask. Her hand was aching and she realized she was gripping the phone. She forced herself to relax.

"Listen. I've decided not to tell the family, not yet anyway. After I know what I'm dealing with, then I'll tell them. I couldn't stand all of them hovering around me. Mom and Dad have really been through it the last couple of months. As proud as they are of my brothers, having most of them in law enforcement has taken its toll. When Dylan was shot on duty, I think they aged twenty years. For a while there, none of us knew if he was going to make it or not. You were there. You know how bad it was."

A shiver rushed down Kate's spine. "Yes, I remember."

"And you saw how the stress affected everyone, especially my parents. Now that Dylan's home and mending, the family's calming down. Just the other day Mom called and mentioned that it had been eight weeks since that nightmare phone call, and she's just now able to take a deep breath. What was I supposed to say to that, Kate? Brace yourself? I've got more bad news for you?"

"You don't know if it's going to be bad news or . . ."

"I know, but it's the not knowing that gets everyone all stirred up. It's better to wait until I find out . . . everything."

"Whatever you want . . ."

"Besides, Dylan is sending Mom and Dad on a cruise."

"That was sweet of him."

"Are you kidding? He just wanted to get them out of his hair. Mom's been driving him crazy, showing up at his place at least once a day with food. He's not used to being pampered."

"What about your sister? I know how close you and Sydney are. Aren't you going to tell her?"

"Have you forgotten? She's in L.A. She starts film school in just a couple of weeks, and she's busy getting settled."

"That's right, film school. I forgot all about that."

"If Sydney knew about the surgery, she'd come home, and I don't want her to do that. If it's bad news, then of course she and Mother will need to know right away."

"Yes."

"But for now it's just you and me. Are you up for this?"

"Absolutely."

They talked for another few minutes and then hung up. Kate stayed in complete control while she gathered up the papers from the table and dumped them into a laundry basket. She wanted to put it all in the trash, but that wouldn't solve anything.

She still had a little time before the roof came crashing down and the creditors were banging on the doors. There was enough money in the checking account to pay the current bills. When she returned from Boston, she would figure out what to do. She wouldn't tell her sisters about the financial disaster until then.

She turned the lights off and carried the laundry basket upstairs to her room. She put it in her closet and got ready for bed.

She didn't start crying until she was under the sheets.

Chapter Eight

JORDAN HAD NEVER BEEN ON TIME FOR ANY-
thing in her life, and today was no exception.

Kate was waiting with her bag at her feet outside the airport doors when her friend pulled up
to baggage claim.

Jordan put the car in park but left the engine
running, popped the trunk, and got out so she
could hug Kate.

"I'm so glad you're here."

"Me too."

"I knew you'd come."

"Of course."

A policeman motioned for Jordan to move the
car. Neither Kate nor her friend said another word
until they were on Harborside Drive heading toward Jordan's apartment.

"How late was I?" Jordan asked.

"Just fifteen minutes."

She glanced at Kate, smiled, and said, "You look like hell."

"You look worse."

Kate was teasing. Jordan always looked beautiful. Though her hair was a deep auburn color, she had a redhead's complexion. She usually had that all-American, freckle-faced, Ralph Lauren model look about her, but not today. There was very little color in her face. Even her freckles looked pale.

"No wonder we're best friends. We're both painfully blunt."

She concentrated on merging onto I-90, then cut over to the middle lane and shot forward. "I wish you'd move here."

"I do love Boston, but . . ."

"I know. You have to keep the home fires burning for your sisters."

"Mostly for Isabel, and just for a little while. She deserves to have some family at home. Of the three of us, Isabel was closest to Mom, and she's had a hard adjustment."

"Is she still headed to Winthrop?"

"Yes," she answered. "She's very excited. It's the perfect school for her." **If I can come up with the money for more than one semester's tuition,** she silently added. "I'm hoping that going away to college will help her grow up a little. Mom always treated her like a baby."

Jordan nodded. "She is the baby in your family,

but she's got a good head on her shoulders. She'll be okay."

"How scared are you, Jordan?"

The abrupt change in topics didn't faze her friend. Her mind worked just like Kate's, bouncing from one thought to another. "Very," she answered.

"What did the specialist tell you?"

"I've gotten three opinions, and all of them have poked, prodded, and taken enough blood to fill a bathtub."

"That's a pleasant image."

"They have to prepare me for the worst."

Kate nodded. "What happens tomorrow?"

"Doctor Cooper will do the surgery. He's gone over all the options with me. He'll do the biopsy . . . and then we'll see."

Kate took a deep breath. She knew she had to keep it together. Her friend needed her to be strong.

They were on Storrow Drive now, and Kate stared out the window at the Charles River. The sun made the water glisten.

"We'll get through this," she told Jordan.

"Yes."

"So what time do we need to be at the hospital?"

"Six."

"We aren't going to be late, even if I have to use electric shock to blast you out of your bed."

Jordan laughed. "You'd do it, too. Dylan threw a soaked towel on my face once to get me to wake up."

"Did it work?"

"Oh, yes."

"Bet you didn't wake up happy."

"You're right. I didn't. I wanted to get even, so the next morning I threw a glass of cold water on him. He roomed with Alec, and you know what a slob he is, and I guess I just didn't think it through. As soon as the water hit his face, Dylan came off that bed . . . I still shudder thinking about it. I've never seen anyone move like that. I had my getaway all planned, but I tripped over one of Alec's shoes and went careening into his bedside table. I cut my knee open and started screaming. I think Alec slept through it all, but poor Dylan ended up carrying me downstairs to Mom. I had to have stitches."

"How old were you?"

"Ten or eleven."

"You sound like a hellion."

"I had my moments. Tell me something. How come you didn't want Dylan to know you sat with him in the hospital?"

"I was there for you, not him."

"Yeah, right."

"And if he knew," she continued, "he'd never let me live it down. Your brother loves to tease and torment."

"All my brothers like to tease."

"Yes, but Dylan's the worst, bless his little ol' heart."

Jordan grinned. "You southern girls mask your criticisms behind the 'bless your heart' you always tack on the end."

"Southern girls never criticize," she said, deliberately exaggerating her accent. "We are raised to be soft-spoken ladies. We always tell the truth but in a kind, genteel way."

Jordan rolled her eyes. "That's a load of . . ."

Kate laughed. "What?"

"I'm cleaning up my vocabulary now that I've got nieces and nephews. I've got to set a good example. That's what Theo and Nick tell me anyway."

"Your brothers are telling you to clean up **your** vocabulary?"

"Speaking of Dylan . . . I think he's kind of sweet on you."

"Dylan's sweet on all women."

"True, he does like women," Jordan said. "But he especially likes teasing you because you embarrass so easily."

"His accidentally walking in on me taking a shower the first time I visited Nathan's Bay didn't help any. I don't think I'll ever live that down."

"Oh, I forgot about that." Jordan laughed. "No wonder he has such a big grin whenever your name comes up."

She turned a corner and spotted a prime spot directly in front of her brownstone. It was an extremely rare occurrence. She also noticed a black Hummer had just turned the corner and was coming from the opposite direction. The driver obviously wanted the same parking spot because he gunned his motor and came racing toward her. Jordan was quicker. She parallel parked like a pro. The driver of the Hummer made an obscene gesture as he drove past, which Jordan and Kate thought was hilarious.

Several years before, the brownstone had been converted into three spacious apartments, one on each floor. Jordan's was on the top. Kate had lived with her during school and was used to the squeaky stairs and narrow corridors.

Jordan had made a fortune for herself with a computer chip she had designed, and she could live anywhere, but she, like Kate, was a creature of habit. She loved her old, worn-out apartment and didn't have any plans to move.

Kate loved the apartment, too. It was warm and inviting even on the coldest of days. It always smelled clean and fresh. Jordan, showing her loyalty to her friend, had placed Kate's scented candles on almost every table. She had Kate's body lotions in the two bathrooms and on the bedside tables as well.

There were three bedrooms. The guest room was at the end of a long hall and was large enough to accommodate the king-sized bed two of Jordan's brothers had purchased for her so they could sleep over when they were in town. Driving to their parents' home on Nathan's Bay was a good two hours with traffic.

The third bedroom had been converted into an office, and bookcases lined all four walls. The shelves were bowed from the weight of Jordan's books. The office was open to the dining room on one side and the hallway on the other.

The hardwood floors were as dark as midnight. Splatters of color came from oriental rugs strewn about. The huge windows in every room were covered with plantation shutters. One of Kate's favorite study spots was the window seat in the living room that overlooked the Charles River.

The only sterile room in the apartment was the galley kitchen. Jordan didn't cook. She lived on carryout or frozen food. If it couldn't be microwaved, she didn't buy it.

Kate immediately went to the guest room and put her bag next to the bed. She cut through the office to get to the dining room. She noticed all the papers on Jordan's desk and backtracked. As cluttered as Jordan's bookshelves were, her desk was always immaculate. Aside from her computer and a stack of Post-its, one or two pencils, and a phone, her work area was usually as sterile as her kitchen counters.

Jordan walked into the office, noticed Kate

looking at the layers of papers on her desk, and said, "It's a mess, isn't it?"

"For you it is," she said. "You always keep a clean desk when you work. You're kind of obsessive about it. You've had a lot of stress lately, though, and I would think paperwork would be the last thing on your mind."

"Most of the papers are legal documents. I'm being sued."

After dropping that bit of shocking news, she turned around and walked into the living room. Kate chased after her.

"You're being sued?"

"That's right," she said as she dropped into an easy chair and swung her legs over the arm.

"You're being awfully blasé about it." Kate stood in front of the coffee table with her arms folded, frowning at her friend while she waited for an explanation.

It didn't come soon enough to suit her. "Okay, I'll ask. How come you're being sued? And how come you're so calm about it?"

"I might as well be calm," she said. "Getting all worked up won't do any good."

She kicked off her sandals and leaned back. "I'm being sued by a man named Willard Bell. He seems to think he came up with the design for my chip before I did and I figured out a way to steal it from him."

Kate sat in the opposite chair and crossed her

feet on the ottoman. "Have you ever met this man?"

"No. He lives in Seattle," she said. "My attorney told me that Bell is a computer geek who makes his living suing people. A very nice living," she stressed. "He doesn't really ever have a case, but it's cheaper to settle than fight because of all the legal expenses."

"What are you going to do?"

Jordan looked exasperated. "What do you think I'm going to do? You know me better than anyone."

"You're not going to settle. Bet your attorney wants you to, doesn't he?"

"You're right, he does. I'm not going to, though. I don't care what it costs. What Bell's doing is wrong, and I'm not going to give him a dime. His attorney is playing hardball," she added. "He's frozen all of my accounts. That just means I won't have money for a while. I'll get them unfrozen soon," she hastened to add. "So there's no need to worry."

"What does Theo think about all this?"

"I haven't asked him for advice. In fact, I haven't even told him about it."

"Why not? He's an attorney, for heaven's sake. You could use his advice."

"Theo's overworked and underpaid, and with a new family . . . no, I'm not going to bother him."

"What about Nick?"

"He graduated from law school, but he doesn't practice," she pointed out. "Besides, I don't want to involve any of my brothers. My attorney is very capable, and any other problems that come along I can handle on my own. All of my brothers have a habit of taking over, but they're going to stay out of this. I'm a big girl now. I can fight my own battles."

"Why do you have to be so independent?"

Jordan smiled. "You make 'independent' sound like a bad word. I'm just like you, Kate. We both like to control everyone and everything."

She didn't argue because she knew Jordan was right. They were overachievers and did like to have complete control over every aspect of their lives. Other people's lives too, when they could get away with it, she admitted.

"How come we're so smart about business matters and so stupid about men?"

"Oh, that one's easy. We tend to date men we can walk all over, and then we don't want them."

"You know what I think?"

"What?"

Kate wrinkled her nose and made a pathetic face. "We're really screwed up."

Jordan laughed. "I'm so glad you're here. Listen, I realized after our phone call that I hadn't really been paying any attention to what you were telling me. You know, when I asked what was going on with you. It was very self-centered of me, don't you suppose?"

Kate grinned. "I do suppose."

"Okay, I'm paying attention now. Did you say your mother gave away your business?"

"Close. I've just hit a couple of bumps, that's all."

"You know that if you ever need anything from me, it's yours, don't you?"

"That's very sweet," she said.

"I know you'd do the same for me."

"I would," Kate agreed. "But don't worry. I'll work this out. You've got enough on your mind right now."

Jordan's face turned pensive as if she were trying to recreate their phone conversation in her head. "And did I hear you say you almost blew something up? All I could think about was the surgery, so I was only half listening. Were you trying to cook again? Lord, I hope not. You could have blown up your house."

Kate protested. "Just because of one little mishap in your kitchen you assume—"

Jordan snorted. "Little mishap? The fire department showed up."

"All this talk about cooking has made me hungry. Do we go out or would you rather order in?"

They spent at least ten minutes deciding and ended up walking two blocks to a neighborhood bistro that Kate thought served the best seafood chowder in the city.

They chose a booth in the back of the restaurant so no one would bother them, but neither of them ate much. Jordan looked worn out.

Kate's stomach ached from the knot that wouldn't go away, but the rest of her body felt numb. She knew if she allowed herself to feel, she'd melt into a pool of tears. She decided to try to take Jordan's mind off her worries for a few minutes.

"Don't you want to know how I almost got blown up?"

Jordan stopped swirling her spoon in the now congealed chowder she'd barely tasted and smiled. "I'm waiting for the punch line."

"It's not a joke. I had a big bump on the back of my head, and haven't you noticed the whopper of a bruise on my forehead?" She lifted her hair away so Jordan could get a better look.

"Of course I noticed, but I just assumed . . ."

"Assumed what?"

"Kate, you've got to know by now that you're kind of a klutz. I just thought you tripped or something."

"I beg to differ. You're a klutz, not me."

Jordan didn't argue with her. "You weren't joking about almost being blown up, were you?"

"No, I wasn't. Do you want to hear what happened or not?"

"I want to hear."

"I guess I should start at the beginning. Have you ever heard of the Wonderbra?"

Chapter Nine

KATE HAD SELECTIVE MEMORY. BECAUSE OF her mother's long illness, she and her sisters had spent what seemed like a lifetime in numerous hospital waiting rooms, and yet Kate couldn't remember what any of them looked like. It was odd, she thought, that she couldn't recall a single piece of furniture, a wall color, or a carpet. She supposed all waiting rooms were pretty much the same, cold and sterile, with mass-produced paintings of mountains and meadows on the walls.

She did remember the people who came and went while she was there, almost every one of them, and she remembered the anxiety. The air was thick with it, and like a virus, it passed from one person to the next, attacking anyone and everyone who walked into the room to wait.

Time and fear, a horrible combination. She remembered the families huddled together, trying to gain comfort and hope from one another. She remembered the young father who looked so lost sitting with his two little girls squeezed up next to him while he read stories and waited to hear if their mother would live or die. He had broken down and sobbed when he was given the good news by the smiling surgeon.

And she remembered the elderly woman who was sitting all alone until Kate and her sisters walked in. She decided to keep them company, told them she was waiting to hear if her husband of forty years was going to survive bypass surgery. She told one story after another and another and wouldn't let anyone else get a word in. Faster and faster the woman talked until Kate's head was spinning. At one point Kate pictured herself sitting there with giant cotton balls stuffed in her ears. It was an uncharitable thought, but the image did make it easier to smile through the woman's endless chatter.

Waiting was always a miserable experience. Today was no exception. Jordan wasn't taken into the OR until a little after ten, and she'd been ready since six-thirty. An emergency had caused the delay. Kate was able to stay with her in preop, but when Jordan was wheeled away, a volunteer who looked about twelve years old showed Kate the way to the surgical waiting room.

She led her down a maze of corridors, and Kate soon became suspicious that the girl didn't know where she was going. It seemed they had made a complete circle and finally found the waiting area by chance.

There were actually two waiting rooms with a desk and a phone manned by another volunteer in between. The larger room was packed, and after giving her name to the woman behind the desk, Kate went into the smaller room.

A family of five, all with red-rimmed eyes, was just leaving as she walked in. There weren't any other people, and Kate was thankful she was alone. She wasn't in the mood to talk to strangers. She sat down in the corner by the window, picked up a magazine, and promptly put it back. She was too nervous to read or sit still.

The truth was that she wanted to sit down and have a good cry, but she couldn't do that, of course.

Kate reached for another magazine and noticed how her hands were shaking. Get a grip, she told herself. Jordan would be okay. It was just a little bump, not a lump, and everything was going to be all right. Except that the surgeon had been so grim about it. According to Jordan, anyway, but then Jordan tended to overreact.

Now who was she trying to fool? Her friend never overreacted. She was too . . . practical . . . and cautious to a fault.

The key to an effective pep talk was honesty,

she decided, and so Kate decided to come up with some honest reasons why everything would be okay.

She paced back and forth while she thought about it. All right then. Jordan had told her that the surgeon had been quite grim. Maybe he had to anticipate the worst so that he would be prepared, and he needed to prepare his patient for the worst, too, didn't he? Wasn't that part of his Hippocratic oath or something?

How convoluted was that reasoning? Time for a little realism. Yes, it was true that one of Jordan's aunts on her mother's side of the family had died because of a lump she had pretended wasn't there until it was too late. And yes, there was a cousin on the same side of the family who had also been given the same diagnosis. But so what? The cousin was in her late eighties, and so was Jordan's aunt, wasn't she? Which meant that statistically the odds were on Jordan's side, and she should and would have a happy, healthy life for the next sixty-five years, give or take a few.

Except that she'd found the lump last week, not sixty-five years from now.

That reminder took the wind out of Kate. She sat down and bowed her head. She was suddenly so tired she could barely think. Early detection was important, right? And Jordan, her sister, Sydney, and their mother had all taken charge of their health. They had the usual examinations—and then some—on a regular basis.

Don't borrow trouble. Kate's mother had often said those very words. Oh, God, she didn't want to think about her mother now. She had enough to deal with.

What was taking so long? Kate was looking at her watch for about the fiftieth time just as her cell phone rang.

Kiera was calling. "How is she?"

Jordan had given Kate permission to talk to Kiera about the surgery but no one else. "Still in surgery," she answered. "They were running late, so she didn't go in until almost ten. It's been over an hour now. Isn't that long enough for a biopsy?"

"No."

"But . . ."

"I'm a medical student, not a doctor, and I'm not going to speculate."

"You're a fourth-year medical student, which means you're almost finished."

"But still not a doctor."

"Come on, Kiera," Kate said in exasperation. "Make a calculated guess. I'm not going to sue you if you're wrong."

"No, I don't think an hour is too long. Remember, the surgeon's waiting for the pathologist's report. And since you didn't go into the OR with her, you can't know exactly when they started."

Kate relaxed. "Good point. They could just be starting now, for all I know. I'll call you as soon as I hear something. How are things at home?"

"Fine. Reece has called here several times."

"Oh?" Kate asked cautiously.

"He's been very polite. Almost too polite. When I tell him Isabel isn't here, he says 'thank you' and hangs up, but then a couple of hours later he calls again. I can hear this edge to him, like he's ready to explode. He's asked for you a couple of times. Once Isabel is well away at school, I suppose he'll get the message."

Kate wasn't so sure about that.

"Oh yes," Kiera continued. "A man named Wallace has called and left a couple of messages. He said he works for a bank. Have you ever heard of him?"

The ever-present knot in Kate's stomach began to swell. "No, I haven't heard of him," she lied. "Did he say what he wanted?"

"No," she answered. "But he wants you to call him right away. Do you have a pen? I'll give you his phone number."

Kate closed her eyes. "No. I'll call him Monday when I get home. Just leave the messages on the machine."

"He said it was urgent."

"Urgent can wait until Monday."

"Aren't you at all curious to know what he wants?"

If the loan officer worked for the bank her mother had used, then Kate knew exactly what he wanted. Everything they owned. And then some.

"Listen, Kiera. Monday we need to sit down and have a long talk."

"It sounds serious."

"We just need to make some decisions about the future. I'm going to hang up now. I'll let you know how Jordan's doing later."

She flipped the cell phone shut and dropped it into her purse just as a white-haired volunteer called her name. Kate saw the surgeon turning toward her when she stood. Then she saw his face. The surgeon was smiling.

Chapter Ten

JORDAN WAS GOING TO BE FINE. THE WONDERFUL news from the surgeon made Kate weak with relief. She felt like hugging the man.

She had thought that she would be able to take her friend home a couple of hours after the anesthesia wore off, but the surgeon wanted to keep her overnight. He explained almost as an afterthought that Jordan had had a very mild reaction to an anesthetic, but there was nothing to worry about, the drug would be out of her system by tomorrow afternoon at the latest, and she could leave the hospital then.

Nothing to worry about. Kate remembered those words when she saw her friend. Poor Jordan was as red as a boiled lobster, had welts all over her face and arms, and was itching like crazy.

Kate did what any best friend would do. She pulled out her cell phone, which happened to have a built-in camera, and took her photo so she could torment her later—maybe even make a screen saver for her computer.

She stayed with Jordan until eight that evening. The rash was still going strong, but the doctor had ordered medication to relieve the itching and help her sleep. Kate waited until she'd fallen asleep again, then drove Jordan's car back to her apartment and took a long, hot shower.

She closed her eyes and let the water cascade over her shoulders. Maybe it would wash away some of the tension. However, each time she tried to clear her mind, visions of her sisters and her company and Reece and mountains of bills swirled through her head.

No, not tonight, she thought. She would not do this tonight. She wasn't going to let herself get all worked up about the future tonight. Tomorrow would be soon enough.

Her stomach began to gnaw at her, and she realized she hadn't eaten anything all day. She toweled off and slipped into her pajamas, a soft gray T-shirt and a pair of gray and navy striped boxer shorts, and headed for the kitchen. Jordan always kept a supply of crackers and jars of peanut butter on hand. There were several old TV dinners in the freezer. Kate was pretty sure they'd been there since Jordan had moved into the apartment. Kate opted for the crackers. She got a fresh box out of the cabinet, put it on the counter, and then opened the refrigerator to get a bottle of water.

She was unscrewing the top when, without any warning at all, the tears started.

Within seconds she was sobbing. She leaned back against the refrigerator, bowed her head, and cried like a baby. The release felt good. She could have kept it up for at least another half hour if someone hadn't intruded. She heard a knock on the door, grabbed a paper towel to wipe the tears from her face, and stood frozen hoping whoever it was would go away.

No such luck. Another knock, more insistent this time. She did not want company. Barefoot, she crept to the door and looked through the peephole. Her heart dropped.

There stood Dylan Buchanan, the bane of her existence. God, he looked good. She shook herself. Stop that. He wore a pale blue shirt neatly tucked into his jeans. The shirt was just fitted enough to show off his broad chest and thick biceps. His dark hair was short, and as usual not a strand was out of place.

All of the Buchanan boys were ruggedly good looking, but Dylan had a little extra something going for him. She thought maybe it was his slow, sexy smile. She only knew one thing for certain. When he turned on the charm, he could melt the most frigid of hearts. Jordan referred to her older brother as the sex machine. Kate thought he had earned the dubious nickname because of all the women he had dated—and no doubt taken to bed—while he was in college. She didn't think he had slowed down much since then, except maybe for a couple of weeks after he'd been shot. The bullet might have slowed him a little.

He looked tired, she thought.

He pushed the doorbell again and leaned against the wall behind him balancing a pizza box and a six-pack of beer on one hand.

Had he heard the floorboard squeak when she'd stepped on that loose one? She moved away from the door, waited a couple of seconds, and then peeked again. Her heart began to pound. It was an instantaneous reaction and one she couldn't seem to control. The conditioned response stemmed from the night he had walked in on her in the shower. He'd had a mighty fine time teasing her about it ever since. She simply wasn't up to sparring with him tonight. In her vulnerable state, he'd eat her alive.

When he winked, she knew he was perfectly aware that she was standing on the other side of the door.

She was going to have to be grown up about this. She would simply open the door and tell him to go away. She looked through the peephole one last time.

The man was a force to be reckoned with, and she was not in the mood tonight. She needed to finish crying and go to bed.

Get it over with, she told herself. She unlocked

the double deadbolts and pulled the door open as she said, "Jordan's not—"

"It's about time. The pizza's getting cold and the beer's getting warm. Move out of the way. Come on, pickle. Move."

She'd forgotten all the silly names he called her. He was partial to food items.

He was already over the threshold and about to step on her toes.

The pizza smelled wonderful and so did he. She got a tiny whiff of his cologne when he strode past her on his way to the kitchen. She followed him and got trapped behind the refrigerator when he opened the door to put the beer inside. He popped the tab on one can and offered it to her. She shook her head. He shut the refrigerator, stepped closer, and pinned her to the counter as he slowly reached over her to get to the pizza.

He was deliberately trying to get a reaction, and from the sparkle in his eyes, she knew he was thoroughly enjoying himself.

"I'll be happy to move."

"No need."

His chest rubbed against hers, and it was then that she remembered what she was wearing.

"Jordan's not here," she told him.

"I noticed."

"You should have called first and saved yourself a trip. I'm not dressed for company."

"Yeah, I noticed that, too. You've got great legs, pickle."

"Dylan . . ."

"I'm not company."

She pushed against his shoulder to get him to step back. When he winced, she realized what she had done. "Oh, Dylan," she whispered as she jerked her hand back. She'd forgotten about his injury. "I'm so sorry. I didn't mean to . . ."

"It's okay."

He left the pizza but took his beer into the living room and dropped down on the sofa. Kate followed him.

"I hurt you, didn't I?"

"Let it go," he said. He knew he'd sounded irritated and softened his tone when he added, "I'm fine."

He didn't look fine. He looked ready to pass out. His complexion had turned gray, but if he wanted her to let it go, then that's what she would do. She went into the kitchen, grabbed the pizza, some napkins, and her bottled water, and then decided to take him another beer as a peace offering of sorts.

There were newspapers spread on the coffee table. Kate put the box down on top and then excused herself and went into Jordan's bedroom to borrow one of her robes. Her friend was taller than Kate, and the pink robe dragged on the floor. It was missing a belt.

She caught a glimpse of herself in the mirror above the sink as she walked past and inwardly groaned. She'd forgotten she'd clipped her hair into a ponytail that was more out than in, and there were mascara smudges under her eyes. "Lovely," she muttered.

She grabbed a washcloth and started scrubbing. By the time she came back to the living room Dylan had finished his third slice of pizza and was reaching for a fourth. He'd also emptied her bottle of water and gotten her another one.

She shook her head. "I wasn't gone that long."

"You snooze, you lose. At least in the Buchanan family you do. Come sit." She must have looked wary. "I won't bite, unless you want me to."

He was smiling at her, and oh, Lord, he was something. Good thing she wasn't interested, she reminded herself. Like the big bad wolf, he'd devour her. No, thank you.

He was sitting in the center of the sofa and took up a fair amount of space, but she didn't ask him to move over. She shoved several pillows out of the way and sat down.

"I was wondering . . ." he began.

She stacked the pillows neatly between them. "Yes?"

He was smiling at her again. She wanted to tell him to stop it, that when he smiled, she lost her ability to concentrate. Wouldn't he love hearing that? He'd have something more to tease her about.

"Where's the remote?"

The question jarred her. "The remote?"

"Uh-huh," he drawled. "The remote."

"You mean the remote for the television. Let me guess. Sports channel."

"I'm that predictable?"

"Afraid so. You're a Buchanan male."

She threw a couple of pillows on the floor and dug between the sofa cushions. She fished out the remote and handed it to him.

"It was nice of you to bring Jordan a pizza. I'll save this for her," she said.

"I didn't bring it for her. It's for you."

"How did you know I was here?"

"Jordan told me." She shook her head. He nodded. "She also told me to keep you company tonight."

Kate was taken aback. "When did she tell you?"

"About an hour ago." She didn't look like she believed him, and so he added, "In the hospital."

"You were there . . . in the hospital?"

"Sure was."

"But . . . but how did you find out she was there?" She didn't give him time to answer but said, "She didn't call you. Did she call you?"

"No, she didn't call me. She didn't call any of us," he added, referring to his brothers, "and I'll be discussing that with her as soon as she's feeling better. We're her family and she shouldn't have—"

She interrupted him before he got all wound up. He was well on his way.

"You still haven't told me how you found out."

"A friend of Nick's works in outpatient and just happened to notice the name on the surgical schedule."

"And called Nick?" She was outraged by the possibility.

He shrugged. "Something like that. She didn't know Nick had gotten married."

"That's unethical."

"What is? Getting married or . . ."

She was going to argue with him about confidentiality and realized he was trying to get a rise out of her.

"You're an extremely exasperating man," she said, and then she nudged him and nodded. He nudged her back and sent her flying off the sofa. He grabbed her arm and pulled her up next to him.

"Nick's sitting with Jordan now, and like I said, I'm here because she told me to keep you company."

"And you do whatever Jordan tells you to do?" She scooted forward and picked up a slice of pizza. The bottom was still warm.

"When it's something I want. You're lucky she didn't send Zack."

Zachary was the youngest. He was still in high school but was already as arrogant and full of the devil as his brothers were. According to Jordan "the baby" wasn't really wild but wanted everyone to think he was. He was giving his parents fits— after raising so many children, they were clearly worn out—but Kate thought Zack was adorable.

"I like him."

"Yeah? Well, be careful. I think he likes you a whole lot more."

She took a bite of the pizza and was suddenly starving. She devoured it and reached for another. Dylan turned on the television, relaxed against the cushions, and yawned loudly.

He wasn't paying much attention to her now. There was some sort of sports recap show on, and he seemed mesmerized by it, so she picked up the empty can and pizza box and took them into the kitchen. She was trying to figure out a diplomatic way to get him to leave.

She decided the direct approach was best.

"You should go now," she said as she returned to the sofa.

He glanced up. "You look worn out. How come you're so frazzled?" he asked.

"I'm not frazzled. I'm tired."

"You were crying before I came, weren't you?"

"No."

"Yeah, you were."

"If you knew, then why did you ask?"

"Why'd you lie?"

"It's been a difficult week," she said. "And I've had a lot of frustration. Crying sometimes helps me get rid of it."

"There are other ways to get rid of pent-up frustration." He wiggled his eyebrows after making the comment.

He was an outrageous flirt. Kate decided it was high time she called his bluff. She was determined to make him squirm.

"You would probably have heart failure if I . . ."

"If you what?"

She took a breath and said, "If I put my arms around your neck and kissed you crazy."

He stared at her without saying a word for a good ten seconds, mostly focusing on her mouth, and said, "Try me."

Oh, Lord. He definitely was not squirming, and she was bombarded with all sorts of nutty thoughts. She suddenly realized what she was doing and decided to get him out of the apartment as soon as possible.

"I'm waiting."

She could hear the laughter in his voice. "Maybe later," she said.

Her mouth went dry. She took a gulp of water. She couldn't understand why she was feeling so nervous, but she was. She didn't want him to know it, though. To give her hands something to do she took her time straightening up the newspapers.

What in heaven's name was the matter with her? She was feeling so unsure of herself—and embarrassed. That didn't make any sense. She'd known Dylan for a long time, and he'd never had quite this effect on her before. She was actually trying to block fantasies about him. She'd never been one to waste her time on fantasies—she lived in the real world, not make-believe. But now one image after another—all involving Dylan's amazing body— was bombarding her.

As she fidgeted with the papers, her robe fell off her shoulders.

"Where did you get all these bruises?" Dylan asked. His hand touched the base of her neck and moved down her arm.

She didn't push his hand away, but she craned her neck to see. "I didn't know that one was there. It must have happened when I fell."

"What about the one on your forehead? And the one on your arm?"

"Same fall."

He was making circles on her back causing goose bumps. She hoped he didn't notice what his touch was doing to her.

"Are you as accident-prone as Jordan is?" He laughed as he thought about that possibility, and then said, "The two of you living together . . . she's always tripping . . ."

"Only when she forgets to wear her glasses," she defended.

"So why were you crying?"

They had come full circle, and he was once again back to his initial question.

"You have already asked me that, and I've answered."

She took the remote from him and pushed a button. A commercial popped on. Turning the volume up, she pretended to be fascinated by a loud salesman dressed in cowboy attire who was shouting into the camera that he must be out of his mind. He was waving a lasso around as his scantily clad female sidekick, showing her patriotic flair with her sequined red, white, and blue ensemble, held up signs with slashed prices on each one. Apparently the salesman was only going to be out of his mind for a one-week extravaganza.

Dylan reached over, pushed the mute button, and said, "It isn't healthy to keep everything all bottled up inside."

Heaven help her, he sounded sympathetic. And that was her undoing. She could feel the tears coming again and was suddenly desperate to get him out of the apartment before she started blubbering.

"You should go home now." Her voice quivered. Why couldn't she control her emotions tonight? What in God's name was wrong with her? It wasn't like her to be so undisciplined.

"Maybe I should stay," he said.

The remote became a Ping Pong ball, going

back and forth between them. He had possession now and was scanning the channels. He turned his head ever so slightly and looked down at her. He had beautiful eyes. And they were looking at her with genuine concern.

"I don't need you to sit with me."

"Okay," he agreed. "Then I guess I'll leave."

"Good, because . . ." She couldn't go on. He wouldn't have understood a word said after that, anyway. She was sobbing. It was mortifying but impossible for her to stop.

Chapter Eleven

KATE JUMPED UP FROM THE SOFA THINKING she would try to regain a tiny shred of dignity and walk out of the room with her head held high, but Dylan had other intentions. He pulled her down on his lap.

For the next ten minutes he didn't say a word to her. He simply wrapped his arms around her, occasionally patted her awkwardly, and let her soak his shirt.

Once the tears stopped, the hiccups started. Her head was down on his good shoulder, her mouth pressed against the side of his throat. She told herself to get a grip and move away from him.

"Dylan?"

He smiled against her. "Yeah?"

"Don't tell anyone."

"Tell what?"

Dylan lazily picked up a strand of her hair and let it slowly slide over his hand. Her hair smelled like apricots. She was so warm and feminine, and he was very aware that the only thing between his hands and her body were a flimsy T-shirt and shorts.

Don't think about it. Yeah, right. Telling himself not to think about it made it all the more impossible not to think about it.

"Don't worry. I don't kiss and tell." He grimaced. His voice was hoarse and a little gruff.

"I haven't kissed you . . . yet."

He needed to regain control of the situation . . . and himself. "Listen. I won't tell anyone you cried. Now get off me."

She kissed his neck, deliberately tormenting him by tickling his skin with the tip of her tongue.

"Son of a . . ."

He jerked back, as though he'd just been struck by lightning.

Kate wiped the tears from her face with the backs of her hands as she sat up.

"You know what I think? You're a fraud," she told him.

Teardrops glistened on her eyelashes and slipped down her cheeks, and he suddenly wanted to kiss every one of them.

"How am I a fraud?" he asked.

She stared into his eyes and said, "You love to flirt when you think you're safe, but now that I'm . . . willing," she whispered, "and taking the initiative, you're shaking in your boots."

"I'm not wearing boots, sugar." He grinned. "And this is me shaking in my socks."

His hand cupped the back of her neck and gently pulled her close. He took his time as his lips gently touched hers. The contact of her mouth on his changed everything. This wasn't a teasing little kiss. It was hot, openmouthed, tongue stroking, and son of a bitch, it was nearly his undoing.

A shiver of longing rushed through Kate. She wrapped her arms around his neck and let him kiss the breath out of her, and she quickly became the aggressor. She felt his hand splayed wide across her back. How he'd gotten under her T-shirt was beyond her comprehension at the moment.

He tried to end the kiss, but she wouldn't let him even as she was realizing that seducing Dylan was a bad idea. A really bad idea. She had never, ever had a one-night stand before, but all she wanted to do now was lose herself in his arms and pretend all was right with the world for one glorious night.

Wham, bam, thank you, ma'am. She didn't really even need a thank-you. It would be one night of escape, pure and simple.

Oh, who was she kidding? There wouldn't be anything simple about it. At least not for her. Sex with the proper stranger who just happened to be her best friend's brother would be filled with problems and regrets. No, she couldn't do it. She would feel too much guilt tomorrow.

Why did she have to be so uptight about sex? Why couldn't she be more nonchalant about the whole thing? Her girlfriends, most of them anyway, didn't think it was a big deal to hook up with a different guy every Saturday night. But Jordan didn't do that, and neither did Kate. Jordan used to say that she had too much respect for her body to rent it out to any guy for a night. Kate felt the same way. There had to be an emotional investment, didn't there? No, no, then there would be strings, wouldn't there? And she didn't want that, either. Kate knew she could come up with at least a hundred other reasons why she was so skittish, but maybe what it really boiled down to was that she was terrified of being hurt.

And that admission tipped the scales. It was definitely safer to abstain.

Now that she had made the decision, all she had to do was implement it. She was going to have to stop kissing him first, of course, but oh Lord, that was proving a difficult challenge. Dylan was an amazing kisser. He could give lessons. He took his time, savoring what he was doing, as he lazily explored her mouth with his tongue.

She wasn't sure when she crossed the line from being smart and sending him on his way to unbuttoning his shirt and kissing nearly ever inch of his neck and chest. He was warm and hard and sexy. Her fingers gently traced the ragged scar on his left shoulder. The bullet had gone clear through, tearing tendon and muscle and just barely missing an artery.

Dylan grabbed her hand and wouldn't let her stroke him. He kissed her again, long and hard, and then tried to end it.

"Kate, we aren't going to do this."

He wasn't sure if she heard him. She was nibbling on his earlobe, driving him nuts. Then she shifted on his lap, and his jeans suddenly felt three sizes too small. It was damned painful. He grabbed hold of her hips to keep her from wiggling again. His voice was ragged when he said, "If we're going to stop, now's the time."

"Yes, of course."

She didn't resist when he lifted her off his lap. She stood next to the sofa and looked away as she tried to catch her breath. Kissing had never caused such a reaction before, but then she'd never kissed Dylan.

He also stood. They were toe to toe but he towered over her. He stared at the top of her head while he waited for her to look at him. His shirt was hanging out and was wide open, but he didn't bother to button it. His priority now was to get the hell out of the apartment before he did something he knew she would regret.

He had no business starting this. Granted, he

had had the hots for Kate since the moment he'd met her. The woman was built, all right. Still, wanting and doing were two different things. Dylan loved women, and flirting with Kate was always fun. She might give others the appearance of being a sophisticated woman, but he saw through that façade. When it came to men and sex, she wasn't all that experienced.

He threaded his fingers through his hair. He was throbbing with his need to touch her. To feel her naked body underneath him . . . to taste the liquid heat . . . to hear her moans of pleasure . . . to . . .

"I've got to go."

"Then go." She reached out and grabbed hold of his shirttails. "Unless you want to stay." She stared into his eyes as she slowly slid her arms around his waist. The feel of his warm skin made her want to do crazy things.

For one night only. Like the commercial . . . a once in a lifetime deal . . . take it or leave it.

"Kate, sugar, listen to me. You know I want you, but . . ." He wrapped his arms around her and hugged her.

"I know," she whispered. "This is a bad idea." She pulled back, but her eyes were still looking up into his.

His mouth settled on hers, his tongue slowly penetrated and then began to stroke hers until she trembled in his arms. Her passionate response fueled his own. He couldn't seem to get enough of her. He slowly eased her T-shirt up.

The second he touched the sides of her breasts he felt her shiver, and he knew then he was lost. He tore his mouth away from hers, kissed her neck, and then moved lower, all the while telling himself to pull away.

He listened to his own warning for a second but then stepped back, lifted her into his arms, and carried her to her bed. His mouth left hers long enough to pull her T-shirt over her head.

"This is crazy," he whispered.

"Crazy for one night."

She was nibbling on his earlobe as she tugged his shirt off. The contact of her breasts against his hairy chest made her shiver again. She helped him get out of his jeans.

Cradling her in his arms, he followed her down onto the bed. His hands caressed every inch of her body. She was just as passionate, as giving, and as frantic to please him. She rubbed against him, cuddled him between her thighs. He loved the feel of her soft body pressed so intimately against his own.

He left her long enough to see to her protection and when he was ready, he drew her into his arms and kissed her again, a hot, searing kiss that made her ache to have him inside her.

Her response stunned him. She became a wild

woman in his arms, and the sexy sounds she made drove him crazy. All he wanted to do was lose himself in her.

Her legs moved restlessly against his. "Don't make me wait any longer . . . please," she whispered.

He tore his mouth away and buried his face in the crook of her neck, inhaling her wonderful feminine scent as he thrust deep. He growled low with such intense pleasure he thought he would die from it. He heard her cry out, realized he might have hurt her, and went completely still. He could feel her throbbing around him, squeezing him, and damn, if he didn't know better, he would have thought this was her first time. He lifted his head and looked into her eyes, saw passion and tears there, but before he could speak, she closed her eyes and arched up against him.

He could feel the urgency in her. "Sweetheart, did I hurt you? Did I—"

Her nails gently scored his shoulder blades as she once again arched up against him.

The pleasure she gave him intensified. He slowly withdrew and then thrust inside her again. She increased the pace, demanding more and more of him until they were both mindless to the world around them. Only the two of them existed, and for that short time, there were no problems, no fears, no insecurities.

She reached a shuddering, heart-stopping orgasm before he did. She cried out and squeezed him, forcing his own climax.

Kate couldn't form a thought, couldn't make herself let go of him. She took deep breaths and tried without success to calm her racing heart.

"Ah, Kate," he whispered. He collapsed on top of her, grimaced when his left shoulder struck hers, and quickly eased the weight to his right side.

He could hear her ragged breathing and lifted up on one elbow. "Are you okay?" He looked into her eyes and laughed. "Damn, you're beautiful."

Before she could respond he ran his thumb across her lips. "Can you feel my heart? It's still trying to jump out of my chest."

Her hand curled around his neck. She leaned up and kissed him, let go of him, and closed her eyes. "You exhausted me."

He kissed the bridge of her nose and rolled away from her. It took every ounce of energy he had to get out of bed, but he finally managed it. Kate heard the bathroom door close behind him. She was still woozy from their lovemaking, but reality was trying to intrude. She rolled to her side, pulled the sheet up, and hugged the pillow to her. She could taste him on her lips. Don't think about it, she told herself. Keep your eyes closed and try to go to sleep.

She tensed when she heard the door open.

Light spilled across the bed, but she didn't look behind her. If he thought she was asleep, he would probably just leave. Had he come to his senses, too? Lord, she hoped he didn't regret what had happened.

She heard him yawn and felt the mattress give as he got back into bed. She tried to roll over to face him, but he wrapped his arms around her waist and hauled her up against him. He kissed the back of her neck.

"Are you asleep?"

His warm, sweet breath tickled her ear. "Yes." She gasped then, for he'd just covered her breast with his hand.

"You don't sound like you're asleep, sugar."

She couldn't believe it, but she actually was embarrassed to look at him. "What are you doing?" she whispered, clutching the pillow tighter as he began to caress her breasts.

"Making love to you. Roll over, Katie."

"But we . . . you're . . ."

"Sure am," he whispered.

"We can't . . ."

"It's just one night, right?"

"Yes."

"Night's not over."

Chapter Twelve

DYLAN BUCHANAN WAS A MAN OF HIS WORD. Their night didn't end until he left the apartment at seven the following morning. Saying good-bye should have been awkward, but Dylan made it easy. Kate was just drifting off to sleep when he leaned over her and kissed her on the cheek.

She remembered that sometime during the night he'd told her he would be tied up for the rest of the weekend, but that he would probably see her Sunday night or Monday. He was either giving her the "I'll call you sometime" line or he actually thought she was back in Boston for good. She didn't correct the misconception. She doubted that after everything they had done she would ever be able to look him in the face again.

So much for being a sophisticated, empowered female.

The doctors kept Jordan until Sunday. She was still too miserable with her splotches to complain about having to stay in the hospital, and when she finally got home, she slept the afternoon away.

Kate picked up carryout for their dinner. They spent a quiet evening together, and both went to bed early.

Jordan wanted Kate to stay a couple more days, but Kate was anxious to get home and tackle the problems there. She also wanted to get out of Boston before she ran into Dylan again. Every time he was mentioned Kate rushed to change the subject. She usually told Jordan everything, but this was different. Way different.

By Monday Jordan was feeling much better and the splotches had faded. Still, Kate wouldn't let her drive her to the airport. She took a cab. It wasn't until she was in the air and on her way back home that she realized how nervous she'd been about seeing Dylan. She sighed with acute relief and decided then never to think about him again. She couldn't change what had happened, but she could force herself never to think about it or talk about it to anyone.

Out of sight, out of mind didn't work. She tried to read, but she couldn't concentrate, and when she closed her eyes and pretended to sleep so the salesman sitting next to her would stop bothering her, all she could think about was Dylan's amazing body. The man didn't have any fat at all. And his thighs . . . oh Lord, those thighs . . .

Stop thinking about him. Telling herself to do

so didn't make it happen, though. By the time she reached Charleston, she was furious with herself. She had the discipline of a nymphomaniac. How could she go so long without sex and then in one night . . .

Stop thinking about it. Those words were becoming a chant in her head.

She took a bus to the long-term parking lot. When she was dropped off, she stood for a second and watched lightning shoot across the ominous sky as she tried to remember where she had parked her car. The bus had just turned the corner when she heard a car coming up behind her. She was standing in the center of the lot and hurried to get out of the way. The driver, she noticed, increased his speed. It was probably some teenager with a lead foot, she thought as she jumped between two parked cars to get out of his way. The car zoomed past. Kate tried to see the driver's face but couldn't. The windows had been tinted a dark gray. She shook her head as she watched him turn the corner on two wheels.

"Idiot," she muttered.

She wasn't just referring to the crazy driver. She was feeling like an idiot herself because she had forgotten where she'd parked the car. She dug through her purse until she found the parking ticket stuck in the back of her billfold. Fortunately, she had remembered to write down the number and the row on the back of the ticket. She was standing in section B, but her car was in D, row three. She headed in that direction, pulling her overnight case behind her.

Her battered, rusted-out car was parked by the exit, wedged in between two huge SUVs. She put her suitcase in the trunk and was just pushing the lid down when she heard the squeal of tires. She turned around and spotted the same white car barreling down the lot one row over. He slowed down a couple of times, then increased his speed again.

Kate had the sense that the driver was trying to find someone. He had to be a teenager, probably joy-riding around the lot, having a fine old time scaring people or, more specifically, scaring her.

The car was heading down her row now. She wasn't certain if the driver saw her or not. He was barreling straight toward her as if he was actually trying to run her down. She dove to the pavement just as the car sped by, and she whacked her knee in the process. Grimacing from the sting, she got to her knees. Her purse had opened and her lipstick was rolling under the Suburban, and she hit her head when she lunged for it.

"Okay," she whispered. "Now I **am** an idiot. A paranoid one at that."

She heard a car honk and thought that maybe the white car was terrorizing someone else. She finally managed to unlock her door and get inside. She felt like she was climbing into a pizza oven.

She quickly rolled down the windows but didn't turn the air conditioner on just yet because the car had been sitting a long while and would stall if she didn't let the motor warm up. Getting it started a second time would be tricky at best.

She looked for the white car as she drove to the booth, and after she'd paid for parking, she told the attendant about the crazy driver. He immediately picked up the phone to call security.

Kate didn't remember to turn her cell phone on until she was waiting at a red light before merging onto the highway. She found it in the bottom of her purse, and about twenty seconds after she pushed the button for power, the phone rang, notifying her that she had voice mail.

The message was from a contractor named Bill Jones. Kate had never heard of him. He explained he worked for the owner of the warehouse she was going to lease, and he wanted to meet her there to go over the design changes she wanted. He also mentioned that the inventory she'd sent over had been stacked in the back of the space and would be out of harm's way during the renovation.

What was going on? Kate hadn't even signed the lease yet, and she certainly hadn't authorized any construction on the warehouse. What had the Realtor told the warehouse owner? She waited until she was at another stoplight to return the call. Jones answered on the second ring. She pulled off the street and into a parking lot as soon as the light changed. She hated talking on her cell phone while she was driving.

"Jones here."

"This is Kate MacKenna."

There was static on the line and what sounded like traffic in the background. The contractor couldn't have been at the warehouse because that was located at the end of an isolated street.

"I'm so glad you called, Miss MacKenna. I need to see you at the warehouse as soon as possible. Time is money, and I've got my crews ready to start."

"I don't understand. Your message said that my inventory was moved over to the warehouse?"

"Yes, that's right. I'm on my way over there now. I'll be waiting for you. It shouldn't take long at all."

"Wait a minute. Who authorized the move?"

There was a long pause, and then he said, "I don't know. The boxes with your name on them were just there when I opened this morning."

That didn't make sense. Kiera and Isabel wouldn't have arranged anything like that, and Kate's two full-time employees were on vacation.

"Mr. Jones, I can't make any changes or authorize any improvements—"

He cut her off before she could explain that she wasn't going to sign a lease. With her bleak financial situation, moving her company now was the last item on her agenda. She needed first to figure out how to keep her company before she did anything else.

"Listen, you're breaking up. Just meet me there," he said. "The side door's unlocked if you get there before I do. Grab a cup of coffee and wait for me. I'm across town, and there's quite a bit of traffic, but I'm on my way."

"Mr. Jones, about my inventory—"

"If you want to move it, we'll move it for you."

Kate was so frustrated she wanted to scream. How many boxes had been taken to the warehouse? It appeared the only way to find out was to drive there and see for herself.

They'd have to be moved immediately. She could stack them in her garage, she supposed, but then she'd have to move them again when the house went on the market. Oh Lord, how was she going to tell Isabel and Kiera?

First things first. She tried to get her sisters on the phone to tell them she'd be late, but the answering machine picked up. She left a message informing them that she was back in town but was going over to the warehouse before she came home.

She was just pulling out of the parking lot to get back onto the highway when she noticed how low she was on gas. Since she was in an unfamiliar part of the city, it took her a while to find a filling station. She spotted a McDonald's across the street and decided to get a Diet Coke. She wasn't in a hurry to get to the warehouse because she didn't want to have to wait for Jones.

She arrived at the warehouse a half hour later. It was located at the end of a long winding street in an area that was earmarked for a renovation by the city There were already several trendy lofts just a few blocks away. Pembroke Street hadn't been touched yet, and there were potholes everywhere, requiring a lot of zigzagging. The empty store fronts with broken windows hadn't been repaired yet, but the projected turnaround in this blighted area of Silver Springs and the expansion that would follow were exactly what Kate had been looking for.

The building was still quite a distance from her house, but the rent was doable—or at least she used to think it was—and she had intended to put in a security system for the safety of the employees.

The employees she might have to let go.

"Stop feeling sorry for yourself," she whispered.

Kate pulled into the lot and parked directly in front of the side door. There weren't any other cars or vans around.

She was about to turn the motor off when her phone rang. She sat back, adjusted the vents, and picked up the phone.

"It's Jones. Are you there yet?"

"Yes," she answered.

"I should be there in about five minutes," he

said. "Help yourself to some coffee while you wait."

"No, thank you."

"You don't drink coffee?"

"No," she replied, wondering why they were having this inane conversation.

"Would you mind turning the pot off? Last time I forgot I nearly burned the place down."

That comment didn't instill a lot of confidence in Kate. "Yes, I'll turn it off," she said. "But about my inventory . . ." she continued impatiently.

"Yes?"

"I'm going to have those boxes moved tomorrow. They never should have been sent over in the first place."

"I'm really sorry if there's been a mix-up, Miss MacKenna. I'll do whatever you want. I'll see you in a few minutes."

He disconnected the call before she could tell him that meeting him was really a waste of his time and hers, that she wasn't going to be making any improvements because she wasn't going to be renting the space. Still, she did want to see how many boxes of her scented candles and body lotion had been moved.

Kate tossed her phone on the seat next to her, but it struck her purse, bounced to the floor, and rolled under the seat.

She unfastened her seat belt and was reaching for the phone when the engine began to make an all too familiar knocking sound. She knew what that meant. She quickly turned the air conditioner off and then the motor so that it could cool down. Otherwise, it would be impossible to start again. She leaned across the console and bent down to get her phone.

She was digging under the seat when the warehouse exploded.

The blast, like a sonic boom, rocked Kate's car and blew out the windows. Had she been sitting in the driver's seat, her face would have been slashed by the razor-sharp chunks of glass flying through the air. The shards pounded the hood and roof of her car and impaled the sides. Next came the wall of fire that blew through the building and rolled across the parking lot. The tires of her car buckled from the intense heat. The dashboard stayed in one piece as it was ripped free and propelled through the back window. It landed on top of the Dumpster across the lot.

Kate lay unconscious on the floor, unaware of the destruction surrounding her.

Chapter Thirteen

"Déjà vu."

Those were the first words out of Kiera's mouth when she was finally allowed to see her sister. Kate had been taken to the Silver Springs hospital and had just been moved to her room and helped into her bed when both her sisters came storming in.

"Haven't you been there and done that already?" Kiera asked with a worried smile. She was so overcome with joy that Kate hadn't been seriously injured there were tears in her eyes.

Isabel was beside herself. "You could have been killed. Why do you have to do things like this?"

"She was just in the wrong place at the wrong time," Kiera said.

Isabel was shaking her head. "That's it, Kate. I'm not going to ever let you leave the house again. I'll even give up college and stay home to make sure you stay put and out of harm's way."

"Isabel, you're not being reasonable," Kiera said.

"Reasonable?" She sounded frantic now. "Is it reasonable to get yourself blown up twice in one week? Is that reasonable?" She looked at Kate, pointed a finger, and stammered, "You scared me." She burst into tears and turned her back on Kate. "I mean it. I'm not going to college."

Kiera walked over to the bed. "She's been like this since we heard, but now that she knows you're fine, she'll stop crying."

Kate's head was killing her, and it was difficult to follow the conversation. She was in a dark room, but when Isabel pulled the drapes open, Kate winced. Isabel noticed and immediately closed them again.

"You were really lucky. Your skull should have been split wide open."

"Oh, that's a picture I won't soon be forgetting, Kiera," Isabel snapped. She grabbed a tissue and wiped her eyes.

"Jordan's called a couple of times," Kiera said, ignoring Isabel now. "She's worried about you."

"How did she know—"

"She called to say hello and Isabel told her what happened and how the fire department had to pry you out of your car. It's totaled, by the way."

"You should be thankful I didn't call Aunt Nora. She's only now unpacking, I bet, but she would have dropped everything and come back here. She'd make sure you didn't take any more crazy chances," Isabel said.

Kate closed her eyes. "When can I go home?"

"Tomorrow at the earliest. The doctor may want to keep you longer."

Isabel's voice shook. "Your face looks sunburned. It's probably from the fire. Kate, do you have any idea how close you came to being killed?"

"You aren't going to start crying again, are you?" Kiera asked.

"Sorry. I can't be a robot like you and keep my emotions all bottled up."

Kiera didn't respond to the comment. "We should go and let you rest," she said to Kate.

"Wait," Kate whispered, surprised her voice sounded so weak. "What happened?"

"You don't remember?"

She started to shake her head and quickly changed her mind. Pain shot up to the top of her skull.

"They think it was a gas leak," Kiera said.

"We heard it on the radio on the way over," Isabel said. "It must have been a gas leak because it's taking forever to put out the fire."

Kiera changed the subject. "You were fortunate the neurologist was here," she said. "I talked to him, and he said he was happy with the scans. It appears you're going to come out of this without any serious injuries."

"Kiera was concerned you jarred something loose in your brain," Isabel said.

"No, you were concerned," Kiera countered.

"Okay, it was me. The doctor was so cute. You know what, Kiera."

"Oh God, here we go again."

"I was just going to say that he would be perfect for you. I know what you're going to say," she rushed on before Kiera could stop her. "He's not interested in you, but you can't possibly know if he is or not until you . . . you know."

"No, what?"

"Make a move. Talk to him."

"Can we not have this conversation?"

Isabel ignored the request. "Maybe if you put on a little makeup and did something about your hair . . ."

Kiera folded her arms across her waist and said, "What's wrong with my hair?"

"You need to get a good haircut and not one of those five-dollar places, either, and you should get some concealer to hide those dark smudges under your eyes. You're sleep-deprived, and you know what? I blame it all on medical school."

"At the risk of sounding like you . . . duh."

Kate started to laugh and then groaned. Her head fell back against the pillows and she closed her eyes. "Stop making me laugh, and take your discussion someplace else. I just want to pull the covers over my head and pretend today didn't happen."

"But Kate, you still haven't told us why you were at that warehouse," Isabel said.

Kate opened her eyes. She started to answer and then stopped. "I don't remember. I mean I feel like I do, but I can't think right now."

"You don't remember anything?"

Kate took a long minute before answering. "No," she whispered. "Isn't that odd?"

"Don't worry about it. It'll come back to you. Get some rest now. I'll be here later to check on you," Kiera said.

Isabel wasn't ready to leave. She went to the side of the bed and asked, "Do you remember going to Boston?"

Kate smiled. "Yes, I do. And I remember coming home. There was a car . . . at the airport . . ."

Isabel patted her hand. "Yes, there was a car," she said. Her voice was soothing, and she was acting as though she was trying to reason with a three-year-old. "You're remembering your car. You drove to the airport."

Kate looked to Kiera for help.

"Isabel, would you hand me the phone before you leave?" Kate asked. "I want to call Jordan."

"Do you remember her phone number?"

"Isabel, the bump on her head didn't turn her into an idiot," Kiera said.

Isabel shrugged. She handed the phone to Kate and patted her hand again. "Tell Jordan we said hello," she said. "And if she wants to come see you, you better tell her not to," she added. "With your streak of bad luck, someone might run over her before she gets to the airport."

"It has been a horrible week, hasn't it?" Kate said.

"It can only get better," Isabel said as she followed Kiera out the door.

Kate hoped she was right. She turned onto her side and fell sound asleep.

A couple of hours later she called Jordan. She tried her best to sound cheerful, but it took effort. The attempt didn't work. Her friend could hear the stress in her voice.

"Tell me about that first explosion again," Jordan said. "Now that I'm not worried about bumps and lumps I can concentrate. Someone was trying to kill that artist, right?"

Kate went through it all again, and when she was finished with that incident, she told her about the crazy teenager joy riding in the airport parking lot. Last, but certainly not least, she told her about her latest mishap.

"I don't remember the explosion at all," she said. "But I keep thinking about coffee. Isn't that peculiar?"

"You don't drink coffee."

"I know. That's what makes it peculiar."

"How hard was that hit on your head?"

"Just hard enough to give me a headache. If I didn't know better, I'd think someone was trying to kill me."

Jordan laughed. "Don't be ridiculous. You've just had a bit of bad luck, that's all. Do you want me to come down there?"

"No, I'm fine. Besides, maybe this bad streak isn't over, and I don't want you hurt in the fallout."

"Don't let your imagination get the better of you. Remember, you're not a superstitious person, so don't overreact. Could I ask you something?"

"Sure."

"Did something happen between you and Dylan?"

Kate nearly dropped the phone. "Why do you ask?"

"He called here looking for you, and when he found out you'd left, he wasn't happy."

"I can't imagine why. So you really don't think someone might be trying to kill me?" she asked, searching for anything that would steer the discussion in a different direction.

"No, I don't think anyone's trying to kill you. I do think you've got an overactive imagination. Get some sleep and call me tomorrow when you're lucid again."

Jordan disconnected the call and immediately called Dylan. The second he answered she blurted, "Someone's trying to kill Kate."

Chapter Fourteen

DYLAN WASN'T IN THE BEST OF MOODS. HE'D just finished another grueling hour of physical therapy for his shoulder, and that had hurt like hell. The muscles were still throbbing, and though he had a prescription for pain killers, he wasn't going to take any. He wasn't trying to be macho. He had tried a couple of the pills last week and had hated the way they made him feel. The pills did dull the pain, but they also dulled his ability to think. He felt as though he was moving around in a thick fog. No, thank you. He'd take the pain over the fog any day of the week.

He was about to strip out of his clothes and get into a hot shower when Jordan called.

After checking the caller ID, he picked up the phone and said, "What do you want?"

"Oh, that's nice."

He smiled. "You're out of the hospital now. I don't have to be nice. And since when have I ever been a nice guy? You're getting me mixed up with Alec."

"No way I'd confuse the two of you. Alec's a slob and you're a neat freak, which is why you two made such perfect roommates growing up, but unlike Alec, you can be a real grouch sometimes."

"If you're finished with the compliments, I'd like to get into the shower."

Jordan was on a roll. "I'll bet you're real nice to the women you want to sleep with, aren't you?"

"Jordan, for the last time, what do you want?" he asked, deciding her comment about his sex life didn't merit a response.

"Kate's in trouble. The problem is, I don't think she realizes she is."

"In trouble?"

"Yes."

He rubbed the back of his neck. "I'm hanging up now."

"Listen to me."

She quickly explained what she knew about the first explosion and said, "If that wasn't enough for poor Kate, when she returned from Boston, someone tried to run her down in the airport parking lot. And then . . . Dylan, are you listening?"

"Yes."

"You don't sound like you are."

"For God's sake . . ."

"I'm right," Jordan continued. "Someone is trying to kill her. There's more, too," she added.

Before she could tell him about the second explosion, he said, "What exactly do you want me to do about it? Talk to whoever is in charge of the investigation? I doubt the detectives in South Carolina would want me looking over their shoulders."

"No, I don't want you to call. I want you to go to Silver Springs and check it out. You're on leave from the department, so you've got the time, and I know you're bored. I can't believe you're hesitating. This weekend you . . ."

"I what?"

"You saw Kate. What is it with you? Out of sight, out of mind?"

Yeah, right, he thought. He hadn't been able to get Kate out of his mind since he'd touched her, and that bothered the hell out of him. She was messing with his mind.

She obviously wasn't giving him a second thought. She'd left Boston without a word, so their night together had been what he and she had wanted it to be, recreational. That attitude should have pleased him. No commitment and no messy good-byes. One perfect night, no doubt about that, with no regrets.

So why was he so irritated she'd left without telling him?

He shook his head. She wasn't easy to forget, and that was all there was to it. It might take a couple of weeks, but then he wouldn't give her another thought.

"Dylan, are you going to go to Kate or not?"

"I'm thinking . . ."

He was in a strange predicament. He'd never been dumped by a woman before, and he didn't know how to feel about it. No, that wasn't true. He knew how he felt. Damned angry.

Had he ever treated a woman like that? Spent the night with her and then vanished? He shook his head. He hoped he hadn't. But had he?

He suddenly pictured her sitting by his bedside in the hospital. To this day she didn't know he was aware of her. He had opened his eyes and looked at her just as she was drifting off to sleep. He remembered he liked her being there.

But then he liked women, he told himself. Still, she'd been there for him, so shouldn't he do the same for her?

Jordan's patience ran out.

"If you don't go, I will."

"Ah, hell. Okay, I'll go."

"When?"

He sighed. "Soon."

"Tomorrow?"

"Yeah, okay. Tomorrow."

"Cheer up, Dylan. If I'm right, you might get to shoot someone."

Chapter Fifteen

ROGER MACKENNA HAD SOME BAD-ASS FRIENDS. They were "casino friends" who'd slithered up his side at the gaming table, introduced themselves, and became his best buddies almost overnight. When Roger won, they helped him spend his money. When his winning streak ended, however, his new best friends turned into sniveling and conniving snakes. They introduced him to a loan shark named Johnny Jackman, and when Roger was over two hundred thousand in debt at fifty percent interest, his friends wooed him back to the tables to lose even more.

All the sharks in town had a hands-off policy toward Roger because they knew, like everyone else in the gambling world who'd run a credit check on him, that when Roger's uncle Compton MacKenna died, Roger would inherit millions of dollars. If anything happened to Roger in the meantime, none of the sharks would get a dime.

Johnny Jackman had quite an investment and had his own crew tailing Roger at all times. This was an asset he wasn't going to let out of his sight. He didn't want Roger reformed either, so when he became infatuated with a pretty little thing named Emma who talked him into attending a Gamblers Anonymous meeting, Jackman became concerned. The next evening sweet little Emma was taken out of town.

Roger was told that Emma had been in an automobile accident. He went to the hospital, took one look at her bruised and swollen face, and went running back to the casino. Emma left town as soon as she was released from the hospital. Roger sighed with relief. He had felt such terrible guilt that he couldn't stomach the sight of her, but now that she was out of his life, he could forget about her. He could also forget all about ever attending meetings for his gambling addiction.

By July, Johnny Jackman was getting nervous. Roger had racked up a debt of an even seven hundred thousand dollars, and if it wasn't paid to the casino by the first of September, Jackman would have to pay it.

Jackman decided he couldn't afford to be a patient, nice guy any longer. He took Roger to dinner that night at Emerald's, let him drink a bottle of expensive wine, and then told him that if he didn't find a way to repay every dollar with interest within thirty days, Jackman was going to start taking body parts as collateral. He toasted Roger and told him he was going to start between his legs.

He made sure Roger knew he wasn't bluffing.

Three packs of cigarettes and a fifth of alcohol a day had aged Roger. He was only thirty-five, but he looked sixty. His hair was thinning and gray. His complexion wasn't gray, though. He had an alcoholic's red-veined nose, but the rest of his skin was yellow.

His nicotine-stained fingers shook as he lit another cigarette. "Where am I going to get that kind of money?" he asked. "You know I'm good for it, but not until my uncle dies. He's sick. It shouldn't take long. According to . . . my source, the old man is dying."

"Who's the source?"

"Someone real close to him. I'm not going to give you the name."

"Okay," he said, deciding not to press. "But your uncle could linger a long time, now couldn't he? If it's more than thirty-one days, you're going to be in a world of hurt."

"If you'll wait, I'll pay you a bonus. And there's a good chance I'll win big the next time I hit the tables, right?"

Jackman shook his head. "Your credit is used up," he said. "You're not welcome at any table until your debt is paid in full. Thirty-one days," he repeated. "If you don't come up with all of it, you're no longer a man. You understand me? You won't get a sip of booze to dull the pain. My associates will take you out in the desert, hold you down, spread your legs, and . . . snip, snip." He made his fingers move like scissors. "I might even tell them to put your balls in your mouth to stop you from screaming while they work on your penis. You do have balls, don't you, Roger?"

Jackman was the most successful loan shark in the city, and when Roger stared into his cold, flat eyes, he suspected that a real shark had more feeling. He didn't have any doubt at all that Jackman would do what he promised. He wasn't a man who bluffed.

Roger began to hyperventilate. He overturned his chair in his haste to bolt from the table. He made it to the corridor before he threw up. Jackman followed him, laughing.

"You're going to get me my money, aren't you, Roger?"

"Yes. I'll get it."

He grabbed his arm and jerked him back. He whispered close to his ear, "Your uncle's going to die real soon, isn't he?"

Roger began to cry. "Yes, he is."

Two hours later Roger took a cab to the airport and flew home on the red-eye. He was too scared and too sick to drink anything. He knew he had to get clear-headed. When he got back to Savannah, he was going to have to pay a visit to his uncle Compton to see for himself just how far gone the old man was and to assure himself the money would be coming soon.

Chapter Sixteen

Kate had wallowed in self-pity long enough and knew it was time to take charge. The trip to Boston had actually helped her get a grip on things. Dylan certainly had taken her mind off her problems, but she was determined never to do anything crazy like that again, and by the time she was released from the hospital a second time she was able to put everything into perspective.

She was going to have to make some huge changes. The first change was the most important to her. There would be no more secrets, and so she called a family meeting and explained to her sisters just how bleak their financial situation was. When she was finished, she put the stack of bills in the center of the kitchen table.

Kiera was rendered speechless. Isabel didn't want to believe any of it. She refused to hear anything that might discredit her mother. Kiera became the peacemaker when Kate demanded that

Isabel open her eyes and stop trying to make their mother a saint.

"How about we all agree that mother did the best she could," Kiera said, "and then let's move on. Arguing won't help us figure anything out, and right now we need to form some kind of a plan."

Isabel finally calmed down. "You're right, Kiera. Mother did do the best she could. We never went hungry, did we? And I got braces when I needed them, and she made sure all of us were educated."

Her sisters were quick to agree. "And Kate, Mom wouldn't have hocked your company if she hadn't needed to, so stop being angry at her," Isabel demanded. "She can't be here to defend herself." She didn't give Kate time for a rebuttal but said, "Okay then."

"Okay, what?" Kiera asked.

Isabel took a deep breath, folded her hands on the table and said, "I guess this," she nodded toward the stack of bills, "means no college for me . . . yet. Since Kiera is on a full scholarship, she should finish her last year of medical school, right? And you and I, Kate, are going to have to get jobs right away if we're going to keep the house."

Kiera was trying not to smile. "Aren't you the little planner? So there is a brain under all that blonde hair."

"No need to be sarcastic," Isabel snapped.

"I wasn't being sarcastic," Kiera said. "I was giving you a backhanded compliment."

"Isabel, your education is far more important than keeping the house. This place has served its purpose. We have to let it go," Kate said.

"But if you got a real good job . . . with your education . . ."

"Do you honestly think she's going to let the bank take her company?" Kiera asked.

"I don't think she can stop them," she said. "And we need money now, don't we? The electric company will turn off the power if we don't pay their bill. How long do we have? Hey, I've got an idea. You know what I think we should do?"

Kate was afraid to ask. Isabel was famous for coming up with nutty ideas. This one turned out to be a real whopper.

"Let's rent out rooms."

Kate wasn't certain if she laughed first or Kiera did. Isabel let them have their moment and then said, "It makes sense."

"Are you . . ." Kiera began.

Kate nudged her under the table. She didn't want Kiera to make fun of Isabel's harebrained scheme now. Their sister had just had the rug pulled out from under her. She was losing her home, and right now she thought she was also losing her college education.

"Even if we rented rooms, we couldn't make

enough money to pay all of these bills and a huge loan," Kiera said. She smiled as she added, "Unless we charged around ten thousand a week."

Isabel ran her fingers through her hair. "Okay, it was a dumb idea."

"No," Kate said. "You're brainstorming and that's good."

"If I were smart like you and Kiera, we wouldn't be worried about this. Kiera got a full ride through college and medical school. The money she gets even pays for her living expenses. I'm the drag on this family."

Kate rolled her eyes, and Kiera shook her head. "Now isn't the time to play the drama princess," Kiera said.

"I guess I'll unpack my stuff." She sounded pitiful. "It took forever to get it all inside Kiera's car. And I'll have to call the school tomorrow and ask them to send back the boxes I've already shipped with all my room stuff."

"Don't unpack the car. You're still leaving for college."

"How can I—"

"The plan hasn't changed. Kiera's going to drive you there in her car, and then she'll drive on to Duke."

"But where will we get the money for my tuition?"

"The initial fees have already been paid," Kiera said. She turned to Kate. "I could take out a loan, couldn't I, to pay the rest of her tuition and expenses?"

"That's a good backup plan, but for now I think I can come up with enough from my business account and the household account to cover the first semester."

"But how will you live?" Isabel asked. "You don't have a car."

"I'll rent a car. Since mine was totaled, the insurance company will be sending me a check."

"You won't be getting much for that old pile of junk," Isabel remarked.

"Could the bank put a hold on the money in the accounts?" Kiera asked.

Kate shook her head. "The bank can't touch the money until the loan is due."

"But that's like in less than a month away," Isabel said.

Kate got up from the table and went to the refrigerator to get a bottle of water. It was a luxury she would soon be doing without. Nothing wrong with plain old tap water, she thought.

She reached for three bottles, handed one to each of her sisters, and said, "When I first opened all of those bills and notices and read the letter from the bank explaining that our mother had signed away everything, including my company, I can tell you, I was extremely upset."

Isabel dropped her head and Kate hurried to add, "You have to stop trying to understand or defend Mom. You said it yourself. She did the best she could."

"Then why did you go and bring it all up again?"

"I'm trying to explain. I was stunned and furious, and I certainly wasn't thinking straight. Now, however, I'm back in control." She circled the table and sat down. "No one's going to take my company away from me."

"How was Mom able to use your company as collateral?"

"She was an equal partner. I set it up that way because at first I was underage and it turned out to be convenient when I was in Boston. She had the authority to sign checks and act on my behalf."

"But how are you going to stop the bank from taking your company?" Isabel asked.

"I'll work something out with the department store, maybe give them a bigger percentage for a lump sum up front. Don't worry."

"But if that doesn't work?"

"I'll follow Isabel's advice. I'll take in renters." She smiled as she added, "Maybe the men will pay more if I throw in a little something something extra."

Kiera laughed. The doorbell rang, interrupting the discussion. Isabel jumped up and headed for the door. "Maybe this is our first renter," she called out, laughing now.

Kate glanced at Kiera as she stood. "You think that could be Reece?"

"No," she said. "He's gone to Europe. He left a message for Isabel that he was leaving, and he hoped she'd think about their future together while he was gone."

Kate replied. "Oh dear. Well, at least he's away from Silver Springs."

"Kate, your first renter is here," Isabel called out from the hallway.

"What in heaven's name . . ." Kate whispered.

Both she and Kiera stood just as Isabel, grinning from ear to ear, walked into the kitchen. Dylan Buchanan was right behind her.

Kate was so astonished to see him she fell into the chair. Isabel introduced him to Kiera, who was moving forward to shake his hand. Kate couldn't find her voice to say hello. Or good-bye.

"We've heard so much about you," Kiera said. "It's nice to finally meet you. It wasn't possible for us to go to Kate and Jordan's graduation. Were all the Buchanans there?"

He nodded and smiled. "There are a lot of us. We probably would have overwhelmed you."

He deliberately ignored Kate as he carried on a pleasant conversation with her sisters, answering questions about Nathan's Bay and Boston.

Kate was still reeling from the surprise. All she could do was stare at him and hope she wasn't blushing. Her face felt warm, though. Was blushing a telltale sign of guilt? But what did she have to feel guilty about? As if she didn't know. How about having hot, amazing sex all night long with her best friend's brother. Yep, that would do it, all right.

Oh my, he looked good. But untouchable, she told herself, even as she was remembering how warm and hard his body had been pressed against hers. Enough. He was untouchable, she repeated. The one-night-only special was over and done with, and the sooner she got him out of her house the better for her peace of mind.

Could a man grow taller in just a couple of days' time? No, he just seemed taller because he towered over Isabel. When Kate was finally able to stop gawking at him, she noticed that both of her sisters were pretty impressed with him, too.

Isabel looked starstruck, and Kiera couldn't stop smiling; however, she was a bit more astute than Isabel. She kept looking back and forth from Dylan to Kate. She knew something was going on, but Kate didn't think she had figured out what just yet.

Isabel was telling Dylan something he found amusing. That lopsided grin of his was outrageously adorable.

Kate finally shook herself from her stupor and stood. "Why are you here?"

When he looked at her, she wished he hadn't. The smile was gone. She couldn't define the exact look on his face, but she would have to say it was somewhere between aloof and homicidal.

"Kate, where are your manners?" Isabel asked, shocked by her sister's surly tone.

Kate circled the table and offered him her hand. "It's lovely to see you again." Her speech took on a pronounced southern accent, but then it always did get thicker when she was nervous. She couldn't help that any more than she could help his effect on her.

He glanced down but didn't shake her hand.

Okay, she'd tried the southern lady approach. Time to get rude again.

"I repeat, why are you here?"

"Kate, what's wrong with you?" Isabel asked. She sounded appalled. "You're being terribly impolite." Turning to Dylan, she asked, "May I offer you something cold to drink? How about some iced tea or perhaps a soda?"

"No thanks," he said.

"Why don't we all go into the living room? That would be so much more comfortable," Kiera suggested as she hurriedly gathered the bills into a stack and set them aside.

Dylan wasn't paying any attention to Kiera or Isabel. He was staring at Kate. He knew he'd shaken her when he'd walked into the kitchen, and it was just fine with him if she felt uncomfortable. She deserved at least that for leaving Boston and not telling him.

As if she could read his mind, she said, "Why didn't you tell me you were coming here?"

"Why didn't you tell me you were leaving?"

"Leaving where?" Isabel asked.

"Never mind," Kate said.

She folded her arms and frowned at Dylan as she took a step toward him. "I spoke to Jordan just a couple of hours ago, and she's doing fine, so I know you aren't here because of her. Did she know you were coming? No, she couldn't have. She would have told me."

"Actually, she sent me," he said with a shrug.

She took another step closer. "No," she said suspiciously.

"Yes, she did," he insisted.

"Then you'll be staying with us?" Isabel asked eagerly. "I'm afraid Kiera and I will be leaving tomorrow, but I'm sure Kate would love to have the company," she continued, casting a warning glance at Kate to cooperate and be hospitable.

"I'm not going to be staying with you, though I appreciate the offer. This is a quick trip. After I talk to Kate, I'm going to check into a hotel. I'll probably be in town only one night."

"You must stay with us," she insisted. "We have the room."

"If he wants to stay in a hotel, we should let him," Kate said with a scowl in Isabel's direction.

"You'll stay for dinner?" Isabel asked. When she smiled, the dimple in her cheek was prominent.

Kate had the sudden desire to stuff a dish towel into Isabel's mouth. "I don't think Dylan—"

"I'd love to stay." He wasn't sure if he agreed because he was hungry or because he knew it would irritate Kate.

"You'll have a taste of southern hospitality," Isabel promised.

"Sounds good," he said.

His cell phone rang. He smiled when he saw who was calling, said, "Excuse me a minute," and walked out of the kitchen as he answered.

Kate waited until he was out of earshot and turned to Isabel. "Will you stop flirting with him? I don't want him to stay for dinner. I want him to go back to Boston."

"But I want him to stay," Isabel argued.

"What's going on with you?" Kiera asked. "From the moment Dylan walked in you've been acting so strange."

"Rude," Isabel offered.

"Nothing is going on with me," Kate explained. "I'm just stressed. That's all. I just need a good night's sleep."

"Do you know what I think?" Isabel asked.

Neither Kate nor Kiera seemed interested in hearing what she had to say.

"Isabel, go set the table," Kiera said. "Dinner's almost ready."

Isabel didn't protest. Kiera waited until she'd gone into the dining room and whispered,

"Something is going on. And don't tell me it's my imagination. I can see the sparks between you two, and the way you look at him and the way he looks at you . . ."

"He looks at every woman the same way. He's got a real fan club back in Boston."

Kiera was trying to signal Kate to be quiet because Dylan was standing in the doorway again, but Kate was looking the other way and didn't notice.

"Women seem to love him," she said.

He leaned against the door frame. "And I love women. No secret about that." His tone was neither boastful nor apologetic. He was simply stating fact.

Not the least bit embarrassed, she turned toward him. "Yes, you do," she agreed. "May I have a word in private?"

"Sure thing, pickle."

"Will you stop calling me that!" she demanded in frustration.

"Would you like something to drink before you have your private word with my sister?" Kiera asked. She pointed her paring knife at Kate as she continued. "You might want to fortify yourself. Kate isn't in the best of moods. She isn't always like this. She can be nice when she tries. When you get to know her better, I'm sure you'll learn to appreciate her as much as we do."

He smiled. He looked at Kate when he said,

"Oh, I don't think I can know her any better than I already do." He was happy to see that Kate looked like she wanted to punch him. "Why do you think I call her pickle? She's sweet one minute, sour the next."

Feeling the tension that was crackling between Kate and Dylan, Kiera said, "I think we'll leave you two so you can talk."

When Isabel walked into the kitchen, Kiera turned her in the opposite direction and gave her a gentle shove back into the hallway.

They were gone before Kate could stop them. She spun around and frowned up at Dylan. "Okay, so why are you really here?"

"Jordan seems to think you're in some kind of danger."

"I'm not in any danger. I've just had a little bad luck lately. Jordan's worrying over nothing."

"She said you were in an explosion. Why did you tell me the bruises were from a fall?"

"They were," she said. "I just didn't mention I fell when a bomb exploded."

"Why didn't you mention it?"

"You didn't ask."

His expression grew darker. "And somebody tried to run you down in a parking lot?"

"That's true, but it was just a teenager acting crazy."

He noticed the fresh bruises on her forehead and moved closer. Lifting the strands of hair cov-

ering the marks, he said, "These weren't there before, were they? These look new."

"They are new," she replied as she backed away
from him.

"Did you fall again?"

"No," she answered. "I was just coincidentally
in the wrong place at the wrong time. It happens,"
she insisted. "Nothing for you or Jordan to be
worried about. There's a perfectly good explanation for all of it."

Dylan turned a kitchen chair toward him and
straddled it, resting his arms across the back.
"Okay then. Start explaining. Why don't you
begin by telling me about this explosion," he said.

"Which one?" she asked.

Chapter Seventeen

"You're telling me there was more than one explosion?" Dylan looked incredulous.

Kate slowly nodded. "That's what I'm telling you. Jordan didn't mention . . ."

"No, she didn't."

"They're not related," she explained. "One was a bomb and the other was a gas leak. They weren't even in the same city," she added. "So you see? Nothing to worry about."

"Start at the beginning."

She groaned. "All of it?"

"All of it."

The set of his jaw told her he wasn't going to let it go until she gave him a quick summation, and so she went through her ordeals from start to finish.

"Okay," he said. "Let me see if I've got the sequence. Explosion in Charleston, hospital, Boston, attempted hit and run in the Charleston airport parking lot, another explosion in Silver Springs, hospital again, and home."

"Don't forget Reece. He was a trauma, too," Kiera said. She was waiting in the doorway for Dylan to finish his rundown.

"He was more of a challenge than a trauma," Kate said. She then related what had happened when Reece had shown up at the door.

"Why didn't you call the police?" Dylan asked.

"What could the police have done? He didn't threaten me or Isabel or Kiera," she said. "And you can't arrest someone for being obnoxious or sinister."

"Did he touch you?" Dylan quietly asked.

She shook her head but immediately contradicted herself when she said, "He might have tried to push me out of the way so he could come inside. He was convinced Isabel was hiding somewhere in the house."

"Touching you in any way is enough to get the police involved," Dylan said.

"She did think about calling them," Isabel blurted out. She had been listening from across the room. "After she told Kiera and me what happened, she said there was still time for her to call the police and make a complaint, but . . ."

"But what?"

Isabel looked at Kate when she answered. "I begged her not to," she admitted. "I felt sorry for him. I mean he's living in this fantasy world, and

I thought that as soon as he sobered up he would realize he needed to move on. Besides, I'm leaving town for a long time, and he's in Europe. I'll just bet he comes home with a new girlfriend." She nodded as she added, "I think he'll give up on me, but I doubt he'll ever forgive Kate. He thinks she's making me go away to college."

"Why don't you both go into the living room," Kiera said.

"You're in the way, Kate. Kiera and I need to get dinner on the table," Isabel said. She was thankful the conversation had turned away from Reece.

Dylan followed Kate. She sat down on the sofa and said, "Have a seat."

She should have been more specific, she supposed. He sat down next to her and was so close their arms were touching. She quickly moved to the end of the sofa.

"Okay," he said. "Let's go through it again."

"Why?"

"You might have forgotten something."

"I didn't forget anything," she insisted. "Go back to Boston and tell Jordan to stop worrying."

"She's convinced you're in trouble."

"And you came all this way to save me?" She pointed her finger at him and stabbed at the air. "I don't need anyone to save me. I can take care of any problems that come my way."

He was trying to be patient. "Kate, what is it I do for a living?"

She knew where this was going. "You're a detective with the Boston Police Department."

"Which is why Jordan asked me to help figure out what's going on. Now, who was in charge of the bomb investigation?"

"Detective Nate Hallinger. Why?"

"I want to talk to him," he said, and before she could argue with him he continued. "Is he convinced that the explosion was meant to kill the artist, Cinnamon?"

"She's in protective custody," she said. "So he must think she was the target."

"Huh."

"What's that supposed to mean?"

He ignored the question. "What kind of explosive device was used?"

"I don't know. I didn't ask," she said. "And I doubt that Detective Hallinger would have told me."

He nodded. His words were more clipped when he asked, "What did he tell you?"

"I don't remember much."

"Sure you do."

She pointed her finger again. "You don't need to snap at me. This isn't an interrogation room, and I'm not a suspect."

He obviously had gotten a kick out of what

she'd said because he looked like he wanted to laugh.

"What's so amusing?"

"You think this is how I interrogate suspects?"

"You had a tone."

Ignoring her sarcasm, he continued. "You were inside your car when the place blew?"

"Yes, I was. One of the paramedics told me that the fire department had to use a can opener to pry me out of the wreckage. Fortunately, I was unconscious. I don't think I would have liked opening my eyes and seeing all that metal pressing in on me. It would be like waking up inside a steel coffin."

He inwardly cringed. "You were extremely lucky."

She shrugged, acting as though what she'd just told him wasn't all that terrible.

He had the urge to wrap his arms around her, but in her present mood he thought she'd probably use that finger to poke him in his bad shoulder if he did. He made up his mind that after they had discussed the more important issues plaguing her, he would find out why she was being so prickly with him. But for now, if she wanted to act as though they barely knew one another, he'd go along with it.

His silence was making her nervous. She crossed one leg, then uncrossed it.

Dylan didn't believe in coincidences, and he didn't think that two near misses could be summed up with a streak of bad luck. Being in the wrong place once—okay, he'd buy that. But twice? No way.

"Did Detective Hallinger give you his card?" he asked. "I'd like to talk to him."

"Yes, he did. I'll get it for you."

Kiera was standing at the sink washing fresh vegetables from the garden. Isabel was folding linen napkins.

"Kiera, what did you do with Detective Hallinger's card?" Kate asked as she entered the kitchen.

Kiera tilted her head toward the refrigerator. "It's under the cow magnet."

"Oops. Kate, don't get mad," Isabel began.

"What is it?"

"I forgot to tell you Detective Hallinger called."

"When did he call?"

"About an hour ago. He'd like to stop by later."

"Did he say why?"

"Not really, and it would have been rude of me to ask."

"Isabel, you've got to learn to write down messages."

"I was using the phone and I got call-interrupted," she explained.

"Dinner's ready," Kiera announced.

Kate took the card back to the living room and handed it to Dylan. "You don't need to call him," she said. "Evidently he's coming over. Dinner's ready. I'll show you where you can wash up."

Dylan had been checking his text messages. He put the phone away and stood.

Kate led the way. "I would appreciate it if we didn't discuss explosions at dinner. I don't want Isabel and Kiera to worry. If they think there's a . . ."

"A what?"

"Problem," she said. "Then they won't leave."

"You're protecting them."

"Yes. Besides, my nearly getting blown up isn't suitable dinner conversation." Never in her wildest dreams could she ever have imagined those words coming out of her mouth.

He laughed as he followed her. "Is that in the etiquette book?"

Dinner was quite lovely by Isabel's standards. The conversation was actually pleasant.

As Isabel cleared the table, Kate and Kiera did the dishes. Dylan had offered to help, but Isabel was vehement in her refusal.

"You're in the South now, and a guest in our home does not lift a finger."

Kiera told him it was pointless to argue, and so after once again thanking them for dinner, he excused himself from the table and went into the den at the back of the house to make a phone call. Kate noticed he shut the door.

The doorbell rang a few minutes later.

"I'll bet that's Detective Hallinger," Isabel said. She put a platter down on the counter and hurried out of the kitchen. "Kiera," she called out, "you have time to go up the back stairs to put on some lipstick."

Kiera was filling the sink with soapy water when Isabel made the suggestion. She bowed her head and said, "She just doesn't stop, does she?"

Kate laughed. "Better you than me."

"The only reason she isn't focusing on you right now is because she thinks you've met your soul mate."

"Meaning Dylan?"

"That's right. I think I understand why she's trying to find someone for me. She doesn't want me to be lonely . . . or scared."

"Which means she is."

"Yes," she said. "She's had a harder time of it, much harder, this past year. She was so close to Mom. So the way I see it, we can't let her think she's on her own. I'll call her almost every day until she adjusts, but Kate, you're going to have to make weekend trips to see her, especially on parents' weekend. If I can get the time off, I'll be there, too."

"Okay, we've got a plan," she said. "Did you happen to notice Dylan was asking Isabel all those questions about Reece?"

"Yes," she said. "He was very smooth about it, too."

"I think he's on the phone now running a check on Reece. You know, finding out if he has a criminal record."

"Oh Lord, wouldn't that be something."

Kate dried her hands, handed Kiera the towel, and went to greet Detective Hallinger.

It was Dylan who actually let the detective inside. Isabel smiled and waited until Kate had made the introduction to say hello.

The two men shook hands. Hallinger was the first to speak. "How long are you in town, detective?"

"Call me Dylan."

Kate was about to tell Hallinger that Dylan would be going home tomorrow, but she never got the chance.

"I'm here for a while. Not sure how long."

The two men were sizing each other up, like two roosters in a henhouse, she thought, and then she realized the comparison wasn't flattering to her or her sisters.

"Where are you staying?"

"Don't know yet," Dylan answered.

"I hope you'll stay with us," Isabel urged. She turned her attention to Detective Hallinger and said, "It's so nice to see you again."

"Nice to see you, too," he replied.

"Won't you come in and sit down," she offered, gesturing toward the living room.

He and Dylan walked in together. Dylan was

talking, but his voice was so low Kate couldn't hear what he was saying. The detective took his notepad out and started writing.

"Did you offer him a beverage?" Isabel asked.

"You were standing right here. You know I didn't. Besides, this isn't a social call."

"Did he tell you what was so important?"

Kate was watching them. "I'm sorry?"

Isabel pulled her toward the banister and farther away from the men. She glanced into the living room and lowered her voice and said, "When Detective Hallinger called, he said he wanted to talk to you about something important. I thought he sounded kind of grim or something. I'm not going anywhere if you're in trouble, Kate. I want to know what the detective says. Maybe I could sit with you and listen. I won't interrupt."

"The detective just wants to tie up some loose ends," she said. "Nothing you haven't already heard." It was a lie, of course, and Isabel didn't look like she was buying it.

"How do you know that? He hasn't had time to tell you anything yet."

Good point, she thought. "I know because Dylan told me. And you trust him, don't you?"

"Yes, of course I do," she said. "But how is that possible? He only just met Detective Hallinger."

"Good heavens, you're suspicious. Dylan talked to someone at the police department."

"Oh . . . okay, then."

Kate was appalled at how easily she could lie. She was getting a little too good at it.

Isabel looked relieved, though. Kate hadn't realized how much Isabel was worrying about her. So maybe in this instance the end did justify the means.

"Everything's fine," she assured her. "And I will offer the detective something to drink. Okay?"

"Mother would want you to remember your manners."

World War III could be going on, but by God no one would be thirsty if Isabel had her way, Kate thought.

"I know."

She tried to go into the living room, but Isabel stopped her once again. "One more thing and don't get mad."

Kate sighed. "Who called?"

"Carl."

"When?"

"This afternoon."

"What did he want?"

"He just wanted to see how you were doing. He was very upset. He told me he was mortified about you getting blown up at his party."

"I did not get blown up."

"You almost did," she said. "Carl also said to tell you he's so sorry about everything, and he hopes you can find it in your heart to forgive him. He's kind of dramatic, isn't he?"

"He can be," she agreed. "I'll call him when I get a free moment."

"Oh, you can't call him. He said to tell you he's going away where no one can bother him. He wouldn't tell me where."

"Then I'll wait until he calls me again. Anything else?"

Isabel looked guilty. "Yes, the box lady called. She said she had something important to ask you." She rushed on. "I didn't tell you about it because she said she'd call back soon." As if on cue, the phone rang. "See?" Isabel said gesturing toward the sound.

Kate glanced at Dylan and Nate, who were deep in conversation, then headed to the den to answer the phone.

Haley George was on the line. To all of her clients she referred to herself as "the box lady." She was one of Kate's most valued suppliers. Her small company, which designed and produced specialty containers, had provided the octagon boxes for Kate's products from the beginning. She never missed a deadline, and Kate had come to rely on her efficiency.

"I'm sorry to call you so late," Haley apologized. "I realize your business is on hiatus right now, but I thought I should call you about this right away so there won't be a delay when production starts again. I know how important the details are to you."

"That's all right, Haley," Kate assured. "What's up?"

"The new spools of ribbon came in today. Your initials were printed in silver as always, but the ribbon color isn't your usual mint green. This one is more of a sage green. If I send it back, it could take another month to get the right color. I want to know what you want me to do."

Kate sighed. With all of her other problems, the color of a ribbon seemed at the bottom of her priority list right now. Nevertheless, the design and color of her packaging had become a Kate MacKenna trademark, and if nothing else, she was a perfectionist when it came to consistency and quality.

"Send it back," she told Haley. "And thanks for letting me know."

"Will do," Haley answered.

Kate hung up the phone. Maybe a slight variation in color wasn't all that important, she thought, but as long as this company was still hers, she would make sure it followed the high standards she had set for it.

Isabel stuck her head in the door. "Dylan's asking for you," she said.

"I'm coming," Kate answered.

"Try to be nice to him, Kate. He's Jordan's brother," she reminded her. "You could show him a little affection."

A little affection? If she only knew, Kate

thought. Affection had reached a whole new plateau in Boston.

Kate joined the men and apologized for making them wait, but neither seemed to have noticed. They were busy sharing war stories about their departments.

Hallinger had spread his notes on the coffee table.

"Nate was telling me the FBI and ATF are both involved in the investigation now, which is no big surprise," Dylan said.

"And that means it's a real circus downtown," Nate said. "Each agency wants to run the show. They're all stepping on each other's toes, and more are on their way."

"And no one wants to share information until they've finished they're reports," Dylan interjected.

Kate knew Dylan was simplifying the situation, but still, so many people thinking they were in charge complicated the situation and made the detective's job much more difficult. Assuming he was still part of the investigation.

"Where does that put you, detective?" she asked.

"I guess you could say I'm at the bottom of the food chain," he answered, smiling. "And please, call me Nate."

She nodded. "What will you do?" she asked.

"My job."

"This is his investigation no matter how many agencies get involved," Dylan added.

The two men had quickly become allies, and Kate thought she understood why. Their jobs put them in the trenches and in the line of fire, and neither one of them appreciated outsiders coming into their neighborhoods and taking over. It seemed to be a territorial thing.

"The FBI's going to give me the most trouble," Nate remarked. "They're all arrogant know-it-alls."

Kate looked at Dylan to see how he was reacting to Nate's comments. He was smiling.

"Did you mention to Nate that you have two brothers who are FBI agents?"

Nate flinched. "No kidding. Look, I'm sorry I . . ."

Dylan put his hand up. "It's okay. Nick and Alec are both arrogant know-it-alls on occasion."

"What do you know so far? Are there any leads? Any suspects?" she asked.

"It's already been determined that the explosive was placed inside a basket of flowers. The investigators can usually pinpoint the origin of the explosion," he explained. "The basket was on the ground in front of a table toward the back of the tent. Your table," he added matter-of-factly.

Kate didn't show any outward reaction to the news. She simply nodded. "I remember the flowers. They were beautiful. I didn't see who delivered them," she added, knowing that was Nate's next question. "I went inside the gallery for just a few minutes, and when I came back to the tent, there they were."

"I just drove back from the airport," Nate said. "I offered to pick up this hotshot expert. He leads the eastern national response team," he explained. "Which is actually part of the ATF. As it turns out, he's a real decent guy. He gave me some useful information. This is all off the record because he'll still go through the site with trained dogs and whatever else it takes, but he told me he knows who it is. He said he's been after this guy for a long time."

"He knows who the bomber is?" Kate felt an instant of relief.

"His signature," he corrected. "He knows his signature."

She didn't know what he was talking about. She looked at Dylan, and he quickly explained. "Every bomber has a signature. They're creatures of habit," he said. "Maybe it's the materials he uses, always the same, or maybe as in this case, where he hides it. This guy likes to hide the explosive in a basket, sometimes more than one."

"Flower baskets," Nate interjected. "They call him the Florist."

"Lovely," she whispered.

"He likes to blow things up in a big way. He's partial to buildings, but he's done cars and houses.

The thing is, no one's ever inside. He seems to go to great lengths to avoid hurting anyone."

"Until now," Dylan said.

Nate glanced at Dylan and then said to Kate, "You've got a good fire department in this little town. They know what they're doing, and one of them noticed the similarities and called Charleston P.D. to find out who was in charge of the Charleston investigation. That's when I found out you were at the warehouse.

"No easy way to say it," Nate said. "Someone tampered with the gas line, but Kate, that wasn't enough to cause the damage done. We checked it out and discovered it was—"

She was beginning to realize what he was telling her. "Another bomb," she finished.

"Yes, and you're the only connection between the two," Hallinger answered. He could see the bewilderment in her eyes. "So now we're wondering . . . who wants you dead?"

Chapter Eighteen

THEY GAVE HER A COUPLE OF MINUTES TO ABsorb the information. Nate was relieved she wasn't falling apart. He hadn't thought she was the type to become hysterical, and he was right. On the surface she was calm and in control.

Kate was screaming inside. She was thinking about the mess her life was in on every possible level, and said, "I don't need this now."

Dylan smiled. "When exactly is it a good time to get blown up?"

She realized how crazy her comment was, and said, "I didn't mean . . . oh, never mind."

"We're early into the investigation," Nate said. "And the leads could take us in a hundred different directions, but for your safety, we have to assume that you're the target and take the necessary precautions."

"What do you suggest?"

Nate looked at Dylan. "How long are you here?"

"For as long as it takes."

"Okay then."

"I'll need a weapon."

"I know. I'll clear it with Bob McCarthy, the chief of police here in Silver Springs. He'll check you out, of course, and he'll want to talk to you. I'll warn you, he's tough, and because he's getting ready to retire, he doesn't care who he offends. He'll give us a hard time, but—"

"Wait a minute," Kate said. She felt like the world had just gone into warp speed. "This is crazy."

Nate turned back to Kate. "Can you think of anyone who has a vendetta against you? Is there anyone who would profit if you were out of the picture, like a partner in your company?"

"I don't have a partner. I do have life insurance, but my sisters are the beneficiaries. The face value is quite small. The only person I can think of who would like to get rid of me is Reece Crowell."

Nate nodded. "Dylan told me about him."

"This has to be a mistake," she said. "I've been away for almost a year, and I just got home. I haven't been here long enough to make enemies."

Kate's back was beginning to throb. She had been sitting on the edge of the easy chair, too nervous to relax. Dylan didn't seem to be having any trouble, though. He looked very comfortable with his arm draped over the back of the sofa and his ankle crossed over his knee.

"Who owned the warehouse?" Dylan asked.

"I'm told it's a corporation," Nate answered. "I don't have names yet." He asked Kate, "How did you find out about it?"

"A Realtor called me. She showed me several spaces, but that warehouse was perfect for my needs."

"How'd the Realtor know you were looking for a bigger space?" Dylan asked.

"Carl Bertolli suggested she call me."

"That's interesting," Dylan said.

"He asked you to get to the reception early," Nate said. "Isn't that right?"

"Yes," she said. "No, wait. Actually my aunt Nora took a phone message, and I just assumed it was from Carl, but now that I think about it, that can't be right because when I arrived and was walking toward the tent, Carl called me on my cell phone and asked if I would please hurry and help set up. He seemed surprised that I was already there."

"He could be checking to make sure she was there," Nate told Dylan.

"Did you interview him?"

"Sure did," he said. "And let me tell you, that was no easy job. He's quite emotional."

"Yeah?"

"He didn't know anything, didn't see anything,

and he says he was on his way to pick up the guest of honor. I checked that out with the limo driver, and he verifies the time. I'll be talking to Carl again after the feds and the ATF get finished with him."

"They'll have to find him first," Kate said.

"Find him?" Nate repeated.

"Isabel told me that Carl called earlier today and told her he was going away. He does that," she quickly added so they wouldn't jump to any crazy conclusions. "When life becomes too stressful, he goes into seclusion. When he comes back, he's refreshed."

"I'm not going to wait until he's refreshed, whatever in God's name that means. I'll find him," Nate said.

"How often does life become too stressful for Carl?" Dylan wanted to know.

"Three or four times a year," she said. "You might want to talk to his fiancée," she suggested then. "Carl doesn't go anywhere without telling her. She has a business to run, so she can't take off as often as Carl can."

She gave Nate the name and phone number and added, "She's a lovely woman but a bit . . . high-strung, I guess you could say, so please try not to scare her."

"She's high-strung, and she's engaged to Bertolli?" Nate shook his head. "Now that's a pair."

"I think you're wasting your time with Carl,"

she said. "He couldn't have seen anything, and if you knew him as well as I do, you'd realize what a kind, sensitive, decent man he is. He's done so much for this community, and he—"

Isabel interrupted by calling Kate's name from the stairs.

"Uh-oh," Kate said. "Detective, would you like something to drink? A soft drink, iced tea, water . . ."

"Iced tea would be nice."

"Excuse me for interrupting." Isabel was standing in the foyer smiling at the men. Kate noticed she'd put on lip gloss and had taken the time to brush her hair.

Kate excused herself and went to her sister.

"Did you want something?" Kate asked when Isabel continued to stand there staring. Had Kate been that transparent around a good-looking man when she was seventeen?

Isabel took a step toward the living room. "Detective Hallinger? Everything's all right, isn't it? Kate said that Dylan told her you're here to tie up some loose ends. There wasn't anything more, was there?"

"I told you everything was all right," Kate said.

"Kate's helping the detective with his investigation," Dylan said. "Nothing for you to worry about, Isabel."

"That's right," Nate confirmed.

"Now will you stop worrying," Kate ordered.

"Who could blame me for worrying? You're so accident-prone . . ."

Kate didn't give her time to get worked up. "Detective Hallinger would like a glass of iced tea."

"He would? I'll get it for him."

"I'll help you," Kate offered.

Dylan was making suggestions when she joined them again. She started for the sofa where Dylan was sitting and then changed her mind and headed back to the chair.

"You do understand why I'd rather Kiera and Isabel didn't know about this, don't you?" she asked. "They're leaving Silver Springs tomorrow morning."

"Dylan filled me in, and I agree," Nate said. "We'll keep this quiet for now."

Isabel carried the iced tea in, handed it to Nate, and then told him it was a pleasure meeting him, and said good night. She shocked Kate when she kissed Dylan on the cheek. "I hope you'll stay in Silver Springs awhile," she said.

"You don't have to stay upstairs all evening," he told her, thinking she was doing so to give them more privacy.

"Oh, I have a few phone calls to make."

"Let me translate that for you." Kate laughed. "She's going to be on the phone for hours."

Nate waited until Isabel was out of earshot, and said, "Okay, Kate. You said you hadn't been home all that long." He was flipping his notepad to find a clean page.

"That's right."

"So it shouldn't be too difficult to retrace your footsteps and tell me where you went, who you talked to . . ."

Kate thought it was going to be easy and quick to recount her activities from the time she'd returned to Silver Springs. Why, it wouldn't take more than ten, maybe fifteen, minutes.

Her estimation was off by an hour. Nate kept making her go back and start over. She knew he was hoping she'd remember something that would lead to some answers.

No such luck. The only lead was still the same. Reece Crowell.

Nate then wanted to talk about her company. She hated doing it, but she had to tell him about the financial mess she'd found. He was extremely interested in the terms of the loan.

"You don't seem too upset," Dylan remarked.

"I was very upset at first . . . I had no idea my mother . . ."

"Yes?"

She couldn't bring herself to say anything that would give Dylan a negative opinion of her mother.

" . . . was struggling so. It was very insensitive of me not to notice how difficult it was for her. I also believe that when she took out the loan and used her assets as collateral, she didn't realize that my company was one of those assets."

"What are you planning to do about it?" Dylan asked.

Now that she'd had some time to think about it, she had come up with several options. She didn't discuss them but simply said, "I'll make some changes and work it out. I've got about three weeks, and that's plenty of time."

Nate asked her a couple more questions and then thanked her for her help.

Dylan walked outside with him and stood in the drive talking for another ten minutes. Then he went to his rental car and got his bag out of the trunk. Kate held the door open as he carried it in.

"Where am I sleeping?" he asked. He locked the door behind him and headed to the stairs.

"Alone," she answered.

"Okay, that's it."

He dropped his garment bag, grabbed her hand, and pulled her into the living room. He let go of her but was still able to back her into a corner by simply moving closer and closer.

"What's going on with you? And don't even try to pretend you don't know what I'm talking about."

The man could be intimidating when he wanted to be. He got that look in his eyes.

"It's . . . difficult . . . after Boston," she stammered.

"Why?"

"Why? Because you're making me crazy."

"Kate, start making sense. How am I making you crazy?"

"You're here," she whispered. "And you shouldn't be. In Boston . . . the night you showed up to keep me company and I came on to you and pretty much pounced on you . . ."

One eyebrow shot up. "You pounced?"

"Lower your voice, please," she whispered. "Pounced, seduced," she said. "Call it what you want." She tried to get around him to put some space between them, but he trapped her with his hands on either side of her. The message wasn't subtle. She wasn't going anywhere until she explained.

"You seduced me?"

"Yes, I did," she said. "I deliberately went after you. I shouldn't have, but I did." She brushed her hair away from her face and looked into his eyes. He was so close she could feel his heat. She had the sudden, insane urge to kiss him again. **Get over it,** she told herself.

"Try to understand," she said. "I had just gotten some awful news, and I felt like my world was crashing in on me. Then there was Jordan's surgery . . . and I was so scared for her . . . and after . . ."

"Yes?"

"I went a little nuts. You were there, and I . . . you know?"

"You seduced me?" He was trying not to smile.

"Yes, I did." She couldn't understand why he was having so much trouble comprehending what she was telling him. Had he already forgotten that night?

"I made the first move. I jumped your bones."

"You're telling me you had a lot to deal with, and you went crazy?"

Hadn't she just said as much? "Yes."

He wasn't smiling now. "Guess I was damned lucky I'm the one who showed up at your door with the pizza. Tell me something. If Nick had knocked on your door, would you have jumped his bones?"

She shook her head. "No, of course not. He's married. You're not."

His expression didn't leave her guessing. He didn't like what she was telling him. Tough, she thought. At least she was being honest.

"What happened was a mistake," she continued, ignoring his frown. "I shouldn't have . . ."

"Jumped my bones?"

She nodded. "That's right."

"I thought it was pretty great. Didn't you?"

"Do you need a testimonial?" She was actually trying to lighten the mood with her question because he was frowning so intently, and she was surprised when he nodded.

"Yes, I guess I do."

"It was wonderful, but . . ."

"Now you regret it?"

"Dylan, try to understand. I shouldn't have come on to you the way I did. You're my best friend's brother. I'm going to be going back and forth to Boston quite a lot, and I don't want it to be awkward when I see you again."

"So what was your game plan?"

She pushed against his chest, hoping to get him to move back, but he wouldn't budge. "Answer me," he demanded.

"I had hoped that I could come home and . . ."

"Pretend it never happened?"

"Yes."

She smiled and looked relieved that he finally understood.

"You don't do this a lot, do you?" he asked.

"Hit on men and take them to my bed? No, I don't. I'm not very with it, am I? And you on the other hand probably can't remember the number of women you've slept with. That's why I thought you'd be . . . safe. You know—no promises, no regrets."

"And you're okay with that?"

"I've upset you."

"No, you haven't."

"You're frowning."

"I'm just trying to get this straight. It's a little surprising, that's all."

"What is?"

"Your attitude."

"Why?"

"You thought that spending the night together and having passionate sex wouldn't mean anything to me?" She opened her mouth to protest, but he shook his head. "As I was saying, you chose me, used me, and now you want me to move on without . . ."

"Any guilt or worries."

He stepped back, smiled, and then laughed.

"Why are you so happy?" she asked.

"Sugar, you're a dream come true."

Chapter Nineteen

THE LETTER ARRIVED BY SPECIAL MESSENGER AT ten o'clock that evening. Everyone heard the doorbell ring, though they were each in different areas of the house.

Isabel was upstairs packing; Kiera was in the kitchen folding laundry, and Kate had spread the papers from the CPA firm on the coffee table to search for a copy of the loan agreement. Dylan had decided to do a home security check and was moving from room to room inspecting the doors and windows.

"I've got it," Isabel shouted from the upstairs landing.

"No, you don't," Dylan replied in a no-nonsense tone of voice as he came from the back of the house. He went outside and pulled the door closed behind him. Isabel watched from the side window.

"Who's at the door?" Kate asked.

"Some man with an envelope. Dylan just made him show him his driver's license. That's kind of odd, isn't it?"

"It's late," Kate offered as an excuse.

"I think he's scared of Dylan. If you could see his face . . ." She jumped back so Dylan wouldn't know she'd been watching when he opened the door.

"One of you needs to sign for this."

"Who would send something this late at night?" Isabel asked as Kate signed the form.

The envelope was marked URGENT. **That can't be good,** Kate thought. She looked at the return address and wanted to groan. The envelope had come from a law firm, and that definitely couldn't be good.

"Who's it from?" Isabel asked.

"Smith and Wesson."

"The gun company?"

"The law firm."

Concerned that the letter was delivering more financial bad news, Isabel snatched the envelope out of Kate's hand so that Dylan wouldn't see it. "Why don't we let Kiera open this," she said as she quickly headed to the kitchen.

Kate didn't follow her. If it was another unpleasant surprise, she didn't want to be the one to break it to the others this time. She returned to her work in the living room. So far, she hadn't found the loan agreement, nor had she found a

ledger summarizing the account since Todd Simmons, the CPA, had taken it over. She was just
about to go through the stacks once again when
Kiera interrupted her.

"Kate, you've got to read this." She held up the
letter. Her face was flushed.

Isabel followed close behind. "It's not about the
loan, is it?"

"No, no. This is from an attorney in Savannah
representing Compton Thomas MacKenna."

Isabel was trying to read the letter, but Kiera
kept waving it around.

"Who's Compton Thomas MacKenna?" Isabel
asked.

"I'm not sure. Maybe he was our father's father
or maybe an uncle. He could even be a cousin."

Kiera stepped over a file box and sat down next
to Kate. Isabel dropped down on her other side.

"Either read it to me or let me read it," Isabel
said. "The suspense is killing me."

Kiera handed her the letter. She read it out loud
and then said, "Isn't this exciting? I wonder what
this Compton Thomas MacKenna wants."

"It appears he wants us to come to Savannah. It
says he requests our presence." Kiera answered.

"I'm not going," Kate said.

"What do you mean you're not going?
Shouldn't we at least think about it?" Isabel asked.

An argument ensued, and Dylan walked right
into the middle of it. "Kate, the back door—"

"I mean I'm not going," Kate said. "You two can do whatever you want, but I don't want to have anything to do with those people. Our father's family disowned him when he married Mother, and I have no interest in meeting any of them now."

Isabel was becoming more and more frustrated. "But one of us has to go, and it should be you, Kate. Maybe this man wants to beg our forgiveness. He said the matter was of the utmost importance. It must be, because he wants us there tomorrow afternoon."

"We're supposed to drop everything and drive to Savannah with absolutely no notice? I don't think so. I'm not going."

"Going where?" Dylan asked.

No one answered him. The sisters were all talking at the same time. It was loud and chaotic, and very much like the home he grew up in, which was probably why he felt so comfortable. He leaned against the door frame, folded his arms, and simply waited for them to finish. Then he was going to give them hell for not locking their doors. Not only was the back door unlocked, but also the side door and the outside door leading to the garage. Damn, he thought, they ought to just put a sign out on the lawn, VICTIMS INSIDE.

Oh, yes, they were all going to catch hell no matter how long he had to stand there and wait.

Kiera yawned loudly. "I can't go," she said. "Isabel and I can't take the time. We should have left here yesterday."

"But we stayed because of you. You just had to go and get yourself blown up again," Isabel said.

"Are you kidding me? I did not . . ."

Isabel looked at Kiera. "Couldn't you drop me off at the dorm and backtrack to—"

She stopped when Kiera shook her head. "I don't have the time. I have to get back. As it is, when we get to Winthrop, I'll have only enough time to help you find your room and unload the car. Once I get back to my apartment, I'll be working twenty-four-seven."

"Do you see, Kate? You're the only one of us who can go."

"I'm not going," she repeated for what she thought had to be the tenth time.

"You're so stubborn," Isabel muttered. She nudged Kiera's foot as she walked past and said, "Make her go."

Kiera laughed. "How do you suppose I do that?"

Isabel noticed Dylan in the doorway and turned to him. "How about you? I'll bet you could make her go."

"No, he could not," Kate said emphatically.

"Go where?" Dylan asked once again.

Isabel realized that Dylan didn't know what any of them was talking about and hastened to tell him what the letter said and to catch him up on their family history. "We've never met any of our father's side of the family," she said. "And this is a wonderful opportunity to find out about them, which is why Kate has to go. We don't even know how many uncles and aunts and cousins there are."

"Why would I want to have anything to do with any of them? Not one relative even came to Dad's or Mom's funeral," Kate argued.

"Sorry, Isabel, but I'm in Kate's corner. If she doesn't want to go, then she shouldn't go," Kiera said. "Except—"

Isabel interrupted. "This man . . . this Compton MacKenna . . . maybe he wants to give us something that belonged to our father. If you don't go, we may never know what he wants to talk to us about."

Kate ignored Isabel. "Except what?" she asked Kiera.

"None of them wanted anything to do with us . . . until now. Wouldn't you like to know why? Besides . . . this would be a great opportunity to get some medical history. Certain diseases run in families," she pointed out. "Don't look at me that way. There could be heart disease and all sorts of genetic problems we're unaware of."

"How about I take one of those forms they make you fill out when you're a new patient in a doctor's office? Or maybe you could make up a list of questions for me to ask them. I could even check their teeth and report back if you want me to."

"I'm serious, Kate. We don't have any medical knowledge about our father's side of the family. It would be good to know something, but if you don't want to go, then don't."

"Okay then."

Isabel was so frustrated with her sisters she threw her hands up and started to walk out of the room. Dylan stopped her.

"Go sit," he said. "I want to talk to you." He added, "Especially you."

"Yes, sir."

"Please think about it, Kate. This could fill in so many holes and answer so many questions about our family," Kiera reasoned.

Kate let out an acquiescent sigh. "Oh, all right, I'll go."

"Good. That's settled then," Kiera said. "I'm going to bed."

"Not just yet," Dylan interjected. No one was going anywhere until he'd had his say about their total disregard for safety. After looking over their house, he had been tempted to submit it for the "what not to do" section of a home security manual.

"Did you want something?" Kate asked.

"As a matter of fact I do. I want to give all three of you hell."

And then he proceeded to do just that.

Chapter Twenty

DYLAN CALLED NATE TO FILL HIM IN ON KATE'S plans to drive to Savannah.

"I like the idea of getting her out of Silver Springs," Dylan told him, "even if it is just for a day or two, especially since it was a spur-of-the-moment decision and very few people know about it, but . . ."

"The letter coming out of the blue."

"Yes," Dylan said. "Kate and her sisters have never heard of this relative, so I've got to wonder, why now?"

"I'll check him out and let you know what I find. Make sure you keep me apprised of what you're doing. I'll call Chief McCarthy to tell him you'll be by his office first thing in the morning. It's his jurisdiction, and as for the legal ramifications, you won't only be on loan from Boston PD, you'll be under his command."

"That's going to be an interesting change. What about the FBI?"

"I'll let the agent running the show know where you're going."

"You don't know who's in charge?"

"I've narrowed it down to three candidates."

It was apparent Nate had an attitude toward the FBI. Dylan couldn't blame him. No detective liked being squeezed out of his own investigation.

Kate sat on the front hall stairs and waited for Dylan to finish his phone call. She was so exhausted she could barely keep her eyes open.

He checked the door locks once again and picked up his garment bag. "What are you doing?" he asked.

She finished yawning before she answered. "Waiting to show you where the guest room is."

"You look wiped out. Didn't you get much sleep last night?"

"I was in the hospital last night."

"Ah, Kate, that's right. You should be in bed."

She led him up the stairs to the guest room. It was the first door on the right and directly across from her room. She opened the door and stepped back so he could go inside. "You'll have your own bathroom. It's—"

"I'll find it. Night."

He shut the door in her face.

She stood there for several seconds staring at

the door trying to figure out what had just happened. He hadn't been rude or angry. In fact, he'd been smiling.

She suddenly felt very foolish. She'd been expecting him to try to kiss her good night, but that apparently was the last thing on his mind.

She went into her room and closed the door. All right then. Her "that was then, this is now" explanation had obviously gotten through to him. And that's exactly what she wanted, wasn't it? So how come she was feeling so disgruntled? And come to think of it, how come he hadn't argued at all when she'd told him it was fine and dandy to move on? Not a single word of protest had he uttered.

She couldn't stop thinking about his behavior while she brushed her teeth and got ready for bed. Women were like fish in the sea, and Dylan was such a playboy he would always have a new catch.

Kate tried to muster up some disgust over his sexual conquests but couldn't quite manage it. So she tried anger. Dylan was an arrogant jerk. How dare he show up on her doorstep without warning. Who did he think he was? Walking in and taking over like that.

She had to admit, however, she did feel safer with him in the house—and the way he talked to Isabel about safety had made an impact. After he had come down hard on all of them because of their lackadaisical attitude about security, his focus had turned to Kate's younger sister. When he was finished with her, Isabel knew everything there was to know about deadbolts, and then some. She wouldn't be walking anywhere on campus without looking over her shoulder or being aware of her surroundings. He had been very candid with her, and yet he hadn't scared her. Kate had watched as Isabel sat transfixed by Dylan's calm instructions.

He'd actually been very sweet. He had no business being sweet. How was she ever going to keep this relationship platonic and forget about him when he went back to Boston if he continued to do caring things for her and her sisters?

Why oh why did she go to bed with him? That had been a huge mistake, and then what had she done to top that? She'd given him the "It means nothing to me and I'm sure nothing to you, so move along" speech.

She got into bed and pulled the sheet up. And how had he responded? She was a dream come true. That's what he'd said all right.

"Great," she whispered. "I'm a frickin' dream come true."

Chapter Twenty-one

Kiera's plan to be on the highway by seven didn't quite work out. Isabel was on time; she wasn't. It was almost eight before they were finally ready to leave. Kate stood by the car for a final good-bye and tried to assure them that everything was going to be fine.

"I hate leaving you with this financial mess," Kiera said.

"We've been over this. We've got a plan, right? So stop worrying."

"You'll let me know what's going on? Don't try to shield me, Kate," Isabel said.

"I'll tell you everything," she promised.

"I'm glad Dylan's here," Kiera said. "You've had such a hellacious week, and it will be nice for you to have company driving to Savannah."

Dylan locked the front door and took a seat on the top step of the porch waiting for the good-byes to end so he and Kate could leave. He'd already packed his rental car and was impatient to get going.

Kate said something to her sisters, and they all turned to smile at him.

Dylan looked at his watch, and when he glanced up, he was momentarily struck by the beauty of the three girls facing him.

Though they looked like sisters, there was something unique about each one. He'd already figured out that Isabel was a charmer and a people pleaser. She was about five-five, and her hair was blond with streaks of honey. Her eyes were as big and as round as Kate's, but the color wasn't the same. Kate's were a vivid blue and were stunning framed by her dark chestnut hair. Isabel's eyes were more of a blue-green, like the ocean. Kiera was taller than the other two, and in the sunlight he could see the streaks of red in her strawberry blond hair. She had freckles on her nose like Kate, but they were on her cheeks, too. She reminded Dylan of a well-scrubbed girl next door who just happened to have a very nice body. She was the most laid-back of the three, and he thought she was also a peacemaker in the family.

Kate was neither a charmer nor a peacemaker. She gave as good as she got, and then some, at least with him, anyway. She stood up to him, and he liked that. He must, he thought, because here he was, back for more.

Kate had a little something extra that drew him

to her. On the surface she was one tough cookie. He imagined she was a barracuda when she negotiated a business contract, but there was a vulnerability he could see that pulled at him. She was talented and a smart businesswoman, but he didn't think she was smart about men. Maybe that was why he had been able to get her into bed so quickly. He knew she regretted their night together, but he sure as certain didn't. The fact was, he couldn't stop thinking about it.

One thought led to another, and it didn't take long before he was picturing her naked in his arms. Not a good idea to be daydreaming about that now, he realized.

"Kate, wind it up. We've got to get going."

She ignored him and waited until Kiera had backed out of the driveway before she finally turned away.

She had tears in her eyes, and she knew he'd noticed. He didn't say anything. He simply walked to the car, opened the passenger door, and waited for her to get in.

"I feel like I'm forgetting something. My purse . . ."

"In the car."

"What about the overnight bag you made me pack in case we have to stay in Savannah, which by the way is totally unnecessary since we'll have plenty of time to get back home . . ."

"You mentioned that."

"I'm sure I left my bag in the foyer."

"It's in the trunk. Get in, pickle."

She gave him what he had begun to call "the look." He translated it to mean, "Call me pickle again and I'll deck you."

"What about . . ."

He gave her a little nudge. "The iron's turned off."

"I didn't turn it on . . . did I?"

"Kate, get in the car."

She stopped arguing. Once she was settled and had clipped her seat belt on, she said, "Why do we have to leave so soon? We have plenty of time."

"No, we don't."

He didn't explain until they had pulled away from the house. "We need to stop at the police station, and I don't know how long that's going to take. Chief McCarthy's waiting."

She gave him directions. The station was only a mile from her house. The parking lot was in the back of a brick, two-story building that looked old and worn. And charming, he thought, if such a word could be used to describe a police station.

Ivy crept up the back of the building nearly to the roof, and the brick path that led to the front door had chunks broken off.

"Is there a jail inside?" he asked.

"I think so, either in the back or upstairs."

The front door had recently been painted a

shiny black. He noticed the white shutters flanking the windows had been painted, too.

He'd never seen anything like it . . . for a police station, that is.

"It looks like a bed and breakfast place."

As soon as he walked inside, though, he felt as though he was back on familiar ground. The floors were an ugly gray linoleum; the walls were a dingy pea green, and the receptionist was just as old and surly as the one back in Boston. The station even smelled the same—must and sweat and Pine-Sol. He loved it.

Chief McCarthy came out of his office to meet both of them. He was a heavyset man with a permanent scowl on his face and the grip of a weight lifter in his handshake.

He offered Kate a cup of coffee and asked her to wait in the outer office.

Kate took a seat on one of the gray metal chairs against the wall and pulled her black smart phone out of her bag to check messages. Haley had called again, probably about the ribbon on back order, she thought. Nothing she could do about it now, so she decided she'd call her from the car.

If she had had her briefcase with her, she could go through some of her other notes. Had she left that at home, or had Dylan put it in the trunk?

The chair was hard and uncomfortable. Kate sat back, crossed one leg over the other, and tried to remain patient. What was taking so long? It seemed that Dylan had been in the office for at least fifteen minutes. She noticed the receptionist was repeatedly glancing at her from behind her computer screen.

Kate looked at her skirt to make sure it hadn't hiked up, then checked her blouse to make certain all the buttons were buttoned.

The woman's head was hidden behind the computer monitor when she said, "I like your candles."

"I'm sorry?"

She leaned to the side. "I said I like your candles."

"Thank you," she said. "I'm happy to hear that."

The receptionist was blushing. "I'm thinking about buying some of your lotion next, but I'm not sure which scent I want. Got any suggestions?"

"Let me see if I have any samples." Kate dug through her purse and found three. "Try these three," she said. "They're all different: Isabel, Kiera, and Leah."

The woman was thrilled. She introduced herself and shook Kate's hand. "You know you're a celebrity around town."

"I am?" she asked, smiling. "My candles?"

"Oh, no, dear. They're lovely, of course, but you're famous because you nearly blew yourself up at the old warehouse."

She made it sound like Kate had done it on purpose. Kate was about to respond to the woman's assessment, but the door opened, and Dylan and the chief walked out of the office. She immediately noticed the gun in a holster at Dylan's side. He had a box in his hand. Probably extra bullets, she thought. Can't have enough of those, can he?

"You're in good hands with this boy, Miss MacKenna. He's got an impressive record and his superior in Boston was mighty aggravated he was doing a job for Silver Springs. He finally agreed but made sure I knew it was temporary. They want him back," he added with a nod.

She couldn't stop looking at the gun. Images of Dylan lying in the hospital bed flashed into her mind. She realized his job required that he carry a gun, and as McCarthy had just confirmed, Dylan was very good at that job, but still, just seeing the weapon made her feel queasy. She smiled at the chief and said, "Yes, I am in good hands with this boy."

McCarthy walked them to the door and held it open. In parting he called, "Try not to get yourself blown up again, Miss MacKenna."

Kate walked ahead of Dylan to the car. "The way people are acting around here you'd think I was some kind of walking detonter—wherever I go there's an explosion," she complained.

Dylan laughed. "I think you've brought a little

more excitement to Silver Springs than they're used to."

He pulled out of the parking lot but stopped at the corner. "Want to give me directions?"

"The most direct route to get to the highway is to take Main Street, which is your next left, but there will be a lot of traffic this time of morning."

"Compared to Boston, this is nothing," he said a few minutes later. "It's nice not to have to be so aggressive. The noise level is so much lower here. I like that."

Kate adjusted the air conditioner vent so it wouldn't blow on her face and tried to relax.

"What did you think of Chief McCarthy?"

"Cranky," he said. "The man is definitely cranky. I don't think he knows how to smile. The way he was frowning at me when he took me into his office made me think he was going to give me trouble, and even after he started complimenting me on my record, the guy was still frowning. It took me a while to catch on." He shook his head and added, "He kind of reminds me of my father."

"Judge Buchanan isn't cranky. He's a dear man. He's always so kind to me."

"He likes you," he said.

"Jordan and Sydney still call him Daddy."

"His sons don't. We call him 'sir.' He was tough with us when we were growing up, but I guess he had to be. Keeping six boys out of trouble couldn't have been easy."

Kate was remembering what Judge Buchanan was like in the hospital when he was waiting with his family for Dylan to come out of surgery. The time had dragged on and on, and the anguish in his eyes was heartbreaking to see. He might have been hard-nosed with his sons, but he also loved them fiercely.

"I hate hospitals."

She hadn't realized she'd whispered the thought out loud until Dylan said, "I imagine you do." Responding to the sadness he heard in her voice, he put his hand on top of hers and said, "What made you think about hospitals?"

She didn't want to talk about it. "I just did," she said without an explanation.

The highway traffic was light. Dylan set the cruise control and sat back.

"I talked to Nate early this morning," he said.

"You did?"

"I let him know last night that you were going to Savannah," he explained, "and I asked him to check out a couple of things."

She turned toward him. "Yes?"

"Remember he had already told us that a corporation owns the warehouse that blew, but he was having trouble finding out who the shareholders were. He finally was able to dig through the layers, and guess who has controlling interest."

"Who?"

"Carl Bertolli."

She certainly hadn't expected to hear his name and immediately thought there had to be a mistake. "Carl? Are you sure? He said Carl? That can't be right."

"You think Nate made it up?" he asked, smiling.

"No, of course not, but . . . Carl? He never said anything to me . . . why wouldn't he tell me he owned the warehouse?"

"Obviously because he didn't want you to know."

"Did Jennifer know?" she asked. "Surely she did. She's a Realtor, for heaven's sake. She'd have to know who the owners were. Did anyone talk to her yet?"

"She and her family are camping, but she's scheduled to be back at work tomorrow morning. Nate could have tracked her down, but he'd already gotten the names of the shareholders, so he's waiting until tomorrow to question her. Nate's guessing Carl instructed her not to tell you."

Kate couldn't wrap her mind around any of it. It just didn't make any sense.

"What would Carl have to gain by blowing up his property? Even if he had the place heavily insured." Her mind was racing. "He doesn't need the money. And tell me, please, what would he gain by killing me? No, it doesn't make any sense."

"You can bet the FBI is digging into Carl's financials right now. If there's a motive, they'll find it."

"The FBI won't find anything."

"You might be surprised. Everyone has secrets, and Carl could have a couple of big ones."

She couldn't accept it. "I've got to think about this."

"I'll give you something else to think about. Compton Thomas MacKenna was, in fact, your great uncle."

"Was?"

"That's right. He died last night, exactly two hours before the letter went out. According to his attorney, Anderson Smith, Compton left specific instructions about the notification of his relatives."

"Then why—"

"You're not going to the attorney's office to meet Compton as the letter implied. You and your sisters have been summoned for the reading of his last will and testament."

She was shocked by the disappointment she felt. "Then I guess I can't ask him any questions, can I? You might as well turn around. I'm not interested in anything the man left."

"Your sisters might be interested."

"I'll be happy to give them the attorney's phone number, and they can talk to him. The next exit is coming up. We can turn around there."

"Kate, you and your sisters weren't the only ones to receive letters. Your cousins will also be there. Now are you interested?"

"Just cousins?"

"I can't answer that. The attorney only mentioned cousins to Nate. Smith also told him that the cousins don't know you're coming. Fact is, he was certain they don't even know you and your sisters exist."

She was even more disheartened. "I'm definitely not interested, then. Slow down. You'll miss the exit."

The exit ramp was a blur as they sped by.

"Dylan, I told you I'm not interested. There isn't any reason for me to go to the reading now. If these cousins haven't been told anything about Kiera and Isabel and me, they certainly won't be able to answer any of my questions, now will they? They were obviously kept in the dark by their parents."

She thought about it another moment and said, "I know Kiera would like medical history, but—"

"There's more," he interrupted.

"Oh?"

"The attorney has photos of your father and other mementos that belonged to him."

She nodded. "Okay, now I'm interested."

Chapter Twenty-two

Roger mackenna came armed with a .45 to the reading of the will.

He arrived at the prestigious law firm of Smith and Wesson twenty minutes before the scheduled appointment, but because it was the lunch hour and the area was filled with trendy, upscale bistros, he had to park three blocks from the square. He got out of the car, leaned against the door, and took one last drag of his cigarette. He'd smoked it down to the filter and could feel it burning his lips as he sucked the nicotine in. He tossed it away and immediately reached for another.

His head felt as though it were going to explode. He was in no condition to walk anywhere today, but he wasn't about to miss this appointment even if he had to crawl to get there.

He had no one but himself to blame for his misery. Upon hearing the glorious news that his uncle had finally died, he'd cried out with joy and then proceeded to get roaring drunk. His private celebration lasted well into the middle of the night.

Walking in the heat and humidity was making him nauseated. He finally reached the square and would have cut across the park, but it was crowded with office workers taking in the sun while they ate their packed lunches.

By the time he stopped in front of the attorney's office building he was exhausted, out of breath, and coated with a clammy sweat. He was anxious to get inside. Pulling the door open, he rushed in. He felt a blast of cold air brush his face a scant second before the alarm sounded. The noise was surprisingly dignified. It wasn't a loud, piercing siren, but a quiet and steady pulsating beep like a heart monitor.

Two armed guards rushed toward him from opposite corridors. Like a jackal, he snarled at them and tried to bluff his way past. The ploy didn't work, and he was given the choice of either leaving the premises or handing over his weapon.

He pulled the gun out of his vest pocket and gave it to the guard standing directly in front of him.

The man glanced down at the weapon, and said, "Is this loaded?"

"Of course it's loaded," Roger snapped. "Why would I carry an empty gun?"

"Did you realize you failed to put the safety

on?" he asked as he lifted the gun to show Roger and then flipped the lever. "You wouldn't want this to go off accidentally, now would you?"

Roger didn't answer. The guard on his left drew his attention when he said, "Sir, do you have a permit to carry a concealed weapon?"

"I most certainly do," he answered indignantly. It was a lie. He'd gotten the gun from his brother Ewan for protection. "I'll want that gun back when I leave."

They didn't ask his permission when they patted him down to make sure the gun was the only weapon he was carrying. Roger was outraged. He was a multimillionaire now and should not be treated this way.

"Do you know who I am?"

He assumed they didn't when neither one of them answered. They stepped out of the way and let him go forward.

He was fuming as he stormed across the tile floor toward the receptionist. He practically shouted his full name so the guards would be sure to hear.

The receptionist asked him to wait while she called upstairs to announce him.

"Mr. Smith's assistant will be right down to escort you to his offices," she said.

Roger didn't have to wait long. He looked up to the top of the winding staircase just as a young man appeared on the landing. He was elegantly dressed in a spotless dark suit, crisp white shirt, and tie. He neither introduced himself nor shook Roger's hand. He simply said, "Mr. MacKenna, if you'll follow me please."

He followed the assistant up the stairs and down a corridor and was shown into the attorney's spacious outer office. The carpet was thick; the furniture was plush, and the paintings on the walls appeared to be originals.

The place reeked of money, and Roger was impressed. Though he'd never met his uncle's attorney, he used his first name when he asked, "Where's Anderson?"

"Mr. Smith will be here momentarily. May I offer you something to drink while you wait?"

Roger ordered bourbon straight up, and as the assistant was leaving to fetch it, he called out, "And bring the bottle. My brothers and I will want to . . ." He caught himself before he said, "celebrate," and substituted, "toast our uncle."

Bryce was shown into the office a few minutes later. He spotted the tray on the coffee table and immediately helped himself to a drink. There was an ice bucket, but he didn't bother. He took a long gulp, expelled a sigh, and finally acknowledged his brother's presence.

They had not seen each other in over six months, and Roger was shocked at the change. The flesh seemed to hang from Bryce's body. A mannequin had more fat than his brother. His eyes had a yellow tinge to them, and his skin was pasty. **Cirrhosis,** Roger thought. **Up close and personal.**

"It's been a long time," Roger said.

"Yes," Bryce agreed. "When was that?"

"Uncle MacKenna's birthday bash."

"Ah, that's right."

"How are you feeling, Bryce?"

His brother immediately went on the defensive. "I'm feeling fine. Why would you ask me that? Don't I look fine?"

Was he daring him to tell the truth? "I heard . . ."

"What? What did you hear?"

"Vanessa mentioned you weren't feeling up to par."

"My wife doesn't know what the hell she's talking about."

Roger shrugged. If Bryce didn't want to admit his liver was going south, he wouldn't argue with him. "Has she moved out yet? Last time we talked you told me she was threatening to leave you."

Bryce poured another drink before answering. "Separate bedrooms, separate lives," he said. "It seems to work for both of us." He swatted the air as he added, "The fact is, we're both too lazy to change anything, and if she left, she couldn't nag me to stop drinking, could she?"

"If she's still trying to get you to stop, she must still care about you."

"She loves me in her own sick, twisted way," he said. "What about you, Roger? How are you doing?"

"I've got big plans," he said. "Investments," he added with a nod and hoped that Bryce wouldn't want to know the details. He was making it up as he went along. "I'm going to make some changes in my life."

His brother didn't seem interested in hearing about his future. "Have you talked to Ewan lately?"

"I spoke to him briefly a while back," he said. He didn't mention that he'd met him in a bar to get a gun from him. Bryce was always so superior, and Roger knew his older brother would look down his nose at him if he heard about the gun, and an argument would be inevitable. Bryce was a drunk, but he was still snooty.

"What's he been up to?" he asked. He didn't really care. He was simply filling time until the attorney got the show on the road.

"He didn't volunteer any personal news."

"Is he still body building?"

"I didn't ask. I would assume so."

"Speaking of the devil."

The brothers turned in unison as Ewan walked in. Bryce greeted him by raising his glass.

Roger thought Ewan looked more fit than ever. He sported a deep tan that came from his sun worshipping hours at the club. From the waist down, he was trim, but his chest and upper arms were huge. He was still lifting weights all right.

The youngest wasn't dressed appropriately, though. He wore khaki pants that appeared to have been purchased at one of those mall chains and a short-sleeve knit shirt that looked like it had been glued to his chest. Ewan had never wanted to grow up. He obviously had loved his college days so much, he continued to dress like a frat boy.

Roger wondered if he still played Jell-O shot games with his juvenile buddies but didn't ask. The least little thing set Ewan off, and Roger wasn't in the mood to put up with his temper today.

Ewan managed to be civil for about thirty seconds. "Nice to see both of you again." And before Bryce or Roger had a chance to respond, Ewan wrinkled his nose and said, "Which one of you stinks?"

"That would be Roger," Bryce said.

Before Roger could protest, Bryce continued, "It's the nicotine oozing through your pores and the smoke all over your clothes. You really ought to give up that filthy habit."

And the gloves came off.

Vanessa walked into the middle of the fray. Dressed in a pale gray silk pantsuit, she was a statuesque woman who was accustomed to turning heads when she entered a room. She wore her raven black hair swept back into a chignon, as only a woman confident in her beauty could. "Isn't this a lovely family reunion," she said sarcastically. She quickly separated herself from the brothers, looked at her watch, and said, "We're all here. Where's the attorney?"

Bryce checked the time and said, "We've got ten more minutes until one."

She tried to open the door to the inner office. It was locked.

"Apparently he doesn't want us rifling through his files," she said.

"We shouldn't have to wait. This is outrageous," Roger muttered. "This outfit isn't going to be handling my share of the money, I promise you that."

"How much do you think there is?" Bryce asked.

"Millions," Roger answered.

"That doesn't answer the question. How many millions?" Ewan wanted to know.

"I'm guessing sixty million," Bryce said.

"That's a high estimate," Ewan said.

"Guessing is rather pointless," Vanessa interjected.

Ewan glared at her. "Why are you here?"

"You two have never gotten along, have you?" Roger said. He sounded like he'd just figured that out.

"That's soft-pedaling the truth," Ewan responded. "I detest her. Her holier-than-thou attitude. She's a snob, and I have no use for her."

"The feeling's mutual," she responded.

"I repeat, why are you here?" Ewan asked again.

"Bryce and I both received letters."

"And you couldn't ride with your husband?" he asked.

"I had a meeting with the art council. It was cultural, so of course you wouldn't understand."

Her condescension infuriated him. He turned to Bryce and said, "How in God's name do you stand her?"

Bryce smiled at his wife. "The question should be, how does she stand me?"

"Oh, please. Your self-loathing became tiresome years ago," Ewan scoffed.

Vanessa was saved from having to listen to any more of Ewan's sarcastic drivel when the door swung open and Anderson Smith, trailed by his assistant, swept into the room.

The attorney's manner was as smooth as alabaster. Without saying a word, he demanded attention, and he got it. He introduced himself and his assistant and shook hands with each one, starting with Vanessa.

He was an older gentleman and quite charismatic. She watched him work his magic on the brothers and was both fascinated and amused, for they were suddenly all on their best behavior.

Terrance unlocked the door, and one by one they filed into the inner sanctum.

Roger spotted the video equipment and asked, "What's all this for? Are we going to see a movie?"

"I wouldn't call it a movie," Anderson responded. "Please make yourselves comfortable. We'll be starting in just a few minutes."

"Why can't we start now?" Ewan asked.

Anderson walked to the office door and was pulling it closed when he answered, "Not everyone is here yet."

Chapter Twenty-three

DYLAN MADE CERTAIN THEY WEREN'T BEING FOL-
lowed, and when they were closing in on Savannah, he left the highway and took back roads into
the city.

He got lost in no time at all, but because he was
a Buchanan male, he wasn't about to admit it or
ask for directions. Kate was filling him in on some
historical facts about Charleston's sister city and
wasn't paying attention to the route he was taking.

"Savannah's called the jewel of the south," she
said. "But you probably already knew that."

"Uh-huh."

"Are you listening to me?"

"Sure I am. You're a jewel."

"No, Savannah's the jewel."

"Yes," he agreed. "But so are you, pickle."

She gave up trying to educate him, picked up
her smart phone, and checked for any new messages.

Dylan still hadn't gotten his bearings. He was certain he'd passed the very same park a couple of times now. He kept driving west. Several blocks later he stopped to let some jay-walkers cross in front of him and happened to look at the number on the door across the street.

Son of a gun, they were exactly where they were supposed to be.

The attorney's office was on the perimeter of a large square that surrounded a shaded park. In the center was a monument to one of the South's revered statesmen, who stood perched on a tall pedestal looking down on the sidewalks and park benches scattered about. Ancient oaks dripping with moss provided shade.

All of the buildings butted up against each other and were once the grand homes of Savannah's finest citizens. Some were still residences, but others had been renovated and converted and now fit into the urban mixture of offices and galleries and restaurants.

Dylan got lucky again when a car pulled out of a prime parking spot near the corner. He backed into the space, put the car in park, and said, "All right."

"We're here?" She looked startled.

"Yes, we're here," he said. "We made good time."

She glanced at the digital clock on the dashboard. "We're twenty minutes early."

"It's closer to fifteen minutes." He unsnapped his seat belt and tried to open the door.

She grabbed his arm. "I don't want to get there early." She sounded panicky now.

"Sure, okay. We won't be early." He reached for the door again.

"Wait."

"Yes?"

"Would you mind if I made a quick call first? I need to talk to Haley about ribbon. It won't take long."

"No problem. While you're doing that, I'll check in with Nate."

Kate was suddenly feeling nervous. She couldn't remember Haley's phone number and had to look it up in her smart phone.

Haley's assistant answered and explained that she had left for a luncheon appointment. Kate left the message that she would be unavailable for a few hours but that she would call Haley later that afternoon.

Dylan got hold of Nate right away. It was a one-sided conversation, and Kate had to wait until he'd flipped his cell phone closed to find out anything.

"Did he have any news?" she asked.

"Some." He didn't expound.

Nate got out of the car, grabbed his suit jacket from the back seat, and put it on so his gun would be concealed, went around and opened her door.

He was acting like a bodyguard, she thought. He was watching the street when he said, "You stay close to me." It wasn't a suggestion but an order.

"I plan to," she said. She gathered her things, stuffed them into her purse, and took his hand.

They crossed the street and walked around the corner. Kate did not want to think about where they were headed. The notion to bolt was gaining momentum.

She needed to stall—to give herself a few minutes to gather her thoughts. She glanced at the park across the street and blurted out, "Look at the park. Isn't it lovely? Did you know that there are over twenty squares in Savannah? All have parks in the center." She stopped and said, "This one is my favorite."

Dylan seemed more interested in the people and the cars. He was subtle about it, but he was making certain that his body protected hers as they walked along.

"Let's go," he said.

She deliberately slowed the pace. "We're building a park like that in Silver Springs."

He glanced over his shoulder, nodded, and said, "I noticed it on our way to the police station."

She walked even more slowly. "And we have three more in the works. They're going to be interconnected when they're finished. The buildings aren't on this grand scale, of course."

Kate saw the door with the names Smith and Wesson engraved on a plaque directly head of her, and stopped. "Let's go sit on the park bench for a little while."

"No."

"I don't want to be early. We still have fifteen minutes."

Dylan didn't know what was going on in her mind, but he wasn't about to stand on the sidewalk and argue with her. She obviously needed a few minutes to calm down and then maybe she would tell him what was bothering her.

"Okay, we won't be early. We'll find someplace to wait."

Relieved, she said, "Thank you." She looked around and spotted a coffee shop catty-corner to the law firm. "Would you like to get some coffee? I'm sure they have iced tea, too."

A few minutes later they were seated at a tiny round table in the back of the coffee shop. There wasn't any air-conditioning, and both front and back doors were wide open. Two ceiling fans were going full speed. Both made a clicking noise that sounded like fingers snapping.

"It's lunch time," she said. "We were lucky to get a table."

"It's hot in here. That's why we got a table. Look around. We're the only ones here."

"We could find somewhere else if the heat bothers you."

"I'm good."

He took his jacket off and draped it over the back of a chair.

Kate waited until the waitress had left with their iced tea orders to ask, "What did Nate have to say?"

"They still can't find Carl. The case is building against him."

"How so?"

"He's in trouble with the IRS."

"Are you serious?"

"Sugar, I never joke about the IRS. He's in trouble," he repeated.

"What kind of trouble?"

"Back taxes."

"But he's . . ."

"What?"

"Rich. He inherited a fortune."

"If he did, he's gone through it."

"I'm stunned."

"He never said anything to you about money worries?"

"Good heavens, no. Carl is every inch the southern gentleman," she explained. "And southern gentlemen never ever discuss money problems. It would be . . . unseemly."

"Is that part of the southern gentleman code?"

He was teasing, but she was serious when she answered. "Yes, it is. Being a gentleman is serious business here."

The waitress had eyes for only Dylan as she placed the iced tea on the table. Kate thanked her anyway, took a sip of the cold drink, and said, "I can't figure this out. Poor Carl, bless his heart. He's always trying to help others."

"How does he help?"

"He gives lavish parties to promote the arts. And he's helped promote my company, too."

"He asked you to bring those gift baskets to his party, didn't he?"

"Yes, he did. He thought it would be good promotion. Oh, I see that look in your eyes. Dylan, Carl was trying to help. I'm telling you, he's a good man. He wanted to buy into my company. I'm sure he thought I needed financial assistance, and of course he couldn't talk about it . . . so he offered to be a partner. If he had such terrible money problems, where would he get the money to help me?"

"When did he try to buy into your company? For God's sake, Kate, why didn't you tell me this?"

"I didn't think it was relevant."

"When?" he repeated.

"Over a year ago."

Dylan checked the time, pulled his wallet out, and put money on the table. "Drink up. We have to get going."

"We've still got time," she said. "What else did Nate tell you?"

"He's doing a background check on your relatives, and I had hoped he'd have something for me by now."

"But no such luck?"

"Not yet. He got pulled into a meeting, but he has people working on it."

"We'll be finding out about them soon enough." Too soon, she thought. Why, oh, why had she agreed to come to Savannah? Guilt, she decided. Isabel and Kiera had guilted her into coming.

"I don't like walking in blind. I want to know what I'm dealing with. You understand?"

Oh, boy, did she. "Yes."

"You're dreading it."

"Yes, I am."

"Why?" And when she didn't immediatcly answer, he asked, "Why are you so worried?"

"I'm not worried," she said. "I just hope . . ."

"Yes?"

She guessed there really wasn't any reason not to tell him. He already knew about her financial situation and her mother's devastating business and personal decisions. "I hope this meeting isn't another surprise my mother left behind. I don't think I could take another . . . disappointment."

"Why do you think that's a possibility? Seems pretty remote to me. You told me your mother never mentioned her husband's relatives," he reminded her.

"The letter . . . by special messenger . . . it

started me thinking. Mother might have borrowed money from this uncle and now the estate wants it paid back."

He looked at her a long minute and then asked, "How long are you going to stay mad at her?"

"I'm not mad. I'm disappointed."

"Yeah, right."

She bristled. "I'm telling you the truth."

"No, you're not. I guess you're just not ready to say it, so how about I say it for you? You're furious with her."

Her spine stiffened. The defiance didn't last long. Tears sprang into her eyes, and she couldn't stop them. She'd already cried in front of him once; she wasn't about to do it again.

"Yes, I'm angry," she said, her voice shaking. "She lied about everything, and she left a mess."

He put his hand on top of hers. "Ah, Katie. It's not about the money."

She pulled her hand away. "Oh? Then what is it about?"

"Your mother got sick, and she died, and no matter how hard you tried, you couldn't stop it from happening."

"That doesn't make sense."

"No, it doesn't," he agreed. He stood and put his suit jacket on. "So maybe you ought to think about forgiving her."

She wanted to argue, to tell him his amateur analysis was way off, but something stopped her.

What if there was a germ of truth in what he was saying? Was she using anger to shield herself from the pain of losing her mother?

He pulled her to her feet. "Come on, sugar. Time to meet the relatives."

Chapter Twenty-four

THE LAW FIRM OF SMITH AND WESSON AND ASSO-
ciates resided in an early nineteenth-century,
three-story home that had been transformed into
offices but had kept its antebellum elegance.

The lobby was wide, and the eye was immediately drawn to the colorful mosaic design on the
tiled floor. A grand staircase in the center led up to
an open balcony that surrounded the lobby and
was supported by white Doric columns.

Dylan half expected to see a southern belle
sweep down the steps in her hoop skirt to greet
them, but instead a receptionist in a dark suit with
a silk blouse and pearls smiled up at them from
her tidy mahogany desk.

Kate waited by Dylan's side while he dealt with
the security guard. The alarm had been triggered
when he'd walked in, but as soon as he showed his
badge, the pulsating noise stopped.

She didn't have to give her name to the receptionist. The young woman already knew who she was.

"Good afternoon, Miss MacKenna. Mr. Smith will be right down. He's most anxious to meet you."

Anxious? Was that a good anxious or a bad one? Kate wondered.

Less than a minute later, the attorney rushed down the stairs. His smile seemed genuine. Still, he was a lawyer, she reminded herself, and from his surroundings, a very successful one at that. Therefore he had to be quite good at masking his real emotions.

Extending his hand, he said, "My name is Anderson Samuel Smith, and I am delighted to meet you, Miss MacKenna. Simply delighted."

He was quite polished, for he quickly put her at ease. He shook Dylan's hand, and the two men exchanged polite greetings.

Speaking to both of them, he said, "I was your great uncle Compton's attorney for twenty years, and I do believe the firm took great care of him. He was quite an interesting fellow. Perhaps we might have dinner sometime, and I'll tell you what I know about him."

"Did you know his brother?" Kate asked.

"Yes, I did, Miss MacKenna. Our firm did not handle his affairs, however."

"Please, call me Kate."

He flashed another brilliant smile. "Kate. A

good name," he added with approval. "And you must call me Anderson."

"If you wouldn't mind, I'd like to freshen up."

"Good idea," Dylan said.

Good idea? What did that mean? She must either look a mess, or Dylan wanted to talk to the attorney alone.

Anderson showed her the way to the powder room and returned to Dylan in the foyer.

Kate washed her hands and checked her appearance in the full-length mirror. Okay, she was a bit disheveled, but she didn't look that bad, did she? She didn't look that good, either. She could make herself a little more presentable, she decided.

She brushed her hair, and since there was some curl, she didn't clip it back again but let it fall around her shoulders. Digging through her purse, she found her blush, and lipstick and freshened her makeup. She checked herself again. It was the best she could do without a complete overhaul.

She wanted to give Dylan another couple of minutes with the attorney. She stopped near the door and gave herself a quick pep talk. Try to be optimistic and stop looking so worried. It was going to be fine. Anderson wouldn't have been so happy to meet her if she owed the estate a lot of money, right? No, that wasn't logical. He could have been thrilled because she had shown up, and he knew he had a good shot at getting her to pay the money back—and she would pay it back even if it took the rest of her life to do it.

Wait, that wasn't optimistic thinking. Kate wanted to latch on to something that would make her feel better. The photos. Yes, there were photos of her father as a little boy. That was definitely something wonderful to share with her sisters, something that would give them a connection to the man who had loved her mother and had given them life.

All right. The pep talk was working. She took it a step further. Maybe she would actually like these cousins. She might.

Straightening her shoulders, she whispered, "Here goes," and opened the door.

Dylan barely spared her a glance as he listened to the attorney who was very seriously explaining something to him. Kate didn't want to interrupt, and so she waited by the receptionist's desk until they finished their discussion.

The smile was back in place the second Anderson spotted her. "Shall we go upstairs?" he said as he led the way.

Kate hung back and whispered to Dylan, "You're frowning. What's wrong?"

Should he warn her? Or should he let her go in cold without any preconceived ideas about the vipers Anderson had just described to him?

He decided to give her a little forewarning. "I don't think you're going to like your cousins."

"Maybe I will," she said, determined to hang on to the burst of optimism she'd mustered up.

He smiled. "I'm pretty sure you won't."

"You can't predict . . ." She suddenly stopped. Oh, who was she kidding? Her bubble of enthusiasm was slowly deflating.

He saw the disheartened look in her eyes and realized he shouldn't have said anything. "You stay tough," he whispered.

"I am tough," she responded.

They had just reached the landing when they heard a man shout a gross obscenity. Kate stopped cold and looked at Dylan. He shrugged as if unfazed.

Anderson looked mortified. "Give me a moment, please," he said.

He hurried down the hall, probably intent on getting his guests to shut the hell up, Dylan surmised, but the damage was done. Kate had gone from worried to fearful.

She grabbed his arm. "Did Anderson tell you why I received a letter?"

"You know why. The reading of the will."

"Yes, but did he say anything more?"

"We didn't talk about the will at all," he said. "I needed to know what we're going to be walking into, and so he filled me in on your cousins. And by the way, he wants to assure you he doesn't represent any of them."

She continued down the corridor. She heard

another obscenity and whispered, "Good Lord. What have I gotten into? Maybe it's not such a good idea to meet any of them just now." **Or ever,** she silently added.

Dylan didn't want her facing the nest of vipers looking worried. If they sensed vulnerability, they'd strike. The cousins needed to see what a strong woman she was.

Anderson opened the door and motioned them to come forward.

"Kate." Dylan touched her arm to stop her.

She looked up and was shocked by his grin. "Yes, Dylan?"

He lowered his voice so only she would hear and asked, "How much do you want to bet Anderson Samuel Smith never uses his initials?"

She didn't get it for a couple of seconds but then put it together. "Good heavens, only a man would think of that." She was laughing when she walked into the office.

The air was thick with hostility, but the shouting and the vulgarities stopped when one by one they noticed the couple and fell silent.

Roger was the first to get past his surprise. "What the—" he muttered. "Who are they, Anderson?"

"Who cares who they are. They don't belong here," Ewan said with a sneer. He took a threatening step toward them.

Did he think he could scare her out of the office? She wasn't going to put up with that non-sense. She looked him right in the eye and kept walking.

Anderson put his hands up. "If you'll calm down, I'll make the introductions. Kate, I'd like you to meet Vanessa MacKenna."

The striking woman was unlike the others clustered together across the room. She didn't seem angry, only curious.

"Hello," Vanessa said politely.

"Vanessa," Anderson continued, "is married to Bryce MacKenna."

The man Anderson gestured to didn't speak. He acknowledged Kate with a curt nod.

"Standing next to Bryce is Roger MacKenna, and on his right is Ewan MacKenna. And now I would like all of you to meet your cousin, Kate MacKenna."

"Our cousin?" Ewan roared. "She has to be a fraud. We don't have any cousins."

"Ewan's right," Bryce said. "We don't have any cousins."

"Obviously you do," Vanessa said with a hint of amusement in her voice.

The brothers ignored her.

"And who is he?" Roger asked. "Is he passing himself off as a cousin, too?"

"Who is he? He's with Kate," Anderson said and refused to explain further.

"Do they think they're going to get a piece of the pie? How absurd," Bryce said.

Anderson held up his hand again. "Your uncle assured me the video will explain everything to your satisfaction. None of you will be left with any questions. He also requested that each of you get a copy of what you're about to see. Terrance, please distribute the discs to everyone." He noticed the sun was shining on the television screen and hurried over to the windows to adjust the blinds. "Is there a disc in the player?"

"Yes, sir. Everything's ready," Terrance answered.

Anderson clasped his hands together and tried to sound enthusiastic. "All right then, shall we get started?"

"It's about time," Bryce said.

"Everyone, please take a seat." His gaze moved to Roger and Ewan. "And try not to comment or interrupt while your uncle is speaking."

Roger slumped into his chair. "We have to listen to that old buzzard lecture us before we get our money?"

He'd addressed the question to Ewan, who promptly answered, "He's still trying to control us, even from the grave. What a hard-nosed bastard."

Vanessa turned on Ewan. "Your uncle isn't here to defend himself. Only you would stoop so low as to defile the dead."

Ewan wasn't fazed by her contempt. He turned to Roger and whispered loud enough for everyone to hear, "Only a bitch could love a bastard."

Kate felt like she was watching a horror movie. How in heaven's name was she going to tell Kiera and Isabel about these vile, contemptible brothers? She was appalled and nauseated that she was actually related to them. They were horrible human beings.

Bryce seemed to be in a hurry to get drunk. He was gulping liquor like water, and the more he drank, the nastier he became. The other brothers seemed to appreciate his twisted wit, and their laughter only encouraged him. How would she describe them to Kiera and Isabel? "Repulsive" came to mind. And creepy. Definitely creepy. No one could become this obnoxious without years of practice.

Her attention turned to Vanessa. She was most curious about her. One could easily assume that the poised, sophisticated woman had wandered into the wrong office by mistake. She seemed so out of place here.

Anderson stood behind Vanessa's chair. He nodded to Terrance, who immediately picked up the remote and pushed the play button.

The bickering stopped as Compton Thomas MacKenna addressed his audience, but the silence didn't last long.

"Did he just say he changed his will some time

ago? Why weren't we informed?" Ewan demanded.

"Shut up and listen," Roger said. "We'll talk
later."

"Start the damned thing again," Bryce
snapped. "I didn't hear a word, thanks to my
brothers' yapping."

And the fighting started all over again.

Kate didn't know how much more of this she
could take. "Oh, my," she whispered.

Dylan heard her. He draped his arm protec-
tively across the back of her chair and leaned
down to whisper, "Do you want to leave?"

Oh, yes, she certainly did. But she also wanted
those photos, and she wanted to know why she
and her sisters had been invited to this freak show.

"I have to see this," she whispered back.

Anderson got them to quiet down, and the
DVD began to play again. The brothers kept
quiet until their uncle gave a history of the family.
One of them groaned then.

Kate was fascinated to hear about her father's
ancestors, and she listened intently. But then he
brought up her mother. In a heartbeat Kate's attitude went from curiosity to outrage. The old
man's words, said so callously, reverberated in her
mind. **No better than a street beggar.** The insults
didn't stop there. His contempt for her mother
was apparent in everything he said about her.

Did the uncle want Kate to see this so he could

slander her mother? Was that his purpose for summoning her here?

She stiffened when he talked about her sisters and was shocked to hear that he had someone checking up on all of them. She couldn't believe the audacity of the man. The comment that stunned Kate the most, however, was his assessment of her. She heard his remark that she was the most like him. Dear God, how could he think such a thing? And he was smiling when he said it, as though he thought it a wonderful distinction to be his spitting image.

Kate didn't think she could be more stunned than she already was. There simply couldn't be anymore surprises, could there?

Obviously there could.

"The bulk of my estate . . . eighty million dollars . . . will go to Kate MacKenna . . ."

No, no, that couldn't be right. She started to stand and fell back. The disc dropped off her lap. She couldn't hear the rest of the video, and she was oblivious to the bedlam going on around her. She sat there paralyzed . . . and sickened.

No better than a street beggar. How dare he say such a thing about her mother.

She shook her head. "No," she said. "No."

They turned on her like a pack of rabid animals. She didn't realize how dangerous the situation had become. Dylan certainly did. He stood and quickly moved in front of her.

Bryce was blubbering and cursing; Roger was screaming and crying, but Ewan was the real threat now. His face was contorted with rage. He came out of his chair like a crazed bull on steroids, and he was completely controlled by his temper as he charged at Kate.

"How did you do it? How did you get that demented old man to change his will?" He tried to push Dylan aside, and when Dylan wouldn't budge, he screamed, "Get out of my way."

Dylan responded quietly. "Go sit down."

Ewan tried to throw a punch at him, but Dylan knocked his fist away and said, "I don't want to do this. I've got my nice suit on, and I'm in this nice office with my girlfriend. I don't want to get into a fistfight."

"You think you can take me?"

He was behaving like a sixteen-year-old bully, and Dylan was not amused. "You're going to sit down, one way or another."

With a roar, Ewan took a wild swing. Dylan dodged the hand, but he was through being nice. When Ewan tried again, Dylan gave a right jab to his midsection. As the man was going down, Dylan shoved him toward the sofa, and Roger got out of the way so Ewan could land on the cushion next to him.

Dylan smiled. "Okay. Now he's sitting down."

"Call the police, Anderson," Ewan gasped. "Have this man arrested for assault. Call nine-one-one. I'm pressing charges. Why aren't you calling? I want the police here now."

"Did I forget to properly introduce Detective Buchanan? If you'd like to see his badge, I'm sure he'll be happy to show it to you."

It was apparent Anderson was having a high old time watching his client's nephews get their just reward. He looked positively overjoyed.

Vanessa hadn't said a word until now. "I cannot believe it. Eighty million?"

"Are you all right, my dear?" Anderson asked.

Ewan turned to her. "And all you get is a house and a measly hundred grand."

"I love that house, and he knew it. I'm thrilled he gave it to me."

Bryce was sneering at her. "You're awfully smug."

"Why shouldn't I be smug? You treated him shamefully. All of you did."

"Forget her," Roger shouted. "What the hell are we going to do?"

"We'll sue," Bryce said. "We'll contest it."

"That could take years," Ewan answered.

Roger was desperate when he said, "I can't wait. I have to get my hands on that money now."

The room erupted in chaos as each brother shouted over the next.

Kate had heard enough. She picked up her purse and stood.

"I don't want it," she said to Anderson. The room suddenly fell quiet.

"I can understand your shock, Kate," Anderson replied. He walked over to his desk and placed his hand on a thick binder. "I'm sure you're beginning to see that your great uncle Compton was a meticulous planner. He arranged the transfer of the estate down to the smallest detail." He patted the binder. "This is a summation compiled by his accounting firm. You are to take it with you today so that you can familiarize yourself with the cash holdings and other assets. He wanted you to understand and appreciate what he accomplished in his life. Tomorrow at three p.m. you are to return here for a meeting with his financial advisors. At that time they will answer any questions you might have and offer you their services to make the transition as smooth as possible."

"But you don't understand," she insisted. "I don't want it. Any of it."

"Give this some time to sink in," Anderson cautioned. "You don't want to make any rash decisions."

"You heard her," Roger argued. "She said she doesn't want it."

Ewan rushed forward. "What happens if she won't take it?"

Anderson was reluctant to answer. "Your uncle was adamant that the estate go to Kate and he was quite confident that she would accept. He did not name a succeeding heir."

"That means if she refuses to take it, then it will go to our uncle's next of kin, right?"

Anderson didn't respond. He turned to Kate instead. "You have until tomorrow to think about this. Please take the binder and look it over. We'll discuss it then."

"That won't be necessary," Kate answered calmly. "I will not accept the inheritance. I want nothing from that man."

Dylan had been standing beside her in case one of the brothers got too close, but she was the one in charge now. She was not about to let them intimidate her, and that impressed the hell out of him.

Vanessa started walking toward the door. She stopped when she reached Kate and said, "He wanted you to have it. I think it would be wise for you to consider this before you give it away." She smiled then and whispered, "Good luck."

"Why aren't you moving, Anderson?" Ewan yelled. "Draw up the papers for her to refuse the money."

The attorney shook his head. "I cannot do that. It is my responsibility to carry out your uncle's wishes to the best of my ability." He picked up the binder and looked at Kate. "I cannot force you to accept the inheritance, but I strongly urge you to at least look at these records so that you can make an informed decision."

"Put the records down, Anderson. She doesn't want them."

Kate's patience had reached its limit. She smiled at Anderson and said, "I appreciate your concern, and I understand that you're simply doing your duty. But you must understand, I'm not going to change my mind. If there are papers I must sign to decline this, please draw them up."

Anderson realized that any further protests now would be wasted. She needed time. "Very well," he said. "It will take me a day or two to notify everyone and to put together the documents. I'll let you know when they're ready."

"May I have the photos of my father now?" she asked.

"Of course," he replied and reached into his drawer to retrieve a large manila envelope for her.

"Thank you," she said. "Could we go?" she asked Dylan.

"Sure thing," he answered. He moved aside to let her walk ahead of him and kept his eye on the brothers as he passed them. They were all but bursting at the seams with the joy of their victory.

"I'll walk out with you," Anderson offered.

The three walked through the outer office and headed for the stairs.

"I'll be in touch with you soon," he said as he

accompanied them down the hall. "I urge you to think about this tonight. Perhaps you'll change your mind."

"It's going to be difficult to explain all of this to my sisters. I knew when I came here that I would meet our relatives, but I certainly didn't expect they would be so . . ."

Anderson smiled. "I know. They're hard to describe, aren't they?"

Kate laughed then. "Yes. At least I have the— Oh . . . I forgot the disc." She spun around and rushed back into the outer office before Dylan could stop her.

She could hear laughter and the sound of glasses clinking together. She reached for the doorknob, but something else caught her attention. She froze. The brothers seemed to be having a grand celebration. They laughed uproariously when one of them made a joke about her family.

Kate stood at the door and listened for a couple of seconds. That was all the time she needed.

When she opened it and marched into the room, the laughter came to an abrupt halt. She didn't spare her cousins a glance, but walked to her chair and picked up the disc she had dropped. Then she swung around and reached for the binder on the desk.

"What are you doing?" Roger demanded.

"You've changed my mind. I'll be needing this

after all," she said as she turned around to face their stares.

With the binder clutched to her chest, she walked back to the door where Dylan stood waiting.

As the door closed behind her, she looked over her shoulder and calmly said, "Oh, don't let me interrupt you, cousins. Please. Carry on. One of you was just calling my mother a whore."

Chapter Twenty-five

"WHAT THE HELL WAS THAT?" DYLAN POSED the question as they crossed the lobby.

"You're going to have to be a little more specific," she said. "Which hell are you referring to?"

Anderson Smith, beaming like a proud parent whose child has performed way beyond his expectations, chased after them.

"Miss MacKenna . . . Kate, Kate, please, wait just a minute."

For a split second Kate considered running from him. She desperately wanted to get away from the relatives with all possible haste, but not at the attorney's expense. It wasn't his fault that his client had been such a foul old man. She also couldn't blame him for the vile relatives. Anderson seemed to be just as shocked and repulsed by their behavior as she and Dylan were.

Forcing a smile, she turned around and waited for the attorney to reach her.

"Yes?"

"I was so pleased to hear you say you have decided to accept your inheritance. Shall I expect you here tomorrow at three? Your uncle's accountants and advisors will be ready to answer any questions you will surely have after you've looked through the report, and they will also witness your signature." He took a breath and added, "And I will of course continue to do my best to guide you until the transfer is complete and until you name a new firm to represent you."

"I have no plans to replace you, Anderson," she assured.

He was obviously thrilled with her decision. He clasped her hand. "Wonderful, wonderful."

"But the eighty million—"

"Actually, my dear, your uncle understated the value."

She blinked. "I'm sorry?"

"Your inheritance is considerably more than eighty million."

"Oh . . . and you will continue to represent . . ." Her voice trailed away.

"Will I see you tomorrow at three?"

He was moving too fast for her. Everything was moving too fast. "I'll need time to read . . . tonight . . . and tomorrow . . ." She looked frantically at Dylan for help. She couldn't seem to get the words out. She thought she must sound moronic.

Dylan thought she sounded as dazed as she looked.

"Could Kate get back to you about the meeting? She could call you in the morning to let you know when to schedule it. Don't do anything until you hear from her."

She was nodding eagerly. "Yes, I'll call you."

Anderson pointed to the binder she was gripping. "You have quite a bit to read tonight and to absorb. I've printed out the arrangements for your uncle's burial in the event you wish to attend, though I would encourage you not to." He patted her hand and stepped back. "As your attorney," he said with a smile, "I want you to feel that you can call me at any time, day or night, with questions or concerns. My card is inside the binder with each of my numerous phone numbers."

"Thank you," she said.

She started to turn away, then stopped. "About this meeting . . ."

"Yes?"

"Will the cousins be there?" She was proud of herself. She'd said "cousins" without flinching or gagging.

He was sympathetic. "I'm sorry to say they will have to be invited. Your uncle's instructions were quite specific. I didn't question his motive when he told me his wishes, but it's my belief he wanted the brothers to see firsthand what they'd be losing. Their presence isn't mandatory, however, because their shares of the estate have already been assigned to them. The same applies to your sisters, Kiera and Isabel. You are the only one who has to be present to sign anything.

"If you had refused the inheritance, I am confident the three nephews would ultimately be the next in line to receive it, since they maintained contact with your uncle while he was alive. His will explicitly limits what he has bequeathed to your sisters, so I doubt they would be able to lay claim to the larger estate. I guess what I am trying to say is that it all rests with you."

He spoke more to Dylan than to her when he said, "I cannot impress upon you strongly enough the importance of continuing to be cautious." Taking her hand again, he said, "I don't want you to be concerned about any of your relatives barging into the meeting with a weapon. There will be sufficient security, I assure you."

She thought he was making a lame attempt at a joke until he addressed Dylan again.

"My security guard has informed me that the serial number on the gun he confiscated had indeed been filed away."

"I'm not surprised," Dylan replied. "Did he call it in, and did he check on a permit?"

"Yes, he did. The police are on their way."

"That's good to hear."

Anderson finally let them escape. They were crossing the lobby when Dylan spotted the security guard anxiously waiting in the shadows near the entrance.

Kate tried to walk ahead to the door, but Dylan grabbed her arm. "Hold on a minute."

The guard rushed over to them. "Detective Buchanan, did Mr. Smith tell you what I found out about the gun?"

"Yes, he did."

"What should I tell them? They're going to be here any second."

Dylan could see the guard was nervous about the procedure. "You don't have to do anything but give them the gun. They'll handle Roger MacKenna."

"Shouldn't they be warned about him?"

"They have been warned," he assured him. "They know what they're doing. You just stay out of their way."

"Yes, sir."

"Anderson is going to try to keep all of them in his office until the police arrive, but if Roger insists on leaving, he'll walk down with him. You won't have to face him alone." The guard still looked worried. "Or you could wait in your office . . ." Dylan continued.

Instantly relieved, the guard answered, "If that's what you want me to do, sir, then I'll wait in my office."

He nodded. "Okay, Kate. Let's go."

She didn't move. Her look of astonishment was priceless, and he almost laughed.

"The gun surprised you?" he asked.

Surprised? Oh, please. She'd gone way past surprise in the attorney's office. Like an Irishman at an Anglican wake, she had this totally inappropriate urge to laugh. The brothers just kept getting worse.

"Roger brought a gun to the attorney's office?" She took a couple of steps toward the door and stopped. "Who would bring a gun to the reading of a will?"

"Apparently Roger MacKenna would, and in fact did. The police will take him to the station and have a little chat with him. They'll run the gun, too," he added. "Hopefully, Roger will do some heavy sweating in jail. That would be pretty sweet, wouldn't it?"

"Shouldn't you be waiting for the police? They might have questions . . ."

"No, we're not waiting. We're getting away from here as quickly as possible. Unless you want to run back upstairs and kiss the cousins good-bye."

She shuddered with repulsion. She'd rather eat glass.

"No, thank you," she said politely. "I'd just as soon leave."

He grinned. "I thought you might."

A clap of thunder greeted them when they stepped outside. It was already drizzling, but the clouds were dark and heavy. A hard rain would come any second now.

"Want to make a run for it?" he asked.

He didn't give her time to answer. He grabbed her hand and took off. By the time they reached the corner, the drizzle had turned into rain.

She was keeping pace with him, which was no small feat. "I would prefer that you bring the car around."

They sprinted across the street as he said, "No way, Pickle. You're staying with me, and we're getting out of here."

They raced along the path through the park. Dylan was scanning the area, looking for anyone or anything that didn't belong. His hand rested on the handle of his gun.

Kate's high heels were taking a pounding and killing her, but pride kept her from complaining or asking him to slow down. She'd keep up or die trying.

When they reached the car, Dylan opened her door and practically tossed her inside. He removed his jacket and, just as he was handing it to her, the skies opened up. He managed to make it to the driver's side without getting completely soaked.

Kate folded his jacket and carefully laid it on the backseat. After placing the thick binder and the envelope on the floor behind her, she sat back and tried to calm her racing heart. She couldn't get the cousins out of her thoughts. She felt as though she'd just spent the past hour whirling in a blender.

Dylan checked the street and the buildings beyond. The rain had chased pedestrians under the awnings and into doorways. Two pickup trucks drove by, but the drivers didn't look their way.

They were safe . . . for the moment.

A police car sped by and turned the corner. It came to an abrupt stop in front of Smith and Wesson.

Dylan started the engine and said, "Okay, let's go."

The windows were beginning to steam up as he pulled onto the street. He flipped on the air conditioner.

Kate wasn't paying attention to where they were going until she noticed he missed the turn that would take them to the highway. When she pointed that out, he nodded but kept going.

It seemed to her that he turned left or right at nearly every corner. She soon lost her sense of direction. She thought they had started out going north, but he'd made so many turns she couldn't get her bearings.

"Where are you going?"

"Nowhere yet. I'm making sure we aren't being followed."

She quickly turned around and looked out the back window. "I don't see anyone."

"Neither do I."

"Then why . . ."

"Just being careful."

The rain was already letting up. Dylan spotted a baseball field and pulled into a parking lot adjacent to a set of metal bleachers. There wasn't a soul around, no doubt because of the weather, but the sun was already moving in, and with it came a renewed wave of heat and humidity. Steam rose up from the concrete path that circled the lot.

Dylan put the car in park, unhooked his seat belt, and loosened his tie. He took a deep breath and slowly let it out.

Kate waited a moment before saying, "Dylan? Do you remember I told you I couldn't think of anyone who would want to kill me?"

A hint of a smile softened his expression. "I remember."

"I believe I could come up with some names for you now."

Chapter Twenty-six

KATE SEEMED TO HAVE A KNACK FOR ALWAYS knowing just what to say to take the edge off. And one of her smiles could cut right through the tension.

Dylan knew she had to be afraid. She'd already been through hell and still carried the bruises as a reminder that someone was trying to kill her, but when she got her back up, she was a force to be reckoned with. She was an amazing woman.

He, on the other hand, was a basket case. Real nice admission coming from a detective.

Her uncle had put Kate in a very dangerous position. Dylan didn't care about the money or what the man's motives had been. Knowingly or unknowingly, Compton MacKenna had given his nephews more than eighty million reasons to get rid of her.

The thought of anyone hurting her enraged him. And terrified him. Not good, he realized.

Not good at all. He'd gotten too emotionally involved, damn it. Too . . . attached. Now how in blazes had that happened?

Kate studied Dylan's face. He was glaring through the windshield at nothing in particular.

"Dylan . . . ?" she began.

"I'm not going to let anyone hurt you." The promise was given with such intensity, his voice shook.

Kate jumped to the conclusion that he needed reassurance. "Do you think I'm concerned about your ability to protect me because you were shot in the line of duty?"

Man, was she dense. He actually laughed. "Yeah, that was my worry, all right."

"I'm aware of all of your commendations," she said. "And I know you're excellent at what you do. I'm not at all worried."

"That's good to hear," he said drily.

That problem resolved, she said, "I'm in a real mess aren't I?"

"Yes, you are," he admitted with a nod.

"For how long, do you think?"

"I can't give you a timeline."

She knew that, of course she did, but she still wanted one. Her entire life had been placed in limbo, and she couldn't get anything done, personally or professionally, until this was settled.

She suddenly realized how foolish her thoughts were. Staying alive was the first priority.

Dylan grabbed his cell phone and opened the door. "I'm going to call Nate. Anderson had given him the names of the relatives, and Nate was going to run a background check on all of them. He should know something by now. You stay put."

He left the motor running and the air conditioner on.

Nate had been anxiously waiting for Dylan to call. He picked up on the first ring and quickly filled Dylan in on what he'd found out about the brothers.

"Might as well start with the youngest, Ewan," he said. "He's a bodybuilder and has one hell of a temper. At last count he had three lawsuits pending, all for assault. He put one guy in ICU a year ago, shattered another man's jaw, and beat the crap out of a bartender for cutting him off. His lawyers have been doing some pretty fancy dancing to keep him out of prison, and Ewan owes them major bucks. A couple of years back he went into business with some investors to produce and sell some sort of new exercise contraption, but that went bust, so now he's banking on the inheritance to come through. If he doesn't get it, he could be bench-pressing in prison."

Dylan could hear him flipping papers.

"Let's see," Nate continued, "Bryce . . . he's the oldest, right?"

"Yes," he answered.

"No criminal record," he said. "But he's still bad news. He started drinking the hard stuff in college, and by the time he graduated, he was a full-blown drunk. He's been hospitalized several times for liver problems. He won't stop drinking, though," he added. "About eighteen months ago he tried to get on the liver transplant list. He didn't qualify because he was still drinking. From what I've been told, Bryce went crazy for a while, even tried to buy himself a liver. He's as whacked as Ewan is," he said. "He did some day-trading when the market was booming, but eventually he lost his shirt. You should see his credit report. It's pages and pages long. His debt is staggering. He doesn't seem to care that his wife is going to end up with all the bills. Anderson Smith said that the specialists give Bryce about six months tops before he keels over."

"What about his wife?" Dylan asked. "I noticed she wasn't wearing a wedding ring. Are they separated or divorced?"

"No, they're still married," he said. "She was going to file, but then she was told that Bryce was dying, and she thought she should be there with him until the end."

"Did you get that from Anderson, too?"

"Yes," he said. "He respects . . . what's her name?"

"Vanessa," he answered.

Dylan could hear the papers turning over again. Several seconds passed and then Nate said, "Ah, here she is. No criminal record, not even a speeding ticket. She's received several awards for her work in the community," he explained. "She's got a small interior design business. The uncle took a shine to her."

"What about Roger MacKenna?"

"I was saving the best for last. You got to meet all of these people, didn't you? You were there in the office with Kate, right?"

"Yes."

"Bet that was interesting. I heard Kate turned it all down."

"The money?"

"Yes," he said. "Sure wish I could have seen the brothers' reactions."

"She didn't want the money. She was ready to sign it all away until she heard Bryce, Roger, and Ewan slandering her family. That got her back up, and she changed her mind."

There was a long pause, then a burst of laughter. Nate was obviously tickled by the news.

"Good for her."

"What did you find out about Roger?" he asked, trying to get Nate back on track.

Dylan paced the parking lot while he waited for Nate to find his notes on the middle brother.

Kate watched him from the car. She couldn't

hear his conversation because the air conditioner was making a racket and he was walking away from her.

Then he turned and smiled at her. The news from Nate must not have been so terrible. Dylan wouldn't be smiling if he was hearing terrible things.

The smile didn't last long, though. She took her eye off him for only a few seconds while she reached down into her purse to get her cell phone, but when she looked at him again, she couldn't believe the radical change. He wasn't calm now; he was furious, so furious in fact he was shouting into the phone.

"Good heavens," she whispered. She thought she heard him yell a man's name—Jack—and wondered who he was.

She turned the air conditioner off and tried to hear more of the one-sided conversation, but other than a roar or two every now and then, she couldn't make out anything he was saying.

She frowned with disapproval. Shouting wasn't very professional of him, especially shouting at the poor, overworked detective, and she was going to tell him so when he got back into the car.

A few minutes later she was screaming into her own phone, and she didn't care.

She had just listened to a message from her box supplier, Haley, and unable to believe what she had heard, she had to replay the message again.

"We keep missing each other," Haley began. "Please call me and give me some direction here. This woman . . . this crazy woman . . . keeps barging into my office trying to change everything. Her name is Randy Simmons, and she insists that she's the new owner of the Kate MacKenna company. I thought it was some kind of sick joke. If you could see her and see how she was dressed, you'd understand why I would think it was a prank. She's very . . ." The message paused for a couple of seconds. ". . . crude. She wouldn't go away, Kate, and when I told her that I had recently talked to you and that you hadn't mentioned anything about selling your company, she explained that of course you wouldn't say anything because you were humiliated and embarrassed. She said you defaulted on your loan."

It was at this point when Kate first listened to the message that she started screaming into the phone. The shock hadn't worn off because she started shouting again the second time she listened.

"You can imagine my reaction," Haley continued. "I was speechless. I think Randy was amused by my reaction. Oh, and get this, she told me not to worry. She didn't have any plans to fire me as long as I did what she wanted. I reminded her that I own my own company and have quite a few clients. I explained in very simple terms that she couldn't fire me because I didn't work for her. I don't think she understood, though. She said she was so excited about owning her own business, perhaps she was being a little overeager to get started. She kept telling me she was going to make big changes. And get this. She said your colors were too quiet.

"I finally got my wits about me, and I told her she would have to prove she was the new owner before she could make any changes. She assured me her husband was taking care of everything, and she promised to have the legal papers on my desk before the month was over. In the meantime she didn't want me to order anything more for you that couldn't be returned. Kate, you've simply got to call me and tell me how you want me to handle this. Oh, and by the way, I don't know how she did it, but she found out the name of the company we use to make your ribbon, and she called them direct to cancel the order. She told them she was the new owner and that she wanted to change the color to something that would get more attention. She's not sure what color the boxes will be yet, but the ribbons will be bright blue with fuchsia trim. The sales rep called me and asked what he should do. Please get back to me as soon as you can. I really need some help here."

Kate was yelling at the phone when Dylan returned to the car. He knew she wasn't talking to anyone because she was holding the phone at arm's length and shouting incoherently.

"Kate, listen to me—" It was as far as he could get.

"She's changing my ribbons. Do you believe that? She's telling people she owns my company. The loan . . . that loan . . . she knew all about the loan my mother . . . it's that weasel accountant, Simmons . . . this must be his wife."

She was so angry she was shaking and talking so fast all Dylan got was something about a ribbon and a weasel.

"You need to listen to me," Dylan said. "Forget about the ribbon—"

"I will not forget about my ribbon. I'm calling a lawyer, and I'm going to nail that little weasel. How dare he . . . and she . . . change my ribbon? She wants fuchsia? Can you believe the gall . . ."

She was waving her phone around while she rambled on. Dylan dodged it once, then grabbed it and placed it on the console.

Once again he tried to get her attention. "Kate . . ."

She was on a roll. "Do you think the loan officer at the bank is in on it, too? If he is, he's going to prison with the weasel. How dare they—"

He cupped the sides of her face and forced her to look at him. "Kate." He didn't shout her name but he came close. He got her full attention. "You've got much bigger problems than ribbon."

He let go of her, sat back, and waited for her to calm down. The impact of what he'd just said cut through her anger. She was suddenly so embarrassed by her raving lunatic behavior she apologized. "I'm so sorry. I shouldn't have shouted . . . it was just a shock, you see. They're trying to steal my company . . . those sneaky—"

He quickly stopped her before she got all revved up again. "But you won't let them."

"Yes, you're right. I won't let them." She was finally able to compose herself.

"Are you ready to listen to me?"

"Yes, I'm ready. What did Nate tell you?"

"The cousins are all bad news. Bryce has racked up a huge debt which will all be dumped on his wife when he dies. He's in liver failure, and the doctors figure he's got about six months."

"No shock there," she said. "He looks like he's dying."

"He's just thirty-five, and he has already destroyed his liver with alcohol."

He moved on to Ewan. Kate wasn't surprised to hear about his violent behavior. She'd seen a glimpse of his temper in Anderson's office. Ewan seemed capable of going into a rage at the least provocation.

"Roger's the gambler in the family."

"Yes," she said. "In the video Compton said Roger had gambled away four hundred thousand. That surely was an exaggeration."

"No, it was pretty accurate," Dylan said. "And apparently Roger hasn't slowed down. He's in to a loan shark for about seven hundred thousand now."

"No," she whispered. "Are you sure? Seven hundred? That's crazy." She shook her head. "No wonder he was crying."

"You haven't heard the bad news yet. Roger borrowed the money from Johnny Jackman. He's the real badass here. He's got connections you wouldn't believe, and he also has a reputation to uphold. He's going to get that money one way or another."

"You sound like you know Jackman. Do you?"

"I've never met him, but I've heard all about him. The feds are going to be happy with this development. They've been trying to get something on him for a long time. Nate can't leave them out of this any longer. He needs them. And so do we."

"What happens now?"

"We keep you alive."

"I want to go home," she whispered.

He was exasperated with her but understood. "You know you can't go home."

She didn't argue. "For how long?"

"Depends."

"I shouldn't have taken the money," she blurted out. "I didn't want it. But then I heard them saying such terrible things about my family . . . my mother in particular, and I wanted to strike back. Taking the money seemed the best way."

"It wouldn't have mattered. Whoever wants

you out of the way couldn't take the chance you might change your mind. Too much is at stake."

"So everything that's been happening to me is tied up with this money?"

"We have to assume it's about the money. You heard what Compton said. He changed the will some time ago, but according to the date on the video, he didn't record his message until a few weeks ago. Since the explosions happened after the video was made, the question now is, who knew about the video?"

"You saw how shocked and outraged those brothers were, and Vanessa looked dumbfounded."

"True. So, either there's a player out there we don't know about, or one of your relatives is a damned fine actor."

Chapter Twenty-seven

KATE DIDN'T WANT TO STAY IN SAVANNAH FOR the night. She dearly loved the city, but because her relatives were there, she was determined to get as far away as possible.

Dylan understood and agreed. He headed northwest, avoided the highway, and stayed on the scenic back roads. He didn't seem worried about where they'd spend the night. He also didn't seem concerned that they were getting low on gas.

"We don't want to run out of gas on a back road," she said.

"No, we don't," he agreed. He glanced at her and asked, "Are you going to worry about it?"

"Yes, I am."

"Okay, we'll stop. Get the map out of the glove compartment, please. Find Bucyrus. The sign we passed a couple of minutes ago says we're ten miles from it."

She hadn't noticed the sign. After unfolding the map and checking their location, she gave him directions. The little town was nestled in a valley, and according to the WELCOME TO BUCYRUS sign, there were 828 residents.

They found a restaurant on Main Street. The parking spots angled into the curb. Dylan pulled in front of the hardware store. He turned the motor off and asked, "Are you hungry? Sure you are," he answered before she had a chance to say anything. "I'm starving."

He made two phone calls while she stretched her legs and tried to shake off the sick feeling in her stomach. She wasn't ill, but every time she thought about the relatives she became nauseated.

She didn't have an appetite until she walked into the restaurant. The aroma of freshly baked bread, cinnamon, and other more pungent spices greeted them, and by the time she sat down, she was ravenous.

The owner had taken time and care with the restaurant's décor and was apparently a fan of stripes. Yellow-and-white-striped curtains hung at the windows. The tablecloths were also yellow and white and so were the stools at the counter. But the motif had not yet reached the booths. Strips of duct tape covered tears in their blue vinyl seats.

"Quaint" or "charming" might be overstated descriptions of the eatery, but it definitely fit into the homey category. On each table were ceramic salt and pepper sets in various animal shapes. The table Dylan and Kate chose had black-and-white-spotted cows.

What the restaurant lacked in ambience was made up for by the food, which was delicious and homemade. They both ordered a shrimp and pasta dish that came with a salad. Dylan ate all of his and half of hers.

The restaurant was empty except for the waitress and the cook, who were occupied with the soap opera that was playing on the small television at the end of the counter. Dylan leaned in so that he couldn't be heard and said, "Tell me more about this weasel and ribbon."

Kate's brow wrinkled into a frown and she shook her head. "You know about the loan my mother took out using my company, among other things, as collateral."

"Yes. And . . . ?" Dylan urged.

"It appears the accountant who managed my mother's finances and his wife are planning to take over my company just as soon as the due date for the payment arrives."

"What does this have to do with ribbon?" he asked.

Kate filled him in on her conversation with Haley, and after she was through, Dylan sat back in the booth and fell silent for a few minutes. He was deep in thought and Kate could tell he was analyzing all the facts of her situation.

"I think we have a lot more to look into," he said finally. He stood, took her hands, and pulled her to her feet. Before leaving the restaurant he got directions to the nearest filling station.

While he filled the gas tank, Kate used her cell phone to try to get hold of Jordan, but the answering machine picked up yet again. Kate left her a message to please call.

Once he was back in the car, Dylan looked at the map for about thirty seconds and said, "Okay, let's go."

"Did you have a destination in mind?"

"How about I surprise you?"

"As long as the rooms are clean, I'll be happy."

"Not rooms," he said. "One room. You're staying with me."

She didn't argue. "Will I have my own bed?"

"If that's what you want."

But what if I don't know what I want? she wondered. **What then?** She thought about the silly that-was-then-this-is-now speech she'd given him and wished she'd kept her mouth shut.

"If you want to make any phone calls, do it now because once we leave Bucyrus I don't want you calling anyone on your cell phone."

"Why can't I use my cell phone?"

"Better to be cautious."

It wasn't much of an explanation. "I should call Kiera and Isabel. I've put it off long enough. Hopefully their answering machines are on. Otherwise, I'll have to go into detail, and I'd rather not do that now."

Kate lucked out. She got voice mail right away. She left the same message for each of them. "The relatives are horrible," she began. "And I've got a video to show you of the great-uncle we've been blessed not to know. I'll explain everything tomorrow. I'm in a rush now and will be unavailable. If you need me, leave me a message."

"How come you didn't tell them about the inheritance?"

She shrugged. "It wasn't important." She noticed his smile and asked, "Why is that amusing?"

"Not amusing . . . just reflective."

"Reflective of what?"

"You."

A sudden worry turned her attention. "What about Kiera and Isabel? They're safe, aren't they? Their inheritance has already been transferred to them. Still . . ."

"Anderson assured us they aren't in line to inherit the fortune. But I already talked to Nate about your sisters, and he's going to make sure they're covered. Hopefully, neither one of them will notice she has a shadow. You don't need to worry about them. All right?"

"Yes," she said. "Thank you."

"Any other phone calls you want to make, make them now," he said.

Kate quickly called Haley and once again

missed her. She left a long message explaining that she still owned the company, and everything would be straightened out soon. In the meantime, she asked her not to say anything to the Simmons woman.

"Please don't let her know we've talked. I'm working on a surprise for her and her husband. I'll explain everything soon," she promised.

She disconnected the line, then tried once again to get hold of Jordan. She left another message before turning her phone off.

"I've been trying to reach your sister, and she hasn't returned my calls. That's not like her," she said.

"You haven't been able to get in touch with her since I showed up at your front door, right?"

"Now that I think about it, yes, that's right."

"She's probably just giving you time to cool down. I'm sure she thinks you're angry with her for interfering."

"By sending you to me?"

"Yes."

"I'll admit for a little while I was irritated. I didn't like the idea of any man coming to save the day, and I found it a bit galling that Jordan, who is beyond a liberated woman, would send her brother to take care of me. I know—she sent you because you're a detective who knows how to handle this sort of thing, but I still want to give her a piece of my mind. Making you come all this way . . ."

"Jordan can't make me do anything I don't want to do."

Ha. Of course she could, but Kate wasn't going to burst his bubble and tell him so. Jordan, like her sister, Sydney, could get all of her brothers to do anything she wanted. When begging didn't work, she used guilt. She'd perfected various other techniques as well; however, guilt had always worked best.

Kate was thankful Dylan was with her. Oh, she knew that Nate and the other detectives in Charleston were capable men, but she was . . . comfortable with Dylan. There was also the trust issue. Hers was absolute.

Dylan's phone rang. The second he read the caller ID he started smiling. One of his women was on the line, no doubt. It was a reasonable conclusion. The man was grinning like an idiot.

Kate couldn't believe how disgruntled she became. What did she care about his love life?

Apparently far more than she wanted to, she admitted.

"Hey, sweetie. What's going on?" he said into the phone.

Sweetie? He called her sweetie? Kate felt like grabbing the phone from him and tossing it out the window. She wondered how sweetie would like that.

She folded her arms and pretended not to be listening as she looked out the side window. The woman on the phone was doing most of the talking, but every once in a while Dylan would interject a word or two of encouragement or praise.

"That's good to hear . . . now you're thinking . . . yes, of course you can call me anytime . . . no, no, you're doing great. I'll talk to you real soon. You take care now . . ."

It was enough to make her want to throw up. How many women did he have dangling, waiting desperately for him to call? **I'll talk to you soon?** How many times had he given that promise? Did he ever follow through? Did he call back? Probably not. It was just a kiss-off line.

She did notice that Dylan hadn't used his flirty voice, that wonderful, sexy tone that melted her defenses. Just bet he'd melted a lot of other women, too . . .

Good God, she was jealous.

"Kate?"

"Yes?" She snapped the word out with bullet speed.

"Isabel says hello."

"What?" If she'd been standing, she would have fallen over. "Isabel . . . what?"

"She said hello. What's the matter with you? Why are you so jumpy?"

If he only knew. "Nothing's wrong with me."

"Your face is red."

"What?"

"I said your face is red."

"Why did Isabel call you?"

"She had my phone number," he said. "And she wanted me to know she changed the dead bolt on her door." He smiled as he added, "She said the lock didn't work, so she went to a hardware store, got what she needed, and impressed her room-mate by doing it all herself."

"Oh. I thought . . ."

"What? What did you think?"

She wasn't going to explain. "Why didn't she call me? I just left her a message about meeting the relatives. Did she mention it?"

"Yes, she did. She wanted me to tell you she's sorry they weren't more hospitable."

Kate laughed. "Hospitable? That's something Isabel would say, all right. She probably thinks they would have been nicer if I'd offered them a beverage."

"Don't sell her short, Kate. There's a brain hiding inside that blond hair. I'll tell you what. She's going to break a lot of hearts."

"I worry about her," she admitted. "She's too trusting."

"You want her to be more cynical?"

"Like me?"

"You're not cynical. You're scared."

"Scared of what?"

"Me."

"Ha." Oh, that was an intelligent, well-thought-out response. "Why didn't you tell me Isabel was on the phone?"

He grinned. "I didn't want to."

"Why not?"

"I was having too much fun watching you get all riled up."

Had her body language been that easy to read?

Kate made the mistake of trying to bluff her way through the awkward conversation. "Why would I get riled up?"

"You thought I was talking to a girlfriend."

Okay, trying to bluff had been a mistake, she realized. Better not to say anything.

"You're not denying it?"

"Would you believe me if I were?"

"Nope."

"Then I won't."

Determined to ignore him, she stared out the window and tried to be fascinated by the scenery. The tarred road they were on wound through a collage of colors. They passed an old, deserted fruit stand, and a few minutes later a black-water lake came into view.

"You know what I find real interesting?" he asked. "You keep insisting that our night together in Boston was a mistake."

"That's right, it was. And it cannot happen again. It was an unusual circumstance, but now that we're back to normal—"

"This is normal?"

She had to wait for him to stop laughing before she could continue. "Apparently I need to explain my actions again."

He groaned. "You're not going to give me the that-was-then lecture again, are you?"

He was beginning to infuriate her. "Do I need to?"

"You seem to enjoy giving that speech," he replied. And before she could interrupt, he added, "What I find interesting is that you don't want me to touch you, but when you thought I was talking to a girl back home, you got all riled up. That's a contradiction, isn't it?"

She needed to stop being defensive and embarrassed. "You enjoy flirting," she said. "And that's fine with me. But you know as well as I do that a relationship with me would be a disaster. Eventually you're going to go home, and you would feel terrible if you hurt me when you ended it, and I'd feel terrible if I hurt you by ending it, and it's just not worth it."

"You forgot to mention Jordan this time."

Rattled, she said, "I what? What do you mean 'this time'?"

"The last time you told me a relationship with you wouldn't work, Jordan was at the top of your list of reasons."

"I've said all of this before?"

"Pretty much."

That took the wind out of her sails. "Then I shouldn't have to go through it again, should I? I value Jordan's friendship . . . did I mention that?"

"Sure did. You also told me you didn't want it to be awkward."

He was sounding slightly patronizing now. "So you were listening and you do understand."

"Yes," he said. "And I agree. Getting involved is a bad idea."

She knew she should be relieved that he agreed with her, and yes, she was relieved, but did he have to agree so quickly?

She wasn't being logical. The problem was, she didn't know what to do about it.

Exhaustion and stress. Perfectly sound reasons for being so contradictory.

"I have every right."

"Excuse me?"

Great. She was in worse condition than she'd realized. Now she was thinking out loud.

"I'm stressed, and I have every right to be stressed, and do you know why?" She continued before he could say a word. "Someone out there is trying to blow me up."

"Katie . . ."

"I'm tired," she said. "Since I came home from Boston, I've felt like a punching bag. I think it's time for me to start punching back."

He nodded approval. "That's good to hear. As long as you know who to punch."

"Oh, I've got a few people in mind."

They rode along for several minutes in silence, and she asked, "Why can't I use my cell phone?"

"I'm probably being overly cautious, but when I heard that Jackman could be involved and probably is, I didn't want to take any chances. A cell phone is easy to pinpoint, and calls, just like regular phones, can be traced if you've got the right equipment."

"You told me Jackman was a loan shark. Would he have that kind of capability?"

"He's a whole lot more than a loan shark, and if he doesn't have the capability, he knows people he can lean on who do."

The man sounded like a monster. A chill ran down her spine. "Have you told anyone where we'll be spending the night?"

"No, not a soul. I thought we'd head to Charleston. I'll find a hotel there, maybe on the outskirts."

"The closer we get to Silver Springs, the happier I'll be."

"We're going to have to figure out what to do about tomorrow. We can't go back to Savannah."

"No, we can't," she agreed. "But until I sign those papers . . ."

Chapter Twenty-eight

THE HOTEL WAS PACKED, YET DYLAN MANAGED to get them a lovely room—all without showing any identification, as far as Kate could see. She waited across the lobby and watched the master at work. The person behind the counter was a young woman, and Dylan was Mr. Charismatic. It took him less than five minutes to get her to blush and hand him the key. Kate thought she might have handed him her phone number, too.

The room was well appointed and spacious and had a breathtaking view of the ocean. There were two queen-size beds which the maids had already turned down for the night.

As soon as the bellman left, she asked Dylan, "What did you have to promise that woman to get this wonderful room?"

"I can't give away trade secrets," he said. He unzipped his garment bag and hung his clothes in the walk-in closet.

She grinned. "You just can't help it, can you?"

She thought he hadn't heard her. He went into the bathroom, put his shaving kit on the marble counter, and called out, "This place is huge. I can't help what?"

He had been listening. "It's second nature to you. I think you were born with this . . . talent. Now that I think about it, all of the Buchanan brothers have it. It must be in the genes," she added as she considered the possibility.

He stood in the doorway watching her. "I've got lots of talents, Pickle."

"Yes, you do."

"What was I born with?"

She really wished she hadn't started this conversation because he wasn't going to let it go. "A tiger can't help having stripes, and you can't help flirting. It's okay," she hastened to add. "You make every woman you meet feel special. It's a gift."

"A gift, huh?"

She couldn't tell if he was pleased by her observation or irritated. "Yes, that's right. Which bed do you want?" she asked, hoping to change the subject.

"The one by the door. You sound like you approve of this gift."

Approve? She wouldn't go that far. "I understand," she said. "And it doesn't faze me."

"So if I were to come on to you, or hit on you, or flirt, or whatever it is you think I do . . ."

"It wouldn't bother me at all. I'm immune now, Dylan."

Ah, man, was he going to have some fun with her. "Good to know," he drawled.

Desperate to change the subject, she picked up her makeup bag and her pajamas and robe. "I'd like to take a shower and go to bed."

"No problem," he said.

She glanced at the clock on the bedside table and was shocked by how late it was. They'd stopped for dinner and must have lingered longer than she realized.

She was walking past him when she remarked, "It's been a long day." She thought he had said something and turned around. "Excuse me?"

"Yeah, okay."

She tilted her head. "What . . ."

He moved fast. His hand cupped the back of her neck and his mouth captured hers.

She didn't even think about pushing him away or stepping back. She might have sighed into his mouth, though. When his tongue swept inside to stroke hers, her body tingled all the way down to her toes.

She was about to put her arms around his neck when he pulled back. Her heart was racing, and she couldn't catch her breath, but Dylan looked unaffected. He reached behind her and pushed the bathroom door open. She didn't budge.

"Why did you do that?"

"Kiss you?"

"Yes."

"You didn't ask me to?" His eyes sparkled with devilment.

"No, of course I didn't."

He gave her a little push to get her to move. "I could have sworn you did. My mistake."

She caught a glimpse of his grin as he walked away.

She shut the door, locked it, and dropped her makeup bag on the counter. There were two sinks. She took the one closest to the wall and tried not to think about the kiss as she took out her toothbrush and toiletries.

She glanced at herself in the mirror and cringed. She looked horrible. Her hair was hanging limply around her face, and the shadows under her eyes had gotten darker. And he'd kissed her. Goes to show you, she thought. Dylan either had very low standards, or he would hit on any woman no matter how bad she looked.

A hot shower made her feel almost human again. She hadn't realized how tense she was or how much the muscles in her neck and shoulders ached until the hot water loosened them.

She worried about Dylan's shoulder. He hadn't had therapy in a while. Were his muscles tightening up? Was he in pain? If he weren't so sensitive and macho about his injury, she would have asked.

She washed her hair and dried it, brushed her teeth, and put on moisturizer. Then she cleaned the bathroom. She knew how much Dylan hated clutter. He liked everything neat and in its place. When she was finished she checked herself in the mirror one last time and opened the door.

"Your turn."

He gave her the once-over as he walked toward her. His gaze lingered on her legs.

She swallowed. Why was she feeling so nervous? After all, she'd slept with him, hadn't she? He'd seen her naked, and she'd seen him.

Don't think about it. Just dive in bed, pull the covers up, and hide like a coward.

He stopped when he was directly in front of her. His hands settled on her hips and he pulled her close. He leaned down, and she thought he was going to kiss her again. She couldn't allow that, shouldn't allow it, she thought as she tilted her head back in anticipation.

"Dylan, I don't think . . ."

"You don't think what? I'm trying to get a closer look at those bruises. The one on your forehead is beginning to fade."

He let go of her and stepped back. She felt like an idiot. "It's better now," she stammered.

"One more thing," he said when she tried to walk past him.

"Yes?"

She looked up just as his hand brushed the side

of her face. And then he kissed her. It was a quick touch of his mouth on hers, and yet it was electrifying all the same.

She wanted more.

She forced herself to put some distance between them. "About that kiss . . ."

"You didn't like it?" He didn't give her time to answer. "Yeah," he said. "I didn't like it either."

Before she could prepare her defenses, he wrapped her in his arms, tilted her head back, and kissed her again. He was serious this time. His mouth was open and hot. How could she not respond? She felt as though she were melting under his touch, and oh it felt so right.

He ended the kiss abruptly and let go. She nearly fell backward, but he grabbed her and smiled. "I like that a lot better."

One kiss and he'd turned her mind into mush. "I don't know how you do it," she whispered hoarsely.

"That's an easy one. I lean in, and my mouth presses against yours, and my tongue— "

"Oh, for heaven's sake. I'm not asking you how to kiss. I just mean that I don't know how you can so easily make me—"

He beat her to the punch. "Want more?"

"Flustered." She nearly shouted the word. "You make me flustered."

"Good to know."

This time she watched him walk into the

bathroom and shut the door. She tried to summon up a frown, to work up a little anger. Self-preservation. That's what it was, she thought. If she could hide behind anger, she wouldn't have to face the truth.

A smile came unbidden, and she was suddenly weak-kneed. She sat on the bed and fell back against the pillows. It was odd, the thoughts that came into your mind when you weren't blocking them. She pictured Dylan lecturing Isabel and instructing her. He'd been so caring with her.

He'd been caring with Kate, too. She remembered the way he'd held her in his arms while she'd wept against his shoulder . . . the way he'd touched her . . .

There was so much more to Dylan than his relentless teasing during those pickup football games on Nathan's Bay. He was strong, and yet he could be very gentle. He was decisive, but still he took time to listen. He was kind and smart and sexy and . . .

"Oh, no," she groaned. She was in love with him.

The truth stunned her. When had this terrible thing happened to her? She tried but couldn't come up with a defining moment. She had a feeling that it would take years of therapy to figure this one out.

Of all the men in the world she could have

fallen in love with, she had to pick Mr. Love-'em-and-leave-'em. She groaned again.

All things considered, however, she thought she was taking the realization quite well. She wasn't running down the hallways screaming or tearing her hair out.

She wasn't jumping up and down with joy, either. But then why should she? She'd lost her frickin' mind.

She reached for the phone to call Jordan. It was an automatic reaction to want to talk to her best friend and pour her heart out. Then she remembered she couldn't call anyone now and knew she shouldn't anyway because Dylan was Jordan's brother. It just wouldn't be right to scream and carry on.

She would have to suffer in silence. She rolled onto her stomach and buried her face in her pillow, thinking that if a scream escaped, the pillow would muffle the sound.

"Kate, are you trying to suffocate yourself?"

Now that's a plan. She was laughing when she sat up. "I always put a pillow over my face when I'm thinking."

He was wearing a pair of khaki shorts that rode low on his hips. They were zipped but not buttoned. His stomach was flat, hard. He didn't bother with a T-shirt. He was sexy, no doubt about it. She refused to look into his eyes, fearing he'd know he was getting to her.

She grabbed the notepad from the bedside table and a pen. "I'm going to write down the names of the people I think would like to kill me."

He stretched out on the bed, adjusted the pillows, and stacked his hands behind his head. "Wouldn't it be quicker to write down the names of the people who don't want to kill you?"

"That's not funny," she said. "People enjoy my company. They do," she insisted when she thought he looked skeptical.

"I sure enjoyed you."

She wasn't in the mood for teasing. Ignoring him seemed to be the only logical course of action. Kate began to write names, and in no time at all, she'd filled two pages and was working on a third. She suddenly stopped. She was struck by what she was doing, and why. Granted, the notepad was small, but still, two and a half pages? Oh, dear Lord.

"Kate, what's the matter?"

"It just hit me . . . what I'm doing. If someone a month ago had told me I would be making this kind of a list, I wouldn't have believed him. Good heavens, Dylan," she cried out, "look at all these names."

He rolled to his side to face her. "You aren't going to panic on me, are you? You're safe now. Right this minute you're safe. Concentrate on that."

She rolled her eyes. "I'm not freaking out, so

you can stop talking to me in that keep-her-calm-until-we-get-the-straitjacket-on-her voice. It all sort of overwhelmed me for a moment, that's all. Two shocks in one night . . ."

"What do you mean, two?"

He would have to zoom in on that slip, wouldn't he? Realizing she loved him was a bigger jolt to her system than her long list of suspects. Maybe because the truth had snuck up on her and then . . . **boom**.

"Kate?"

"It's work related," she lied. She rotated her pen between her fingers while she once again concentrated on the list. "I'm not going to sleep until I've crossed off at least one of these names. I'd feel like I was making some progress," she explained before he could ask a third time. "You could help, you know."

He was on his back again staring at the ceiling. He looked half asleep.

She thought he was ignoring her until he said, "I guess you could cross off the artist, Oregano."

"Cinnamon," she corrected. "Her name is Cinnamon. I'll bet she'll be devastated to know the explosion wasn't meant to kill her. She was getting a lot of mileage out of the publicity." She sighed as she added, "I didn't put her name on my list so I can't cross her off."

She read him the names she'd written. All of the MacKenna brothers made her list, and she had even included Anderson and his assistant. She couldn't remember his name.

"Terrance," he supplied.

"I honestly don't think Anderson or Terrance or Vanessa MacKenna is involved, but I included them because they were in the office when the video was played. I also put Carl's name on the list, but I can surely cross him off, can't I?"

"No, you can't. He's guilty until proven innocent."

"That's not how it works. It's the other way around."

"Not when it comes to your life. He's involved in some way," he added. "I just don't know how yet."

She tucked a strand of hair behind her ear and studied her list for another minute or two.

She couldn't believe she'd forgotten to add Jackman. She wrote the name and was putting the pen down when he added, "And his associates."

She was becoming more and more frustrated. "I'm going to put a name down and then I'm going to cross him off, got that? What about Reece? Should I put him on the list?"

Her voice was becoming shrill. She knew she needed to calm down before she lost it. She just wasn't sure how.

"Why are you so relaxed about all this?" she demanded.

"Waiting's always tough. I've got good people

gathering information for me. I have to be patient, and so do you."

"Easier said than done," she said. "Are you sorry you got involved?"

"No."

The answer was abrupt, almost angry. Kate thought she might have offended.

"What about the weasel's wife who took your ribbon? Would you feel better if you put her name on the list and crossed it off?" he asked.

"She didn't take my ribbon. She and her husband are trying to steal my company."

"But you've got a plan to stop them, don't you?"

She was able to smile again. "Yes, I do. And when I'm finished with them, I assure you they'll want to kill me."

He laughed; she'd sounded so gleeful. "That's my girl."

She tossed the pad and pen on the table and turned the lamp off. The room was suffused in moonlight filtering in through the sheers.

"Good night," she whispered.

He didn't respond. Had he already fallen asleep? Or was he faking it so she'd stop talking and give him a little peace?

She knew she wasn't going to get any rest. All she could think about was Dylan. She wanted to sleep with him, and for a minute or two she was actually able to pretend that she only wanted to be held in his arms, but she was deceiving herself and she knew it. She wanted it all. She wanted to feel him moving within her, to touch every inch of him.

She thought about his mouth, his hot, sexy mouth, and what he could do with it . . .

"Kate?"

She nearly came off the bed. "Yes?"

"What's wrong?"

"Nothing's wrong."

"I thought I heard you groan."

"Oh. Maybe I did. I can't sleep."

"You just turned the lamp off. Don't you think you should give yourself a couple of minutes before you decide you can't sleep? Is there anything I can do to help?"

If he only knew. "Like what?"

"You're going to have to tell me."

She was certain she heard amusement in his voice. Did he know what his nearness was doing to her?

Hold on a minute. What about him? Was she affecting him the same way? He was the sex maniac, not her . . . until recently, anyway, or more specifically until she'd spent the night with him. Was he toying with her?

"No. I can't think of a thing you could do to help me."

She waited for a reaction and was disappointed when she didn't get one. Several long minutes passed in silence. She couldn't even hear him breathe.

And then a long drawn out sigh. "Katie?"

"Yes, Dylan?"

"Am I coming over there, or are you coming to me?"

Chapter Twenty-nine

MORNING CAME ALL TOO SOON, AND SHE awoke with no regrets. After the night they'd shared, she probably should feel a little awkward around him, and when she thought about all the things he'd done to her and she'd done to him, she should at the very least find it difficult to look him in the eye. But regrets? No, there were no regrets.

She was thankful she woke up before he did. He was sleeping on his stomach with one arm hanging off the bed. The pillows and sheets and blankets were on the floor. It had been a wild night, all right. And glorious.

Kate didn't start worrying until she was in the shower. Had she said something she shouldn't have in one of those passionate moments when he was driving her out of her mind? Had she told him she loved him? Dear God, she didn't, did she?

She couldn't remember. She prayed she hadn't. But if she had . . . what then? Pretend she hadn't? She couldn't think of anything better to do, and so she settled on that. Senators did it all the time, and under oath no less. They pretended they hadn't known . . . whatever. And if lying was good enough for a congressman, by God, it was good enough for her.

Okay, it had finally happened. Dylan had made her completely crazy.

She'd never get out of the shower if she didn't stop thinking about him. There was so much she needed to get done today. She had promised Anderson that she would look through the binder. He wanted her to understand how the uncle had amassed his fortune, she supposed. And his advisors and accountants would be on hand to answer questions. No choice, she decided. She had to read the thing.

But there were also the photos of her father. She'd been too weary last night to look at them.

Kate hurried to get dressed. She packed her makeup and toothbrush in her bag and opened the door.

Dylan was just getting out of bed. He didn't look awake, though. His hair was tousled and he was naked. As he walked toward her, her stomach quivered.

"Good morning," she said cheerfully.

He grunted a reply. Obviously not a morning person, she decided.

He passed her, grabbed her arm, and before she had time to prepare, he kissed her. She wanted to put her arms around him and lean into him. His body was so warm and . . .

She pulled back. Her thoughts were going to get her in trouble. "I've got reading to do, and you need to wake up."

With the least amount of coaxing she would have gone back to bed with him. She rushed to the table and grabbed the binder and the envelope of photos. She heard the bathroom door shut, and she relaxed. She was safe from acting out her lustful thoughts, and hopefully when he came out of the bathroom, he'd be dressed.

She went to her bed, kicked her shoes off, and sat with her back against the headboard. Ready now, she opened the binder and began to read . . . and became sick in no time at all. That horrible old man had documented each acquisition with boastful notes in the margin, and after reading about fifteen pages word for word, she understood the pattern and skimmed over the rest.

He made his fortune buying companies, stripping them, and selling off what was left.

If Anderson had told her that Compton had been a shrewd businessman and had carefully built his portfolio by buying and selling properties, Kate probably wouldn't have thought much

about it, and she doubted she would have been repulsed. Lots of clever, driven men and women
made their fortunes wheeling and dealing, and
Kate would have assumed Compton fit into that
category. But seeing what he had done, and how
he had done it, on paper, made all the difference.
He used deceit and false promises, anything, it
seemed, to get what he wanted. He certainly
didn't have any scruples. The number of lives, the
dreams he'd destroyed over the years, the jobs
and security of faithful employees he'd snatched
away . . . all that meant nothing to him, nor did
the families of those who were dependent on the
income of the companies he closed. The human
element wasn't his concern, and compassion
wasn't in his nature.

The only thing Compton MacKenna ever
cared about was money, and how to make more.

What he had done wasn't criminal. But it was
immoral. And he had gone to his grave proud of
his accomplishments. Had he compiled this testimonial to his conquests just to impress her?

Dear God, he believed she was like him.

Reading his financial history validated her initial decision. She could not and would not spend
a single dollar of his money on herself, her family,
her company, or her future.

Compton MacKenna was a selfish, cruel man.
She was not like him, and she meant to prove it.
Whatever she decided to do with the money had

to be perfect, and when she was done, she hoped Compton would roll over in his grave.

Shoving the binder aside, she reached for the envelope and opened it. Her mood immediately improved. There were ten photos, all black and white.

Her father had been a handsome boy. He looked dashing in his school uniform. He was definitely a child of privilege, she thought, as she studied one photo of him in a polo outfit standing so proudly in front of a horse. In another photo he was about four or five years old, and he was standing on a lawn, smiling into the camera. In the background was a house—no, not a house, a mansion. Had he lived there?

There weren't any photos of him with his parents or other relatives. She thought that was odd and wondered if there were other pictures of her father packed away somewhere. She made a mental note to ask Anderson to find out.

She was just tucking the last photo back into the envelope when Dylan joined her.

"You ready?" he asked.

"Almost."

She put the envelope and binder in her overnight bag.

Dylan was folding linens and placing them back on the bed with the pillows he'd already picked up. He noticed what she was doing and asked, "Don't you want to take that binder in the car so you can look it over?"

"I've already looked through it."

"Were you impressed? I got the idea that whoever put it together for you thought you would be."

"I wasn't."

She checked the bathroom and closet to make sure she hadn't left anything behind, but Dylan had already straightened them. Even the damp towels in the bathroom had been folded and left on the vanity.

They stopped for breakfast at the hotel coffee shop, but neither one of them was very hungry. As soon as they were back in the car, he checked the map again so he could avoid highways as they made their way toward Silver Springs.

"I should call Anderson," she said. "I don't want him to plan on seeing me at three."

"But you might see him at three," he said. "It all depends on how we work things out."

"We're going back to Savannah? Won't that be dangerous? That's a terrible idea. I'm warning you now. If we walk into that office and I see a basket of flowers anywhere in the vicinity, I won't be responsible for my actions. I'll do something terrible. I just know I will. I don't know exactly what that will be, but I assure you I cannot endure getting blown up again, and I won't let you get hurt.

No, it's out of the question. We simply can't go back there. My mind's made up."

He did try to interrupt her during her tirade, but she was on a roll and wouldn't be stopped. When she finally had to take a breath, he said, "We don't know yet if we have to go back to Anderson's office. He might be able to bring the papers to us."

"Oh."

"Oh? That's it?"

"I might have overreacted . . ."

"Might have?"

She reached behind her seat for the briefcase. "If you had mentioned this sooner, I wouldn't have gotten upset." She found the file folders she was looking for and pulled them out.

"What's all that?" he asked.

"Loan papers my mother signed. I want to read them again. The other folder is from one of the hospitals. In the last year of her life she spent more time there than at home."

Kate took the next twenty minutes to read each paper, each bill, and each receipt, and she at last understood. Tears clouded her vision. What little insurance her mother had, had run out, and in desperation she'd signed away everything so that her daughters wouldn't be saddled with her debt.

The hospital bills alone were astronomical.

How she must have worried, but in silence, telling no one and keeping the heartache and fear inside.

Tears streamed down Kate's face. She turned away so Dylan wouldn't notice. She found a tissue in her purse and quickly wiped the tears away.

"Kate, do you want to tell me what's going on?"

"I need information," she said. "And fast."

"All right."

"Do you think Anderson is ethical? If he's going to become my attorney, I'll need to know he has scruples. Is there a way to find out quickly?"

"I've already got someone looking at him. We'll know something soon."

"I like him. But he did represent Compton MacKenna, and that worries me."

"He's an attorney and obviously a good one or your uncle wouldn't have hired him. It's naïve to think Anderson had to like or respect him or any of his other clients."

"There are other people I want checked out. Who would give us the name of a good investigator?"

"I could do it for you. This is about your company, isn't it?"

"Yes," she said. "But you've got enough to deal with, and I need this information soon."

He didn't argue. "Let me think about it," he said.

She put the folders in the briefcase and sat

back. Her mind was racing with details she needed to take care of.

"After you sign those papers, what are you going to do with all that money?" he asked.

The question reminded her of yet another errand. "I need to go to a bank in Silver Springs."

He thought she meant she would transfer the money there. "Anderson will do that for you."

"You don't understand. I need to get a loan."

Chapter Thirty

DYLAN HAD THE UNEASY FEELING THAT HE WAS forgetting something. He kept replaying conversations in his mind and going over various details again and again, and still he couldn't figure out what was bothering him.

He knew he was missing something, but what? What wasn't he seeing?

Kate noticed how preoccupied and withdrawn he had become. It didn't take long for her to catch on that he didn't want to talk—his abrupt one-word responses were a dead giveaway—and for over an hour neither of them said a word. The silence wasn't awkward, though. Had she become that comfortable with him, she wondered, that she could feel so at ease?

They had reached the outskirts of Silver Springs. When he suddenly took an unexpected turn, she asked him where they were going.

"Somewhere safe," he answered. "And quiet."

"It's quiet at my house now," she said. "We could go there."

He shook his head. He bypassed her neighborhood and continued down Main Street to the Silver Springs police station.

He drove around the corner to once again park in the back lot.

"What are we doing here?"

"I need to check in," he said.

He got out of the car and came around to open the door. "I don't understand," she said. "Why do you have to check in?"

He offered her his hand. "Even though this is a temporary assignment, I'm working for Chief Drummond, and I answer to him, so it's my job to keep him informed. I don't want to do that over the phone. I was also thinking that the chief could be a big help to you with your company problems."

"He could? How?"

"You said you wanted an investigator to check out the weasel. Drummond's got the resources, and I know he won't mind helping. You'll have to explain why you want the information, but he'll keep whatever you tell him confidential. I know how worried you are."

"It would be wonderful if I could get something in my life straightened out. Thank you," she said, overcome with gratitude.

"The chief's helping me out, too," he said. "I've already called him several times and given him names to run for me. Hopefully, he'll have something by now."

She was smiling. "You must have really impressed him. I remember what Nate told you about the chief."

"Yeah? What was that?"

"He said he was tough . . . or difficult . . . and because he was retiring soon, he didn't care who he offended."

"He is retiring," he said. "I don't know how old he is or how long he's been at the job, but I'll tell you this. He hasn't lost his edge. After I met with him to get the badge and gun and we talked, I made a couple of calls of my own. I wanted to know that, if I had to, I could trust him."

"And can you?"

"Yes," he said emphatically. "He's got an impressive record, and he's a good man. I respect him," he added, "and I definitely trust him."

"Okay. Then I'll trust him, too."

They started to cross the parking lot, but Kate turned back. "I'll need my briefcase. The chief might want to look at some of the papers in my mother's file . . . if he has time to help."

"He'll make time," he assured her as he retrieved the briefcase.

After he'd handed it to her, she whispered, "And you're certain he'll keep this confidential?"

"I'm certain," he said. "You shouldn't be embarrassed about—"

She interrupted. "I'm not embarrassed. I'm just trying to protect my mother's reputation. I know you think I'm being silly. My mother wouldn't care. I just don't want anyone to think less of her." They started toward the path again. "I'm glad the chief is helping you," she said.

"I'm trying to take some of the load off Nate's shoulders," he explained. "He'd do whatever I asked him to do, but he's overworked as it is. He's trying to track down Jackman, who seems to have vanished from Las Vegas, and he's also keeping a tail on Roger and the two brothers. I doubt he's asking for any outside help. He's new to the Charleston department, and I know he wants to prove himself. The FBI is focusing on the bomber, and from what I understand, they've got a couple of solid leads there. They're also searching for Jackman, and according to Nate, everyone's still tripping over everyone else. It would look real good on his record if Nate brought Jackman in." He glanced at the station and said, "It will be less chaotic here."

Chief Drummond must have spotted them from the window. The back door swung open and he beckoned to them.

"Don't you listen to your messages?" he asked Dylan in lieu of a greeting.

"I was just about to do that," he replied.

"When you do, you'll hear me tell you to call me. We've got a real interesting situation here," he announced.

He tipped his head to Kate and said, "Good morning, Miss MacKenna."

"Good morning to you too, Chief Drummond, and please call me Kate."

"All right then."

Southerners, Dylan was learning, were always polite, no matter what the circumstances.

"You have a situation?" Dylan asked, trying to get his attention.

"Real interesting," he said. He stepped out of the way so Kate and Dylan could go inside first, then made sure the door locked behind him.

"A fella came in here about a half hour ago. Said his name was Carl Bertolli."

"Carl's here?" Kate asked.

The chief nodded. "You heard right. He's here." He led the way up the stairs to the first floor.

Kate waited impatiently for him to explain, but he didn't seem to be in any hurry as he proceeded down the back hall and pushed open the door to his office.

She hurried inside and turned to face him. "Why is he here?" she asked.

"He said he drove all this way to pay you a call,

Kate, but you weren't home, and so he decided to come on down here and turn himself in. Please, take a seat."

She dropped into one of the chairs facing his desk. "But what is Carl turning himself in for?" She was thoroughly confused.

Drummond made himself comfortable in his old squeaky chair. He folded his hands on his desk and said, "He told me he was responsible."

Kate looked at Dylan, who had closed the door behind him and was leaning against it with his arms folded across his chest. He seemed to be taking the news in stride. She wasn't. She was flabbergasted.

She carefully placed her briefcase and her purse on the floor next to her chair, her mind racing with questions.

"What is Carl saying he's responsible for?" she asked the chief.

Drummond shifted his weight and tilted his chair back on two legs. "That's a good question. I thought I would give him a few more minutes to settle down, and then I'd try once again to get an answer out of him."

"Settle down?" Dylan asked, not understanding.

Drummond nodded. "I want to question him, I sure do, and just as soon as I can figure out a way to get him to stop crying, I'll start in."

Kate now understood why the chief looked so

bewildered. He'd obviously never encountered anyone quite like Carl.

"He's . . . dramatic," she said.

"Yes, he is," the chief agreed.

"And he can be temperamental. He's an artist," she hastened to add, so Drummond wouldn't think she was criticizing her friend. "He majored in drama at the university, and he's been in several local theater productions. And as I'm sure you know, some creative artists are high-strung and . . . emotional."

"He's emotional all right."

"How do you suppose he knew you were looking for him?" she asked Dylan.

"I'm guessing his fiancée," he answered. "The police questioned her about his whereabouts. She must have gotten word to him."

"You want to take a shot at him?" Drummond asked Dylan. "He should be calming down about now."

"I'll talk to him," Kate said.

"I don't know about that," Drummond said.

Dylan was shaking his head, but she ignored him as she stood, picked up her things, straightened her skirt, and asked the chief to please take her to Carl.

When he didn't immediately hop to, she said, "Where is he waiting? In a conference room or a lounge? Chief, if I have to open every door on every floor to find him, I'll do it."

"We do have a nice conference room, and we've got a lounge with a soda machine, but Carl isn't in either one of those rooms. He's in a cell."

"You locked that dear man in a cell?"

He didn't give her time to get all worked up. "Now hold on. I didn't want to put him there. It wasn't my idea."

"Then whose idea was it?"

"His," he answered. "He insisted that I lock him up."

That didn't make any sense to her. "But why did you arrest him?" she asked.

"I didn't."

"Excuse me?"

"I didn't arrest him. He wanted me to lock him up, so I did. I figured a cell was as good a place as any for him to calm down."

"Where are the cells?"

"Upstairs."

"Will you please take me to him? He must be beside himself with worry."

"No, I'm not taking you to his cell, but here's what I will do. I'll bring Carl down to the first floor and put him in the interrogation room. You can talk to him there."

"Thank you," she said.

"Don't thank me yet. You've still got to get around him," he said, nodding at Dylan.

"I'll talk to him," Dylan said. "And I'll tell you what he had to say."

"She could stand on the other side of the two-way mirror and watch and listen," Drummond suggested. "We just had it installed," he announced proudly.

The chief was clearly on her side, and that made her like him all the more.

"Kate has something she would like to talk to you about," Dylan said. "Now would be the perfect time."

"Oh, that can wait until after I talk to Carl."

"I plan on being here all day," the chief said.

She took a step toward Dylan. "Carl and I are friends. He'll talk to me. He isn't going to hurt me, and if that's your reason for not wanting me to talk to him, then come in with me. Just don't—"

"Don't what?"

She sighed. "Scare him." He looked exasperated. "And don't intimidate him."

"How old is this guy? Ten?"

"He's sensitive," she muttered. "Unlike you."

Dylan had to move out of the way so the chief could open the door and leave. Kate seized the opportunity and slipped past Dylan on Drummond's heels.

Drummond pulled a huge round key ring with only three keys dangling from it off a wooden peg attached to the wall and headed toward the open staircase. "The interrogation room is the second door on the right. You two wait in there, and you better decide who's talking to him and who's listening, and then get on with it because, Dylan, you know you've got to call this in to Charleston and let Detective Hallinger know Carl's here. And he'll have to let the FBI know, and that means that you've got about an hour tops after you make that call before they all come tearing in here to snatch Carl away."

"They're going to have to wait," he said. "I'll make the call after I find out what Carl knows. I also want to run a couple of things past you," he explained.

"After **we** talk to Carl," Kate said.

He finally relented but with conditions. "If I think he's playing you, you're out of there. Understand?" Before she could agree or disagree he continued, "And if I don't like the way he's talking to you, you're out of there." He let her go ahead of him, and when they reached the interrogation room, he added yet another condition. "And if I think he's becoming belligerent or threatening . . ."

She turned around. "Let me guess. I'm out of there?"

"That's right."

"Would you like to know what I think?"

He grinned. "Not really."

"You're going to listen anyway. If he plays me, I'll know it and I'll tell him to knock it off. And if I don't like the way he's talking to me, I'll tell him to stop. Should he threaten me, I'll threaten back."

The interrogation room was tiny. There was a small oblong table and four chairs, two on either side. The two-way mirror was on the wall opposite the door. Dylan pulled out a chair for Kate, but he remained standing as they waited.

Carl turned out to be a surprise. Dylan had made a couple of snap judgments about the man, but as soon as Carl walked into the room, he knew he was wrong.

Carl was extremely happy to see Kate, and before Dylan could stop him, he hugged her.

"Thank God you're safe. This is all my fault, darling. I'm so sorry."

She quickly disengaged herself and made the introductions. Once the formality was dispensed with, she sat down, and Carl took the seat across from her. She put her hand out and he clasped it.

"You look tired," she said.

"I am tired. That's why I went away. I need to rest and rejuvenate, but I've been so worried."

Kate was sympathetic. "It must have been upsetting for you to find out that the police were looking for you."

"Yes, it was most distressing." His eyes welled up with tears. "But not nearly as upsetting as it was for Delilah. My fiancée worries about me, you see," he added. "I should call her. I'm allowed one phone call, aren't I?"

Dylan pulled out a chair next to Kate and sat down. "You can make as many phone calls as you want. You're not under arrest."

"Am I a suspect?"

"Yes."

"No," Kate said at the same time.

"Depends on what you have to tell me," Dylan explained.

"I should be arrested. I'm responsible for everything that's happened to Kate." He looked at her and summoned a weak smile. "It's so good to see you."

"It's good to see you, too," she said. "Would you like something to drink?" Oh my, she was sounding like Isabel again.

"A decaf latte would be lovely, but I don't suppose there's a Starbucks close by."

"No, sorry, not yet."

Dylan had had enough of the chitchat. "Tell me why you think you're responsible."

"Because it was my idea."

"What was your idea?" His voice took on a sharp edge. He wanted some answers now.

"It was my idea to display Kate's products at the event I was hosting. All of Charleston's elite were going to be there. They wouldn't dare miss," he explained. "And I thought it would be a wonderful opportunity to present her."

"Present her?"

"Launch her."

"Still not getting it."

"Though I know this is going to sound egotistical, it's a simple truth that if I endorse a product, it skyrockets."

He was right. It did sound egotistical.

"That makes you a very powerful man, doesn't it? You can make or break a career."

Carl shook his head. "I have never tried to destroy anyone. It would be vulgar. If I don't approve of a product or a person, I keep silent."

So he only used his power for good? Did he think he was Superman? Dylan suppressed a laugh.

"And what did you have to gain from this?"

"Satisfaction," he said.

"What about the warehouse? Why didn't you want Kate to know you owned it?"

"I'm only one of the owners," he corrected. "But I do have controlling interest."

"Answer the question." Dylan was tired of being accommodating. He was about to tell Kate to leave, but Carl surprised him by beating him to the punch.

"Kate, darling, would you please give us a moment alone?"

She didn't want to leave; she wanted to stay to make sure Dylan didn't tromp all over Carl's feelings, but she knew it would be rude to refuse. "Yes, of course."

Both men stood when she did, and Dylan

opened the door for her. She gave him a warning look as she walked past and whispered, "Be patient with him."

The audio control for the interrogation room was on the wall in front of him. Dylan decided to turn it off.

Carl had resumed his seat and arrogantly gestured for Dylan to do the same.

"If Kate knew what I was about to tell you, she would be embarrassed, and so I would appreciate your discretion. In return I shall be completely frank with you. Now then, I didn't want her to know that I owned the warehouse because I was going to offer it—through a Realtor, of course—at a substantially reduced price. I was trying to help Kate," he explained. "She is the dearest lady, and what I have seen happening to her this past year has been heart-wrenching. She was on the fast track, you know, and she had such grand plans. She was going to move her company to Boston. She has so many connections there. Within a year, I guarantee you, her company would have become a giant in the industry. Within five years, her products would have been sold all over the world. She could have accomplished unparalleled success."

He carefully adjusted the collar of his white shirt before continuing. "She won't move her company now. She's responsible, you see. Always responsible. Everyone comes before Kate. She will stay in Silver Springs because that's the responsible thing to do. For a long while she stayed for her mother, and now she'll stay for her sister. Isabel is the youngest, but of course you know that, don't you? Kate will stay here for at least another two, perhaps three, years.

"I would love it if she stayed permanently and expanded her company from here. She could put Silver Springs on the map. It would probably take her longer to achieve international success from here, but with her drive and her determination I have no doubt she'll get it . . . if that is what she wants. She'll do magnificent things wherever she is, but this is where Kate belongs."

"How did the other owners feel about reducing the price of the warehouse?"

"I don't know. I didn't ask them. I have controlling interest," he explained. "And the others will do whatever I want them to do. Together we own several blocks, and now that the renovation is under way and the rebirth has begun, they know they'll make a fortune. Silver Springs is a small community, and because it offers people a slower pace and a safer environment, it's becoming the place to live and play. We want to attract local business, so helping Kate by reducing the price will be seen as goodwill."

"I'll need the names of the other owners."

"Yes, of course."

"So you reduced the price because it was a smart business move."

"Yes, but also because I knew Kate was in financial trouble."

Dylan sat back. "Oh? How did you know that?"

Carl ran his fingers across the smooth surface of the table while he thought about the question. "I'm not sure how I knew," he admitted. "Someone told me. Yes," he said, nodding. "Someone must have told me, and now you'll want to know who that person was, and for the life of me, I can't remember. There have been so many cocktail parties and dinners, and people tell me things—in the strictest confidence. I hear things, often secondhand, and everyone knows how much I love Kate. I boast about her company all the time so I can get people talking and buzzing about her lovely candles and her body lotions. My Delilah adores them. Her signature perfumes are divine, and there's a new one coming in December that I believe is the most divine of all. It's called Sassy." He bit his lower lip to restrain his emotion.

Dylan had never questioned anyone quite like Carl before. He was prone to digression, but Dylan was determined to keep him on track. "If I were to ask you to write the names of the people who knew you owned that warehouse . . ."

"Impossible," Carl said. "I've been heavily promoting the area. I swear I've told half of Charleston and Silver Springs and Savannah—"

"Why Savannah?"

"I have many friends," he explained. "I spend a great deal of time there."

"Have you ever met any MacKennas in Savannah?"

"Not that I recall. I believe Kate and her sisters are the only MacKennas I know, but then I do meet so many people and I don't always catch the names."

"You still haven't explained what makes you responsible for the explosions."

"Consider the circumstances," he said. "I invited Kate to my estate, and I insisted she bring her products, and **boom**, she's nearly killed. And through a Realtor I encourage her to look at my warehouse, and **boom**, she's nearly killed again. I own both properties, you see. I am responsible. I just don't know how or why. I'm hoping you'll be able to figure that out."

The only thing Carl might be guilty of was telling everything he knew to anyone who would listen. Someone used him for information.

"What's your financial situation?" Dylan asked.

"Dismal at the moment. Abysmal. I've completely over-extended myself. But it's temporary," he assured him. "I'm building a gallery on my property—which will be magnificent when it's completed—and I've sunk the rest of my money into this latest project. But I have no doubt the return will be well worth the risk."

Dylan was a little surprised by Carl's candor. He was an unusual character and a complete contradiction. On the one hand he was pretentious and arrogant, and on the other he was straightforward and considerate. One thing was certain, he wore his heart on his sleeve for everyone to see, so there was little pretense when it came to his feelings.

"How did you meet Kate?" Dylan asked. It seemed such a curious friendship to him.

Carl smiled. "I met her at the hospital. It was several years back. She was there with her mother, and I was visiting my sister, Susannah. Kate was in high school, but she was already a beauty. And such a presence. Do you understand what I mean?"

"Oh, yes." He understood perfectly.

"She could start pulses racing even back then. My sister actually introduced us. Kate was waiting for her mother to come out of X-ray, and my sister was waiting to be taken in, and they began to chat. They became dear friends in no time at all. Susannah was two years younger than Kate," he thought to add. "Kate told her about the candles she was making with all the strange scents, and she asked Susannah if she would give her opinion of some of them. My sister was thrilled. Kate made her feel very important.

"Susannah was ill for quite some time—in and out of the hospital so often she called it her home away from home." He paused with a melancholy smile at the memory. "Kate's mother went into remission, so Kate didn't need to come to the hospital anymore, but she never forgot Susannah. She visited her often, and even after she started college, Kate would make a point of seeing her when she came home for vacations. And no matter where she was, every week, she would send a little something to Susannah. A candle, a special lotion, a flower . . . a gift to tell her she was thinking about her. Each time Kate started working on a new product, she would call to get her input. I know Kate didn't really need Susannah's opinion, but she asked for it just the same. It gave Susannah something to look forward to, especially in her last days when she was so weak." Carl's voice cracked when he said, "We lost Susannah in September. But Kate, my dear, dear Kate, still hasn't forgotten her. She told me she wanted to do something special in her memory, and so she's developed a special perfume that will be named after my sister. Susannah was her given name, but we called her Sassy."

Chapter Thirty-one

DYLAN WASN'T ABOUT TO LET KATE WALK INTO the Smith and Wesson building to sign any papers until he was absolutely certain she would be safe. Figuring out all the details and coordinating security measures with Nate and the Charleston PD, the FBI, and the Savannah PD would not only take time but would also be a logistical nightmare, and that meant that the three o'clock meeting this afternoon would definitely have to be rescheduled.

One solution would be for the attorney to bring the papers to Kate. The Silver Springs police station would have been a good location, but anywhere away from the heart of Savannah and the MacKenna brothers would have been acceptable.

Unfortunately, the location for the meeting couldn't be moved. When Dylan got Anderson on the phone and suggested other arrangements, the attorney was most apologetic as he explained that a change of venue wouldn't be possible.

"I must follow Compton MacKenna's instructions. He insisted that the meeting take place at Smith and Wesson. He liked to direct every facet of his affairs. He signed his new will in the conference room on the second floor, and that is where he wanted the transfer of his estate to take place. He even went so far as to assign seating. Kate must first listen to his advisors and his accountants as they explain how Compton accumulated his fortune, and when they are finished, she can sign the papers."

"Is that a mandatory condition?"

"I'm afraid so, yes."

"What was his reason for setting it up this way?"

"There were several reasons," Anderson said. "He expected Kate to follow in his footsteps, and he therefore believed that his advisors would guide her in future decisions that would increase his fortune. It is not a condition of the will, however, that Kate continue to employ them, and as her attorney I will strongly recommend that she fire the lot."

Before Dylan could ask why, Anderson continued. "I also believe Compton wanted to impress her, to brag, if you will. In his mind Kate was a prodigy, his prodigy."

"She won't like hearing that."

"After having spent a very brief time with her, I have already judged her to be nothing like Compton . . . or his advisors," he added.

"You'd think someone who was going to hand over that much money to one person would want to get to know her," Dylan surmised.

"I mentioned that very thing to him a few months ago, but he became indignant at the suggestion. He felt his investigation told him everything he needed to know about Kate and her sisters. He was quite the recluse at times—I suppose one would call him eccentric. He had difficulty establishing any sort of personal relationship. I think, as long as he kept his transactions on a strictly business level, he could control them. I was his attorney for the last seven years and found him to be extraordinarily inflexible. He preferred to work through his financial associates."

"How many are there?"

"Six in all," he replied. "Four advisors and two accountants. I've already given their names to Detective Hallinger."

Dylan was walking back and forth in the hall of the police station while he talked to Anderson on his cell phone. The door to the lounge was open. The tiny room was furnished with a synthetic leather sofa and a soda machine. Dylan went in and dipped into his pocket for some change as he continued his conversation. He asked the attorney to e-mail him the names and phone numbers so he could do a little checking on them, too. Just to be on the safe side. Who knew, maybe he'd find out something Nate had missed. Remote possibility . . . but still . . .

"Did Compton also want to control the time for the meeting from his grave, or can that be rescheduled?" he asked and then quickly answered his own question. "It has to be rescheduled. There's just no way it can take place this afternoon."

"I understand," Anderson said. "Compton was more flexible about the time. He realized people do get sick and there are emergencies. I believe the only reason he wanted the meeting scheduled two days after his death was to make certain his advisors and accountants would be in Savannah in time for his funeral. It was his way of making sure someone besides me showed up. What about tomorrow evening at seven? Would that be convenient for Kate?" Anderson asked. "Or the day after that? The others are coming in from out of town. They'll stay in Savannah for as long as necessary. But, you know, the sooner those papers are signed, the better for everyone's peace of mind."

And better for her chances of survival, Dylan thought. "How much notice do you need?"

"Whatever you can give me."

"What about notifying the MacKennas? You said they had to be invited? Right?"

"When I know the time, I'll call them, though I doubt any of them will show up."

"Why did Compton want them there?"

"He didn't say, but I think it was out of spite. Perhaps he wanted to rub their noses in what they had lost."

"Let's try for tomorrow at seven, and if I can't make it happen, I'll call you to reschedule."

Dylan realized he was making decisions without Kate's input. He would have to run his plans by her and get her approval.

He disconnected the call and then went through the rest of his voice messages. Nate had called four times trying to find him. With each message he became angrier. Dylan understood why. Nate felt responsible for Kate's well-being, and not knowing where she was would naturally infuriate him. Dylan didn't particularly care how angry he was. The fewer people who knew her whereabouts, the better.

He knew he couldn't avoid Nate much longer. He got two sodas out of the machine, popped the tab of one, and took a drink. And then he called Nate.

And got his voice mail. "Okay, I'm calling you back. So call me on my cell phone."

That ought to piss him off, Dylan thought.

Kate was in the chief's office. Dylan decided she had had enough time to talk to Drummond about the weasel problem, and went downstairs to join them.

She was stuffing papers into her briefcase when he walked in and handed her the other can of soda. Drummond was making notes on his legal pad.

"I'll get right on this," he promised. He looked at Dylan and said, "Kate wants to stay the night at home. I think we could make that happen. Don't you? I could get some men to sweep the house and get a couple more to patrol the grounds. She lives in a cul-de-sac, and that will make the job easier."

"Did you put him up to this?" Dylan asked Kate accusingly.

"I might have mentioned that I would like to be able to sleep in my own bed tonight."

"You did a bit more than mention it to me," the chief countered. "You out and out begged me to get Dylan to agree."

She closed her briefcase and placed it on the floor. "I don't beg," she said. Turning to Dylan, she asked, "Did you know that Chief Drummond was a detective in Los Angeles? He retired after twenty years of service and moved here because he got tired of all the traffic."

"I think she's trying to convince you that I'm qualified for the job."

"We've already talked, Kate," Dylan answered. "He knows all about my background, and I know a considerable amount about his. I think the chief knows how much I respect his experience."

Kate stood. "Then I can go home now."

"Sit right back down," the chief ordered. "You aren't going anywhere until your house has been swept. And the street," he thought to add. "Is the attorney going to bring the papers here for Kate to sign?"

Dylan had previously talked to Drummond about the possibility. "No. It was nonnegotiable. If Kate agrees, we'll try for seven o'clock tomorrow evening. That should give us enough time to get organized."

"In Savannah?" the chief asked.

"Yes."

"That's too bad. You're going to have everyone but me taking charge then."

"Everyone?" she asked.

"Savannah's in another state," he reminded her. "The FBI isn't going to be left out. This really should be their case. And then you've got Charleston PD wanting to stay in charge. The first explosion did take place in their jurisdiction, and now you also have to include Savannah PD, especially if you think something might happen."

"The Savannah police? Why would you want to involve them?"

"Because you'll be in their yard," the chief said. He looked at Dylan and added, "Think how they're gonna feel if there's gunfire or something gets blown up and they're not consulted."

Dylan nodded. "We'd never hear the end of it."

They were joking . . . weren't they? If all those people showed up, there wouldn't be enough room inside the Smith and Wesson building.

And then it hit her. If there was gunfire or a bomb—which did seem to be the favored weapon of destruction—some of those people could die.

"No," she blurted. "I don't want anyone to go to Savannah with me. I'll go alone."

"I'll let you handle this," the chief said to Dylan as he pushed his chair back. "I've got things to do."

After Drummond left, Dylan leaned against the desk waiting for Kate to explain.

She was waiting for him to argue with her. When he remained silent, she demanded, "Did you hear what I said?"

"I heard."

"And?" she was frowning up at him.

What had set her off? "Sure," he said. "If you want to go alone, you can go alone."

She immediately became suspicious. This was too easy. "Thank you."

"How are you going to get there?"

"I'll drive."

"Wasn't your car blown up?"

How could she have forgotten that? "I won't drive my car."

"I guess not."

"I'll rent a car."

"Kate, what's this about?"

You, you big dummy. You're what this is about. You could get killed. Oh, God, she couldn't even think about that. And what about all the other detectives and policemen? All of them could die in one big boom. She shook her head, letting him know she wasn't willing to explain.

He didn't take the hint. "What's this about?" he repeated.

She gave in. "It just struck me. People could die protecting me . . ."

Tears pooled in her eyes. Dylan must have seen them because he pulled her to her feet and hugged her. "It's okay. You're just a little overwhelmed."

"I guess I am," she said. She waited for him to give her a few words of comfort, to say something, anything, that would make her feel better.

He didn't seem inclined to do more than hold her, and after a moment she realized that was all she really needed.

Chapter Thirty-two

KATE LIFTED HER HEAD FROM DYLAN'S CHEST. "What about Carl?"

"What about him?"

She put some space between them. "Are you convinced that he had nothing to do with any of this?"

"Yes, I'm convinced."

"Then he can go home?"

"No, not yet. He's going to have to convince some other people first."

Two FBI agents and another detective from Charleston PD who were helping Nate out arrived at the police station an hour later and took turns questioning Carl. After they had finished with him, they let him go home. He kissed Kate on the cheek, squeezed her hand, and whispered, "Be brave, darling."

They questioned her next. She was weary of having to go through every little detail again,

starting with that first explosion, but she cooper-
ated and answered every question as thoroughly as
she could. By the time they ran out of questions,
she had run out of patience.

Drummond came to get her. "Come on, Kate.
It's time to go home. Your house has been
searched from top to bottom, and is clear."

"Where's Dylan?"

"He's waiting for you in back."

She collected her purse and briefcase from his
office and followed him to the back door.

He put his hand on her shoulder. "You're going
to get through this just fine," he said. If she wasn't
sure of his good intentions, she might think he
was chastising her with his abrupt order.

"I'll be over later with dinner," he added.

"You don't have to go to all that trouble—"

"Yes, I do. I looked inside your refrigerator. I'll
bring something," he said curtly.

She was glad hadn't protested when she arrived
home and looked in the refrigerator. There really
wasn't anything there she wanted to eat. Her
stomach was grumbling. Neither she nor Dylan
had eaten anything since breakfast, and it was already after six.

"Time flies even when you're not having fun,"
she remarked as she walked into the front hall.

Dylan followed her up the stairs carrying
their bags.

"You're not having fun? I guess we'll have to do something about that."

He didn't ask her if she wanted him to share her bed. He put his bag in the guest room and dropped her bag on her bed.

She was not going to ask him to sleep with her. Absolutely not. She went into the bathroom, locked the door, and took a long shower, hoping that would revive her.

It didn't help much. She put on her favorite pair of old jeans and a T-shirt and actually did feel a little better then. She combed her hair and went downstairs.

Dylan was in the backyard talking to a police officer. She watched him from the kitchen window while she chewed on a wilted celery stick. He looked tired, she thought. And wonderful. He certainly seemed to be coping better than she was. There were moments when she felt she was going to fall apart.

Not wanting him to catch her staring at him, she forced herself to turn away. She listened to the messages on her home phone. Most of them were for Isabel, and none of them were important.

She was feeling out of sorts and restless. She got a bag of potato chips out of the pantry and put it back unopened.

She knew what was wrong with her. Dylan. How long was it going to take her to stop loving him, she wondered. Was it even possible, or was she doomed to live in misery the rest of her life? There was no one to blame but herself for her unhappiness. She had known from the very beginning what she was getting into with him—he loved them and he left them. He didn't make any excuses about the way he lived. He was what he was.

And she was what she was—a complete idiot because she had fallen in love with him.

Definitely melancholy tonight, she decided. Stress was putting her on edge. That's what it was, all right. Stress. And feeling completely helpless.

The doorbell rang, and she was forced to stop feeling sorry for herself. She assumed it was Drummond with dinner, and she was suddenly ravenous. It wasn't Drummond, though. It was Nate, and when she opened the door for him, he looked astonished to see her.

He was quick to recover. "What are you doing opening this door?" he demanded.

His glare made her flinch. "You rang the doorbell. Answering it seemed the proper thing to do. Please, come in."

"Are you alone in here?" he demanded as he stormed past her. "What the hell's wrong with you? Don't you know someone's trying to kill you? Or don't you care?"

"Yes, I know, and yes, I care," she said softly. "Please stop shouting at me. My ears are ringing."

He took a deep breath before continuing. "I've got to yell at someone. Where's Dylan?"

"In the backyard. There are deputies in the front and the back," she said. "So it was all right for me to open the door."

"That's not why I'm angry," he snapped.

She chased him to the kitchen. "Then why are you?"

"Because I didn't know where the hell you were last night. Not good," he snapped. "You two just . . . vanished. What if I had vital information? What then? Dylan wasn't answering his cell phone, and you weren't answering yours . . . what the hell's the matter with him? He knows better. Where is he?"

Nate was on a rampage. "I just told you," she answered.

"Tell me again," he demanded.

"In the backyard," she said. "Have at him."

"Don't you dare open that front door again. Understand me?"

He didn't wait for an answer but tore the kitchen door open and went outside. The door slammed shut behind him.

He's just lost his dinner invitation, she thought. How dare he shout at her. She wasn't a child he could scold.

But he was right, she reluctantly admitted. They should have let him know where they were going. It wasn't deliberate; they weren't trying to hide from him. They hadn't been sure where they would spend the night, and once they had checked into the hotel, one thing led to another, and they had become occupied.

Oh, that's a great excuse. Sorry we didn't call. We were too busy having sex. Nate would understand. Sure he would.

The chief arrived a few minutes later with enough food to feed half the town.

"What's going on out there?" he asked as he set the bags on the kitchen counter and looked out the window. "Looks like Hallinger is giving Dylan hell."

Kate quickly explained.

The chief glanced out the window again. "Dylan doesn't seem contrite. Fact is, he's giving it back." With a shrug he added, "They'll work it out. Let's eat."

The chief was right; they did work it out. Nate didn't ask if he could stay for dinner. He grabbed a plate and helped himself.

"I'll get some men here in an hour and let you off the hook, chief," he offered.

"No reason to do that," Drummond replied. "We're all set. You've got enough going on trying to get everyone in place for tomorrow's meeting."

"Is that a for-sure thing?" Nate asked. "She signs the papers tomorrow? No more changes?"

"Seven o'clock tomorrow night unless you

change the plan," Dylan said. "We just went over this in the backyard."

"I'm making sure. No one's going to disappear on me again. Got that?"

"You need to let that go."

"And you need—" Nate began.

Drummond put his hand up to stop him. "That's enough. Kate needs all the help she can get, so stop bickering and get with the program."

Nate nodded. "Yes, sir."

The three men went over strategy for the next day while they ate.

"What did you find out about the video?" Dylan asked Nate. "Any idea who taped it?"

"No. We know that it and the packet of photos were delivered by messenger to Anderson Smith's office. He claims no one there even knew a video existed until it and Compton MacKenna's instructions showed up on his desk."

"Someone knew about it," Dylan insisted. "When Compton was talking into the camera, he would glance beyond the lens every so often. Obviously, someone else was in that room. What about servants, staff?"

"No, there's no one we can find who knew anything about it."

Dylan glanced over at Kate, whose eyes were half closed.

"Kate, why don't you go upstairs to bed," he suggested. "We're almost finished here."

She was happy to oblige. It had been a very long day. She could hear the men talking as she put on her pajamas, and a few minutes later she heard Nate and Drummond leaving.

She was tired, but she decided to call Isabel to check on her before going to bed. Her sister surprised her by answering. Kate said hello and didn't get another word in for about fifteen minutes. Isabel must have assumed that the reading of the will had turned out to be a big nothing because she didn't ask Kate about it. Her social life seemed to be the only thing she was interested in talking about, and Kate had to remind her she was there to study. She was relieved, however, that Isabel was happy . . . and safe.

"Have you heard from Reece Crowell?" Kate asked.

"He should still be in Europe, but don't worry. If he comes back and starts bothering me again, I can handle him," Isabel replied, and then she moved on to more immediate topics.

While Kate was listening to Isabel's description of the young man who sat next to her in her sociology class, the call was interrupted. Thinking it could be important news, Kate cut into Isabel's chatter.

"Isabel," she said, "I've got another call. I have to hang up now. You be very careful, okay?"

She was surprised by the voice she heard when she switched over.

"Kate, this is Vanessa MacKenna."

Kate was slow to respond, unsure of how she should react. After an awkward pause, she said, "Vanessa, hello, what can I do for you?"

Vanessa was a bit stiff as she began the conversation, but she quickly loosened up and actually became quite gracious.

"Anderson called and told me how much you loved having those photos of your father," she said. "He asked me if I wouldn't mind looking around Compton's house—or rather my house now—and see if there might be others. The attic is packed full of boxes, and I decided I might as well get started clearing things out. As luck would have it, I found a box full of things I believe belonged to your father. There are photos but also trophies and school papers and a couple of report cards. I'll pack it all up and send it to you, or I could drop it off at Anderson's office if you'd prefer. And I'll keep looking for more," she promised. "I'm staying at the house now because Bryce went back into the hospital last night, and this will make it a shorter commute to see him. You know, you could stop by and see the old place . . . if you're interested. I'd love to show you around."

"Yes, I'd like to see it someday," she responded.

"Just let me know when it's convenient. Perhaps next week or the week after? I'd like to get to know you, Kate. You seem so . . . different from Bryce and his brothers, refreshingly different."

Kate felt a pang of guilt after the conversation ended and she'd hung up the phone. She hadn't asked Vanessa how serious Bryce's condition was, but then she realized an expression of sympathy or concern would have been hypocritical.

Dylan walked into her bedroom as she sat cross-legged on her bed with the phone still in her hand.

"I just received a call from Vanessa Mac-Kenna," she announced. "She invited me to come to Compton's house. She said she has more things that belonged to my father."

Dylan stopped at the foot of the bed and scowled. "You're not going anywhere near that house or any of the Savannah MacKennas until we've caught whoever is out to kill you," he ordered.

"No, of course not," she assured him. She wasn't in the mood for a lecture now. She'd had enough pressure in one day to last a lifetime, and so she moved away from the subjects of bombs and killers and money.

"I also talked to Isabel," she said. "She seems happy. I didn't tell her you were here. I didn't want her to know . . . you know . . ."

"Know what?" he prodded.

"I told her everything was fine, and if she knew you were here, she'd start asking questions. What are you doing?"

"What does it look like I'm doing? I'm taking my clothes off, and then I'm going to get in the shower."

"There's a shower in the guest bath . . ."

She stopped talking when he shut her bathroom door. A second later she heard the shower.

She could be more forceful and send him to the guest room to sleep, but she didn't want to, and that was the problem. In her heart she knew she was going to attack him as soon as he opened the door.

"I need help," she muttered. She was thoroughly disgusted with herself. She pulled the covers back and stretched out on the bed. This is all Jordan's fault, she decided. Jordan sent Dylan, and she knew . . . oh, yes, she knew what would happen.

Kate rolled onto her side and picked up the phone. Jordan couldn't avoid her forever, and she decided she would leave a message that would guarantee she'd call back.

Voice mail picked up. Kate waited for the beep and then she said, "Just thought you should know I—" She suddenly stopped. What if someone else listened to the message and heard her say she'd slept with Dylan? "Never mind," she said.

She was hanging up the phone when she heard someone say, "She should know what?"

It was a man's voice. "Who is this?"

"Michael Buchanan. Is this Kate?"

Thank God she'd come to her senses. "What are you doing in Boston?"

"I'm on leave. I got in early, and I'm staying with Jordan until next weekend. Then I'll move over to Nathan's Bay. Mom and Dad will be home by then."

Michael had graduated from Annapolis and was training to become a Navy SEAL. He was a real daredevil, and of all the Buchanan brothers he was the most competitive.

"When are you coming back to Boston?" he asked. "I want a rematch."

"Why? You'll only lose again."

His laugh was just like Dylan's. "We'll see about that."

"Did you know Dylan's here?"

"Yes. Jordan told me he's helping you with a little problem."

A little problem? "Yes, that's right."

They talked for another minute. She promised to tell Dylan that Michael was home, and Michael promised to make Jordan call her back.

She'd just hung up the phone when Dylan came out of the bathroom. He'd put on his khaki shorts and was going downstairs to check on the police officers to make sure they were where they were supposed to be. Kate thought he was being a little obsessive-compulsive.

He didn't come back upstairs for a long time.

Kate tried to go to sleep, but her mind wouldn't rest. She kept thinking about the "little" problem of figuring out who was trying to kill her. It had to be one of the MacKennas, but which one? Maybe all of them. Wouldn't that be something? Vanessa could be in on it, too. At this point anything was possible.

Chapter Thirty-three

KATE HAD BEEN TOSSING AND TURNING FOR what seemed like hours when Dylan finally came to bed. It was well after midnight.

He didn't ask her if he could sleep with her. He simply took off his shorts and slid in next to her. He was awfully sure of himself, she thought, and she was about to tell him so when he pulled her into his arms.

"You awake, Pickle?"

"I'm too nervous about tomorrow to go to sleep."

"Good," he said. He lifted her hair off the back of her neck and began to nibble on her soft skin.

Shivers coursed down her legs, and she moved restlessly against him. "Why is it good?" she asked breathlessly.

"It's good because I won't have to wake you up to make love to you."

He might have said something more to her; she couldn't remember. The way he was touching her demanded her full attention, and forming a coherent thought simply became impossible.

Their lovemaking was different tonight, more passionate, far more intense. And when at last they had both found fulfillment, he continued to hold her in his arms and stroke her back. His chin rested on top of her head, and every once in a while he would kiss her.

As soon as the haze of passion lifted, she was miserable. She wanted to tell him how she felt, but she couldn't. Why? Because the quickest way to get him to disappear would be to admit that she wanted to be with him forever.

She did want that impossible dream with all her heart. How would he respond if she told him she wanted him forever? He'd probably pass out on her. She was actually able to summon up a smile as she thought about how crazy those three little words would make him.

Good thing she knew CPR.

Dylan turned over on his back and stared at the ceiling. "Kate, how come you want to get a loan? You did say that was what you were going to do. Were you joking?"

"No, I was serious. I need a loan to pay off a loan. It's a temporary solution that will buy me some time."

"You do know that as soon as you sign those papers tomorrow, you're going to be a millionaire, don't you?"

"Yes, I know," she said. "But I won't be a millionaire for long. When I go to the bank and fill out the application, I'll have to list the money as an asset . . . a temporary asset," she stressed.

He yawned. "They're gonna think you're nuts."

She snuggled up against him and whispered, "Maybe I am."

He didn't think she was too worried about the reputation of her mental state because she fell asleep less than a minute later. Dylan pulled the sheet up over them and tried to clear his mind so he could sleep. That proved to be impossible. He couldn't stop thinking about tomorrow and all the things that could go wrong.

Kate slept hard that night, but she didn't feel rested when she got out of bed the following morning. She so dreaded the day ahead of her. She hoped to heaven none of the MacKennas would come to the meeting. Bryce was probably still in the hospital, and she felt a little ashamed hoping he hadn't been released yet. Roger and Ewan were the biggest worries. She didn't think she had the stamina to put up with their vulgarity again, and if they began to slander her mother, she didn't know what she would do.

Dylan was downstairs in the kitchen talking to

someone. She thought she heard Chief Drummond's voice, but she couldn't be sure.

Nine o'clock. She couldn't believe the time. She'd never slept this late before. No reason to rush, she decided. The meeting at Anderson's office wasn't until seven that evening, and she assumed that she and Dylan wouldn't leave Silver Springs until the middle of the afternoon.

Anderson wouldn't be back from the funeral until at least five, maybe later. For some unknown reason, Compton MacKenna had insisted that his funeral begin at precisely two o'clock in the afternoon. He'd written out a schedule of "events" and had even included the names of the mourners he wanted to speak on his behalf. Kate wondered if Compton had also written the eulogy.

She thought about that crazy old man while she showered and dressed for the trip. Just in case they had to stay the night in Savannah, she packed her overnighter again.

She carried the bag downstairs, left it in the foyer, and went into the kitchen.

"Good morning," she said.

Dylan was drying his hands. He draped the towel on his shoulder as he walked toward her. He kissed her with a good deal of gusto, and when he moved back, he was pleased with her reaction. She was actually blushing.

He pulled a chair out from the table, kissed her again but so quickly this time she wasn't at all ready, and then gently forced her to sit.

"What do you want for breakfast?" he asked. "I'll fix it for you."

"Toast would be nice. Who were you talking to? I thought I heard Chief Drummond."

"You did hear him," he said. "He just left. White or wheat?"

"I can make my own breakfast."

"You're getting wheat."

He didn't ask her if she wanted orange juice. He poured a glass and put it on the table in front of her.

"As soon as you finish breakfast, we need to get on the road."

He was leaning against the counter facing her, one ankle crossed over the other, looking absolutely gorgeous, and she was suddenly feeling overwhelmed by him.

The toast popped up. "Here we go."

He put the dry toast on a plate and handed it to her. Cooking obviously wasn't one of his talents. She picked up a slice and tore a corner off.

"Why are you in such a rush?" she asked. "We have plenty of time."

"There's been a change in plans."

"What change in what plan?"

"We had a plan, and we changed it," he explained. "Come on, Kate. Eat your breakfast. Did you pack a bag for tonight?"

"Yes. It's in the foyer."

"I'll put it in the car," he said, and as he walked out of the kitchen, he ordered, "eat."

The second he was out of sight, she dumped the toast in the disposal, gulped the orange juice, and rinsed the plate and the glass.

The kitchen sink looked brand-new. Dylan had obviously scrubbed it. He may not be much of a chef, but he certainly knew how to clean. He'd be a good man to have around . . . for all sorts of reasons.

She ran upstairs to get her purse and laptop. She hadn't had a chance to answer her e-mails in heaven knew how long, and she hoped there would be time this afternoon or this evening after the meeting. She slipped the laptop behind the cushioned divider in her briefcase and went back downstairs.

Chief Drummond was getting into his car. He had parked his Jeep behind Dylan's rental in the drive.

"You should have told me he was waiting. I would have hurried."

"I asked you to hurry," Dylan responded.

"That was different."

He wasn't going to try to figure out what she meant. "The chief wanted to go over the car just to make sure there weren't any surprises waiting for us."

"You mean like a bomb?" she asked but didn't wait for an answer. "Did he find anything?"

"No. We're okay."

"Is he coming with us?"

"No," he answered. "But he wrote out instructions. We're going to be taking some roads that aren't on any map."

Kate had grown up in Silver Springs and thought she knew the area better than anyone, and she'd driven to Savannah too many times to count, but several of the back roads Dylan took she had to admit she'd never seen before. Some of them weren't roads at all. They were gravel ruts.

The drive was scenic, and every now and then Dylan would point out something he found fascinating. He loved the weeping willows and the wildflowers growing in clusters in untended fields. He didn't know what any of them were called and was impressed that she did.

"How could you ever want to leave this?" he asked. "It's beautiful here."

"I won't be leaving for a long time . . . if ever. I think I'm meant to stay here."

"I could do it. I could live here."

She didn't want to get her hopes up that he might stay in her life, and so she tried to think of all the reasons he should leave.

"You'd be bored."

"I don't think so."

"You'd miss Boston. There's such energy there."

"Yes, I would miss Boston," he agreed. "But I'm ready for a change. Besides, Charleston is just down the road from Silver Springs, and it has all the big-city advantages and problems. You want energy, drive there. I certainly wouldn't miss the traffic," he added. "I wonder what the crime rate is in Silver Springs."

"Before or after I moved back home?"

"Okay, we made it," he said. "Read the sign. We're officially in Savannah."

Kate assumed they were going to meet at one of the Savannah precincts.

"I don't want to sit in a police station until the meeting," she said. "Couldn't we go on to Anderson's office? I could get some work done while I wait."

"Good idea," he said.

Fifteen minutes later he was pulling up in front of Smith and Wesson. "You were planning on driving here anyway, weren't you? Does Nate know?"

"Yes, he does."

"We can just walk in?"

As she asked the question, two police officers exited the building and waited for Dylan and Kate to get out of the car. Yet another officer came from across the street. "You can leave the car here," he said. "I'll make sure no one touches it."

Dylan turned the motor off but left the keys in the ignition. He followed Kate inside, and once the door was shut behind him, he said, "Which one of you checked the building?"

"The bomb squad just left. The place is clean," one of the officers said. "We've got a man watching the door and a couple of security guards, one inside and one out back. The two of us are assigned to you. Where do you want us?"

"Right here in the entry is good. Who's in the building now?"

"Almost everyone is either at a funeral or on vacation. The receptionist's here, and so is Smith's assistant, a guy named Terrance. He's upstairs in Smith's office. You want him out, we'll get him out."

"He can stay."

Terrance must have heard all the commotion. He came rushing downstairs. "Miss MacKenna, I'm afraid Mr. Smith isn't here just yet. The funeral—"

"I know," she interrupted. "We're quite early. I was wondering if I might have a desk to use. I'd like to do some work until Anderson returns."

He seemed nervous, and smiling at him didn't put him at ease. She finally figured out why he was so jumpy. Dylan was making him apprehensive. Terrance was watching him out of the corner of his eye, acting like he expected Dylan to grab him.

"I'd like to see the conference room," Dylan said.

Terrance led the way up the stairs and down a long hallway on the right. The conference room was one door down from Anderson's office.

"I was just putting name cards in front of each chair," Terrance said.

"Would you mind if I worked in here?" Kate asked. "If I could plug in my computer . . ."

"Yes, of course." He pulled the chair out at the head of the table and showed her where the outlet was located.

Dylan left the door open and continued down to the end of the hallway. To the left was an alcove with a fire door wired to the alarm. A small red light was blinking, indicating the system was on. A wide metal bar crossed the door in the center. Dylan assumed that on the other side of the door were fire escape stairs leading to the ground.

The carpeted back staircase was to his right. He descended a flight to the first floor where a guard was stationed in front of the exit that led to the parking lot. Dylan showed him his identification and talked to him a few minutes before going back up.

Satisfied with security, he returned to Kate, who had her laptop set up on the conference room table and was answering e-mail. When they heard someone shouting Dylan's name, his hand immediately went to his gun, and he took a protective step toward her.

Dylan recognized the voice when his name was shouted again, and he relaxed. A couple of seconds later Nate came running into the room. His face was flushed and he was smiling.

"It's over," he announced jubilantly.

"Over?" Kate asked. "Really over?"

"That's right. You two can start breathing easy again and get on with your lives. The case is closed," he added. "Or will be," he qualified. "As soon as all the paperwork is done."

"Tell me," Dylan demanded.

Nate was enjoying the moment. His eyes lit up with excitement. "Roger MacKenna. Just as I thought. The bastard was behind it all. After seeing that video, I was sure he was the number one suspect. I had requested a search warrant, but now that's not necessary. We have all the proof we need. Roger was quite the busy little planner. He had help, of course."

"Jackman."

"Yes," he confirmed. "And Jackman had all the connections to get the job done. The loan shark didn't really have a choice. He had to help Roger. It was the only way he would ever see the money Roger owed him."

"How did you ever get Roger to confess?" she asked. "He doesn't seem the type to cooperate with the police."

"He didn't confess. He killed himself."

She hadn't expected to hear that. Stunned, she said, "He what?"

"Killed himself," he repeated. He looked at Dylan as he continued. "We had a tail on him, but our guy didn't hear the gunshot. Roger lived in a high-rise," he explained. "Our detective was in a parked car out front, and he'd watched him go inside. He told me he heard about it on the scanner. A woman called, said she heard a gunshot. He went inside then and found Roger on the floor. One head shot," he added. "He also found incriminating evidence and lots of it. He didn't touch anything, of course. He said it was all sitting out on the table in plain sight. I think Roger wanted the police to know that Jackman was involved. I can't wait to get over there and have a look."

"Is Crime Scene there yet?" Dylan asked.

"They're on their way. Do you want to meet me over there? His apartment is only about a mile from here. Or I could drop you off. I've got to check in with Savannah PD first. Then I'll head over."

"Yeah, I want to see it, and I don't want anything moved until I get there. Make that happen."

Nate smiled. "FBI said the same thing. CSU will have first priority. The sooner we get over there, the better."

"Yeah, okay. Where did Roger get the gun?"

"I don't know yet."

"He had a gun when he came to the reading of the will," Kate said. "Remember?"

"The police wouldn't have given it back to him," Nate said. "Roger had just made bail. He was carrying a concealed weapon without a permit."

"Did he tell the police where he got that gun?"

"Yes," he answered. "He said Ewan gave it to him and that Ewan had bought it on the street."

"Where's Ewan now?"

"He's voluntarily turning himself in. He's on his way to the police station, no doubt with an attorney ready to bail him out. That's why I'm headed there now. He'll find out about Roger when he gets there. I checked on Bryce's whereabouts, too. He'll never hear about Roger. He's slipping in and out of consciousness. His wife is by his side and will stay until the bitter end, which is going to be real soon."

"What about Jackman?"

"FBI in Las Vegas picked him up for questioning. He's their problem now." Nate started toward the door as he said, "I'll see you over there."

"It's really over, isn't it? I still can't believe it," Kate said. Dylan was nodding, but she didn't think he was paying attention. "Is something wrong?"

"No, but I want those policemen to stay until you've signed those papers."

He walked downstairs with Nate, and together they checked in with the officers on duty, who assured them they would stay as long as Kate was in the building.

When Dylan came back into the conference room, she said, "I thought you wanted to look at the evidence."

"Yeah, I do."

"Go," she said. "I'll be fine."

"Yeah, but—"

"Go on, and shut the door behind you. I'm not going anywhere."

Chapter Thirty-four

KATE HADN'T QUITE ABSORBED THE NEWS YET. The man who tried to kill her was dead, and his accomplice was in custody. And here she sat diligently answering her e-mail as though nothing out of the ordinary had occurred.

She would probably fall apart tonight when she was all alone. Dylan could very well be on his way back to Boston by then. She felt an instant rush of panic and became angry with herself. Why should she be upset? She'd always known he was going to leave. No surprise there. And she would get through it just like everything else in her life that had been painful.

But Dylan wouldn't go until tomorrow, she decided. He'd drive her back to Silver Springs, spend the night with her, and early the next morning while she was sound asleep, he'd leave.

She knew he cared about her. It had taken a considerable amount of coaxing just to get him to leave her alone to work on her computer while he went to the crime scene with Nate. He'd even suggested she go with him.

She realized she wasn't going to get any work done if she continued to think about Dylan. He'd only just left, and she was already missing him.

She forced herself to go back to work. She'd answered several more e-mails before she was interrupted by Anderson's assistant. He timidly knocked on the door and stepped inside.

"Miss MacKenna, there's a phone call for you on line one. The gentleman wouldn't give me his name, but he insisted he was a friend."

Who would be calling her at the law office? The only people who knew where she was had her cell phone number.

"Should I tell him you're unavailable?"

"No, I'll take the call," she said.

Terrance picked up the phone from the credenza and placed it on the corner of the table. "Would you like me to help you with anything? Get you anything?"

"No, but thank you for asking."

"If you need me, I'll be in the library. Just push the intercom button."

She thanked him again, and as he was pulling the door closed, she answered the phone.

"Is this Kate MacKenna?" a man asked.

She didn't recognize the caller. The voice was pleasant, though.

"Yes, it is," she said. "And who is this?"

"I don't think it's a good idea to give you my name. I want to help you," he said. "And I mean you no harm. I have information for you," he rushed on. "Will you please listen to what I have to say?"

"Yes," she replied cautiously. "I'll listen, but first, please tell me why it isn't a good idea to tell me your name."

"I'm wanted by the police," he answered. He hurried to add, "I've never killed anyone . . . at least on purpose." He laughed, and then he snorted. "Just kidding . . . really, I've never killed anyone."

Kate didn't know what to make of him, but the call was beginning to unnerve her. She glanced around. She was alone, and the conference room door was closed.

Before she could ask him why he was a wanted man, he continued. "The authorities don't know my real name, and I would prefer they never find out. Will you promise to remain calm? I want to help you, and in order to do that, you have to be able to hear what I have to say. You can't become hysterical."

"Of course I'll remain calm," she told him. "Just tell me who you are." She could hear the apprehension in her own voice.

He laughed. "Nice try. I won't be giving you my name. But I'll tell you what I will do; I'll give you the name the police call me."

"And what's that?"

"The Florist."

Kate nearly dropped the phone. Her immediate response was disbelief. "That's not funny . . . I don't believe . . . why would . . ."

"Now, you promised to stay calm . . ."

Kate looked at the closed door again, willing it to open and Terrance—anyone—to walk in so she could signal him. Maybe someone could trace the call.

"This is a twisted prank," she said.

"It is not a prank," he insisted. "I'd never prank you. I **am** called the Florist, and I do want to help you."

"Help me? If you are who you say you are, your bombs have nearly killed me twice." She pressed the intercom button hoping that someone would hear the conversation, but the phone would not allow her to access the intercom as long as she was on the line.

"I didn't try to kill you," he said, exasperated. "I only made the explosives."

"This is crazy," she said.

"You need to hear what I have to say." He didn't sound crazy. He sounded reasonable. Was he going to offer her an apology?

"I'll listen. Start explaining."

"I like blowing things up."

Okay, so he was crazy after all. She thought she should say something in response. "Do you want to tell me why?" If she could keep him on the line, she might be able to summon help.

"Why isn't relevant," he said. "I've made quite a nice income. I bought a big-screen TV with surround sound last month. You wouldn't believe how it makes the Nature Channel come alive . . . but I digress. Truth is, I enjoy the extra income, and it allows me to do something I love doing."

"Blowing things up."

"I like building explosives, and in the past I never let anyone else near them. Until recently. A friend of a friend of a friend . . . you know how it goes. I was lured by the money, and I was hoodwinked. I was told the explosives would be used in the desert. There was a lot of talk about caves and underground facilities. Oh, yes, I was spun an elaborate lie, and I believed it. I was extremely naïve and greedy.

"I took the money and went back to my day job. I didn't think another thing about it until I opened the newspaper and saw a photo of an explosion at a gallery. It made the national news. I recognized my work right away. I was outraged because I had been hoodwinked, and after I read the article about how you had narrowly escaped death, I was scared, and I felt really bad for you." He snorted again. "Really, I did . . . heh, heh . . . I thought about sending you flowers.

"I tried to get hold of my contact, but he had

disappeared. Then I read about another explosion that destroyed a building and nearly killed you again. I knew then that you were the target."

She heard him take a deep breath and let out a long sigh.

"This is a dangerous business."

He was just now figuring that out? "Yes," she said.

"I've decided to quit."

"You're calling me to tell me you're retiring?" she asked suspiciously.

He didn't answer the question. "There's a gentleman who has been pursuing me for several years now. His name is Sutherland, and he works for ATF. I would appreciate it if you would call him and tell him to go home."

"Because you're retiring."

"Yes."

This was the most bizarre conversation she had ever had. "I think you should tell him. I'm sure he would love to meet you, even if only by phone."

"Oh, we have met, several times, in fact. He just doesn't know it."

She bet Sutherland was going to love hearing that. She spotted her purse on a chair next to the window. Her cell phone was in it. If she could get it, she might be able to contact someone.

She needed to keep him talking.

"May I ask a question?" she asked as she stood

up and moved the phone to the end of the table as far as the cord would allow so she could reach for her purse.

"Certainly. If I can answer it, I will, and no, I'm not really a florist. If you could see my garden, you'd—"

"That's not the question I was going to ask. I was told that you always put your explosives in baskets. I was curious to know why."

"That's a common misconception. I don't put them in baskets. They are the baskets. It's quite intricate work. I like to think of myself as a virtuoso. The Beethoven of bang, if you will." He chuckled.

"Why did you really call me?"

"I need to get serious now," he said as he stopped his laugh with a sigh. "I want to save your life."

"How do you plan to do that?"

"By giving you important information. The first explosion tore out a hill."

"Yes." She grabbed the purse handle and pulled it to her.

"You walked away and barely suffered a scratch. Do you know the statistical odds for that?" He didn't wait for an answer. "The second explosive took down a building, and you survived that as well. That's phenomenal, just phenomenal."

"Yes," she said again. Where was this leading?

She fished to the bottom of the purse for her phone.

"The odds are becoming positively astronomical. I'm quite worried about you. You just can't survive another one."

"Another one?"

"Yes. You see, I made three."

"What?" She stopped. "What did you say?"

"There's one more bomb out there, and you need to listen carefully . . ."

Kate was concentrating so intently on what the bomber was saying, she didn't hear the door open behind her.

Chapter Thirty-five

ROGER MACKENNA'S APARTMENT SMELLED LIKE forgotten garbage. Roger smelled like he'd rolled around in it before he killed himself. He was lying on the floor in the living room, flat on his back, the gun still clutched in his hand. Blood had pooled around his head and upper shoulders and had formed what appeared to be a perfect black chalk outline. Death had captured his expression of despair. One eye was closed, the other was somewhere in the back of his skull.

He wasn't a pretty sight.

The FBI was there in force, and the agent in charge, Joel Kline, turned out to be surprisingly accommodating. He was about Dylan's age, but he already had deep creases at the corners of his mouth. His tall, thin frame was hunched at the shoulders as though permanently bent from stooping over too many crime scenes.

Once Dylan had diplomatically let him know

that he was in no way interested in usurping his position, Kline handed him a pair of gloves and told him to have a look around. He'd be happy to get his input.

The medical examiner was a middle-aged man named Dr. Luke Parrish. He was kneeling beside the body. Dylan squatted next to him, introduced himself, and showed him his badge.

Parrish liked to chat. "I used to live near Silver Springs," he said. "Real nice area. Not enough homicides to keep me busy or interested, so I moved here. Savannah's real nice, too," he added. "With that accent of yours I'd say you're from the northeast. Am I right?"

"Yes," he said. "Boston."

"You relocating?"

"No, this is a temporary job."

They both turned to look at the body. "This one knew what he was doing," Parrish said. "One clean shot took care of it. Most of them don't know where to aim."

The weapon was a Glock. Parrish bagged it and handed it to a hovering agent. "Damn, he stinks. I don't think he ever took a shower. He hasn't been dead long. He had this stench on him when he was alive. How could anyone live like this? Look around. The place is a pit. You'd think anybody who could afford expensive furniture like this might try a little to keep it nice. That leather sofa alone had to have cost a couple thousand."

Parrish wasn't exaggerating about the apartment. It was a pit. There were overflowing ashtrays on tables and chairs, and empty whiskey bottles scattered about. The sofa looked like it was ready to be carted off to the city dump. The cushions were all broken down, and there were cigarette holes along the arms.

The coffee table was the only clean surface in the apartment. The papers on top were organized.

"Did you find a suicide note?" Dylan asked.

Kline crossed the room to join him. "No, not yet. But he left us all these papers. I think he wanted to help us get Jackman."

"Is there enough to prosecute him?"

"We're not through looking."

In other words, no, Dylan thought. "Tell me what you do have."

"We've compared what we found here with the information we'd already gotten from Nate Hallinger. He's gonna love seeing all this evidence when he gets here.

"It looks like Roger knew just about everything there was to know about Kate MacKenna. He had all of her phone numbers, her work and home addresses, the make and model of her car, the license plate number, her business associates' phone numbers and addresses, her sisters' cell phone numbers. He even had Isabel MacKenna's exboyfriend's name and phone number."

"He had Reece Crowell's name?"

"And he'd underlined Carl Bertolli's address and had the date and time for the gallery party. He had the address for the warehouse, too."

"My God, he had it all, didn't he?"

"I'm just getting warmed up. We already bagged the calendar we found in the kitchen next to the phone. It was covered with prints. It looked like someone else besides Roger had made notes. There were two distinct handwritings. I sent it to the lab over an hour ago and put a rush on it. We should have a preliminary report any minute now. Besides times and places, there were flight numbers. Kate's flight numbers. He knew when she was going to Boston, and he knew when she was coming home."

Dylan was having a difficult time controlling his anger. How long had the son of a bitch been stalking Kate? Had he been inside her house? It would have been easy for him. She never locked the damned doors.

"Have you looked at his car yet?"

"Yes," Kline answered. "It's a white Ford with tinted windows. This has to be the car Kate described to Hallinger, the one that tried to run her down."

"Getting all this information took a lot of time and care." Dylan rubbed the back of his neck. "What else?"

"There were two dates heavily circled on the calendar."

"The dates of the explosions."

"That's right," Kline said. "Roger made a lot of notations. One was real interesting. 'Jackman got the baskets.' 'Two hundred thousand' was written next to it. That has to be the amount he paid for the explosives."

"Nate told me Jackman's been picked up."

"Yes," he replied. "Right now he's sitting in an interrogation room in Vegas waiting for his attorney."

"Roger's notes aren't going to be enough to hold him long, and you still don't know who was behind the camera when Compton MacKenna filmed his farewell address."

"We know it wasn't one of the nephews because he didn't trust any of them, and he didn't want them to know what he was up to," he said. "That was real apparent in the video. There are a couple of people looking good to us, though. One's the housekeeper. We just found out she made a fat deposit in her account about six weeks ago. We're bringing her in to have a little talk." He added, "And we're also interested in Compton Mac-Kenna's attorney. I'm not worried. We'll find whoever it was."

Dylan took his time walking around the apartment and studying the papers and the handwritten notes. Nice tidy package, he thought. Roger couldn't have been more accommodating if he'd tried. He'd left just enough hints to connect Jackman, but not hard evidence to nail him.

Something didn't compute. Dylan made a second examination of the information the agents had collected, but each time a question was answered, another one popped up. What was Reece's name doing in Roger's notes? Why did he leave information for them to find and yet leave no suicide note? Where did he get another gun so quickly? There was nothing orderly in Roger's life, so why was this so organized?

One perfect shot . . . knew just where to aim.

The paramedics had come in to bag the body. Agent Kline moved out of their way and noticed Dylan staring down at the papers, frowning. "Something bothering you?" he asked.

Dylan nodded. "This doesn't feel right. It isn't working for me."

They both watched the body being carted away. "What you've got here is a nice, tidy package," Dylan said.

Kline shrugged. "It can happen this way . . . all of it coming together . . ."

"Yeah? Since when does it happen this way? Everything laid out nice and easy for you? The only thing missing from the table are arrows pointing to the evidence on those papers." He shook his head. "I don't like nice and tidy, and do you know why? It makes me think that maybe all this was staged."

Chapter Thirty-six

DYLAN HAD STAYED AT THE CRIME SCENE MUCH longer than he'd intended, and he was anxious to get back to Kate. He took the stairs at Roger's apartment building and called her cell phone on his way down to let her know he was returning to the law office. He was only ten minutes away, but he needed to hear her voice. He heard her voice mail instead. What the hell? Why hadn't she answered? Where was she? Trying not to panic, he quickly called Smith and Wesson.

"Miss MacKenna is on another line. Would you like to hold, or may I take a message?" the receptionist inquired.

He didn't leave a message, but he did relax. It was okay. Kate was where she was supposed to be.

He was crossing the busy street heading to his car when his phone rang. Nate was on the line.

"We've got a problem. Ewan MacKenna hasn't shown up at the police station. His attorney's still

there waiting for him, and he swears he doesn't
know where his client is. Can't find Ewan's car, either. We've sent some men to his house. No car,
no Ewan. He left in a hurry, too, because his front
door was wide open. Police went in and searched.
Nothing."

"What happened to Ewan's surveillance?"

"Evidently some idiot pulled it when Roger
was found with all that evidence. I've got some
guys checking a couple of Ewan's favorite health
clubs."

"You better get someone over to the hospital to
make sure Bryce and Vanessa haven't disappeared."

"I was just about to send someone. I'll talk to
you later."

Dylan pulled his car key out of his pocket and
was inserting it in the door when he saw Agent
Kline rushing across the street waving to get his
attention.

"Glad I caught you. Ewan MacKenna's missing," Kline said as he caught up to him.

"Yeah, I heard," Dylan answered.

"Well, there's more. I just got a call from the
lab. They found a match to the fingerprints on the
calendar, and they just happen to belong to Ewan
MacKenna himself. Maybe you're right. Maybe
the crime scene was staged. So now I guess we've
got a whole new kettle of fish to deal with here."

Kline folded his arms, looked at the ground for
a second as he thought, and then said, "Here's my

original theory: Someone the old man trusts films the video and makes himself an extra copy. He sells it to Roger. Roger watches it and knows he's got to get rid of Kate or he's not gonna see a dime. So what does he do? He calls Jackman and cuts him in because he needs his connections. This all makes sense, right? But now I've got to consider that either Ewan is in on it with Roger and Jackman, or maybe the video is sold to Ewan. Roger doesn't know anything about it. Ewan watches it, and he cuts Jackman in, and the two of them set Roger up to take the fall. It could have happened that way because, I'm telling you, there sure as certain isn't any brotherly love going on in that family."

Dylan draped his arms across the car door and listened to the agent's hypothesis.

Kline continued to think out loud. "Still nice and tidy, right?" he asked. "Now I've got to wonder about the timing. Why did Roger kill himself when he did?"

"I don't think he did kill himself," Dylan said.

Kline's shoulders hunched a bit more. "Yeah, maybe."

Dylan got in the car and rolled down the window. "Hopefully, evidence will prove it."

"If Roger was murdered, Ewan becomes the number one suspect. He's capable of murder."

"In that family . . . they're all capable of murder."

"I'll let you know when we find Ewan," Kline said. He jogged back across the street and into the building.

Dylan couldn't get rid of the uneasy feeling that he was missing something. He was looking at it but not seeing it. He locked in on Kline's comment about timing. Maybe that was it. The timing was wrong. Yeah, that's what was bothering him.

At the first stoplight he dug through his pocket, found Anderson's cell phone number, and called him.

The attorney, who had forgotten to turn off his phone, answered in a whisper. "May I call you back?"

"No, you may not," Dylan said firmly. "You need to answer a question for me right now."

"I'm paying my respects—"

"This can't wait."

"Let me just step outside this door . . ." His voice became louder. "All right. What do you want to know?"

"I've got some puzzle pieces missing," Dylan answered. "I need you to help me create a timeline."

Chapter Thirty-seven

TIMING REALLY WAS EVERYTHING, AND THE phone logs at Smith and Wesson would confirm what Dylan had finally figured out.

The truth didn't set him free; it enraged him. How could he have been so blind? And why had it taken him so long to see what was there the whole time?

He realized he was driving like a maniac. He didn't care. Panic was building inside him, and all he could think about was getting to Kate. He needed to see her and know that she was all right. She didn't realize the danger, and she was so trusting. She was sitting in the middle of a hornet's nest. The bastard knew where she was, and he would be coming for her.

He turned the corner on two wheels, slammed on the brakes, and hit the ground running. He had a plan. After he made sure Kate was safe, he was going to kill the son of a bitch.

Dylan sprinted into the building. Two policemen were hurrying down the stairs toward him.
As soon as he saw their expressions, he knew
something was wrong.

"Where's Kate?" he demanded.

"Gone . . . she's gone," one of the officers answered.

The other rushed to add, "We've searched the
entire building. She left in a hurry."

They both talked at once.

"Phone was off the hook, purse and briefcase
still there . . ."

"The alarm on the back door . . . someone dis-
armed it . . . couldn't have been her . . ."

A security guard rushed forward, visibly
shaken. "This is all my fault. She went out the
back door. I got called on the intercom to come
up to the entrance, and I didn't question it. I
thought it was one of the cops."

"We called it in as soon as we realized . . . The
FBI is on the way. Agent Kline says to wait here."
The first policeman said.

Dylan was too late. The son of a bitch had her.

Chapter Thirty-eight

LIGHT SLOWLY CREPT INTO THE BLACK VOID. Kate struggled to open her eyes. It was such a difficult task, and when she finally managed it, the room she was in refused to come into focus. Thoughts were spinning in and out of her mind, and nothing was making sense.

She was lying on something hard and cold. What was it? A table? A slab? She couldn't be on a slab. She wasn't dead. She could feel herself breathing. Had she been in an accident? She couldn't remember. She wasn't in pain, but she didn't think anything was broken. She gingerly tested her arms and legs to make sure. Good, she could move, but it was difficult. She felt so weak and lethargic, and she couldn't understand why. What had happened to her?

Oh, no, she didn't get blown up again, did she?

Panic jolted her awake. Isabel. Oh, God, Isabel

was in trouble. Someone had taken her. Kate remembered running. She had to get to her before he hurt her . . .

Where was her sister? Kate tried to call out to her, but her voice wouldn't cooperate.

Drugged. She had been drugged. She remembered the peculiar smell pressed against her face. And then a pinch. Yes, someone had pinched her arm.

She didn't know how long she'd been unconscious. Her mind was clearing now, and she could feel her strength coming back. She managed to sit up. A wave of nausea gripped her, but it quickly passed.

The room finally came into focus. She was sitting on a hardwood floor. There were books on shelves against the wall and a desk in front of her—a library. Why did it look so familiar? The video. Yes, that was where she'd seen the desk. Compton MacKenna had been sitting there. She was in his library. The painting that had been behind him in the video was still there hanging on the wall. A hunting scene . . . with kilts. A countryside somewhere in Scotland.

What was she doing here?

She made a feeble attempt to stand and nearly toppled over. Gripping the arm of the chair to balance herself, she was about to try again when she heard a door slam. Then she heard voices getting closer.

"Are you sure you gave her enough? I'm worried she'll wake up before I'm ready."

Kate froze. She recognized the voice. Vanessa.

Who was she talking to? Kate heard another voice, but too far away and muffled.

Vanessa continued to speak. "I'll need at least fifteen minutes. Twenty would be better. And that's enough time? Okay, I'll stop worrying. We still need to hurry, though. Drag him into the library." Another door slammed shut. "And hurry. You need to get back before you're missed."

Vanessa was just outside the door now. Kate dove to the floor and rolled onto her back. Her heart was pounding. She heard a crash. It sounded like glass breaking. Then laughter.

"Don't worry," Vanessa said. "Nothing in this rat trap is worth anything. Can you believe that senile old man thought I'd be happy with this house and a measly hundred thousand dollars? And he thought he could give his fortune to a stranger. I swear, I almost killed him with the camera. That stupid fool. I didn't put up with a drunk just for this dump. By the way, sweetheart, Bryce should be expiring any moment now. He was too drunk to know how many pain pills he was taking. I told the doctors I was worried about him accidentally overdosing." There was the sound of feet shuffling and then, "My hands are full. Could you get the door for me?"

Kate felt a slight draft as the door opened. She heard a skirt rustle. Vanessa was walking toward her. She stopped and nudged Kate's foot, and Kate knew the woman was staring at her. And then Vanessa kicked her thigh. Hard. Kate was certain Vanessa was watching her face. She didn't dare flinch.

"She's still out cold," Vanessa said smugly. She walked to the desk.

What was she doing? And where was "sweetheart"?

Then she heard him. He was dragging something. He dropped whatever it was to the floor with a heavy thud.

A phone rang, and Vanessa let out a slight gasp. "That has to be your cell. Mine's in the car. We need to hurry. Go. Go. I'm right behind you. Oh, I almost forgot. Here, take the desk phone out with you. I'll lock the door—just in case."

Quick footsteps, and the library door closed. Then another door shut. Kate thought it might be the front door. Were they really gone? Or was it a trick? It was deadly quiet. She didn't move for several seconds. Finally, she dared to open her eyes.

They were gone. But she wasn't alone. Ewan MacKenna lay on the floor facing her. His eyes were closed. Was he dead or alive? She crawled close and put her hand on his chest. He was breathing. Had he been drugged, too?

She had to get help. She made it to her knees and reached for the top of the desk for support. Then she saw it. A basket of flowers.

Chapter Thirty-nine

THE ELEVATORS WERE TOO DAMNED SLOW. NATE raced up the three flights of stairs to the ICU. He crashed through the double doors, spotted the nurses' station on his right, and headed there.

A technician and a nurse were working behind the counter. "Where's Vanessa MacKenna?" he demanded, panting for breath. "Her husband, Bryce, is a patient here."

The two of them shared a worried look, and the nurse moved closer to the counter. "Sir, are you a family member?" she asked. Her voice was soothing, as though she were comforting a distraught relative.

"No, I'm Detective Hallinger," he said. He showed his badge. "Now answer my question."

"Mrs. MacKenna isn't here," the nurse said. No more soothing pretense. She was all business now. "She received a call here at the station."

The tech nodded. "I answered it. A man was calling. He said he was Bryce MacKenna's brother, Ewan. I remember the name because he said it a couple of times. He was upset and said it was urgent that he talk to Mrs. MacKenna. I went and got her, and she talked to him. Whatever he was saying upset her. I heard her tell him several times to calm down, and when she hung up the phone, she was very distraught. Wasn't she, LeeAnne?"

"Yes, she was."

"She told me there was an emergency, and she had to leave."

"Did she tell you where she was going?" Nate asked urgently. He watched the second hand on the clock behind the counter. He knew he had to hurry. "Think," he demanded.

"No, she didn't tell me where she was going," the tech answered.

"It's not too far away," LeeAnne interjected. "She told me it wouldn't take her any time at all to get back if we needed her."

"She also said she wouldn't be gone long," the tech volunteered, trying to be helpful.

"Compton MacKenna's house is close by," he said. "Did she mention his name?"

"No, she didn't."

"Call her," he demanded. "You have her number. Call her and see if she's there."

"We did try to call her, but she didn't answer. I even had her paged here at the hospital—"

"Try her again," he said. He shoved his hands in his pockets as he waited.

The nurse didn't argue. She found the number and made the call.

"It's ringing," she whispered.

"How's her husband doing?" Nate asked the tech.

"Mr. MacKenna expired a few minutes ago. That's why we were trying to get hold of Mrs. MacKenna. She had hoped to be by her husband's side. She's a devoted wife. And he was so self-destructive. But she knew he was dying—she's prepared for it."

"Voice mail answered on the fourth ring," the nurse said. "Should I leave a message?"

He shook his head and reached for the phone. "Get me an outside line. I've got to call this in."

Chapter Forty

Vanessa was about to become a terrified woman, running for her life.

She needed to look the part. She ran halfway down the hill, turned toward the driveway, closed her eyes, then threw herself on her left knee and struck the cement. The skin split just as she'd hoped, and the cut began to bleed. Stumbling to her feet, she kicked one shoe off and deliberately fell into the shrubbery. She instinctively protected her face with her arms, but when she looked, there were cuts and scratches everywhere. She rolled over and made sure there were twigs and a blade of grass or two in her hair and dirt on her face. Her knee was throbbing—a small price to pay for the millions she would inherit. She checked her watch again just to see how much time she still had.

She hadn't thought to rip her clothes, but when she staggered to her feet, she heard her skirt tear. Nice touch, she thought, tearing it just a bit more.

It was almost time to make the call. She'd already moved Ewan's car to the end of the drive at the bottom of the hill, and she'd parked her car behind his. It had to be out of harms way when the house blew, and she'd be able to tell the police that Ewan blocked the drive and she couldn't get any closer. There was so much detail to the planning. Nothing could be overlooked.

It was ironic that she really did fall down when she was just a few feet away from her car door. She even bumped her forehead on the fender.

She got the door open and slid into the driver's seat. Her gaze locked on her watch as the seconds ticked by. Less than three minutes remained. Perfect timing. She glanced up at the old Victorian brick mansion at the top of the hill and laughed to herself. To think that she'd ever want such a monstrosity was ludicrous. The old man hadn't done anything in thirty years to update or maintain it. It was just a huge, ugly monument to his mean and selfish life.

She knew she was supposed to wait until after the explosion to make the call, but she thought it would be more convincing if she were on the line pleading for help when the house exploded.

Two minutes to go. Now, she thought. She pushed 9-1-1.

An operator answered on the first ring.

"What is your emergency?"

"Please, please help me," she cried out. "He's

got a bomb, and he's going to kill her. I got out, but she's still inside the house with him, and I can't . . . oh, please . . ."

"What is your address?" the calm operator asked.

"Four-seventeen Barkley Road. Please hurry," she screamed.

"We have two cars in your area, ma'am. They're on their way. Just stay on the line with me until they get there. What is your name?"

Vanessa was sobbing and panting for breath and hoped she sounded hysterical. "Vanessa MacKenna. They've got to get here now. Don't you understand? He's going to kill her."

"Who, ma'am? Who are you talking about?"

"Kate MacKenna. My brother-in-law Ewan has her."

Less than a minute to go.

The operator continued to ask questions.

"Where are you now, ma'am? Are you away from the house?"

"Yes. He looked the other way, and I ran. I'm at the gate at the end of the driveway—by my car. Oh, I hear sirens. They're coming."

"Just stay with me until they get to you, okay?"

"Yes, I will. Oh, please, they have to stop him." She took the phone from her ear and turned it toward the house.

Five . . . four . . . three . . . two . . . one.

Time ran out . . . and nothing happened.

Chapter Forty-one

Dylan's heart dropped to the pit of his stomach. How could he have let this happen? Kate . . . oh, God, Kate . . . .

No sooner had he absorbed the news that she had disappeared than he heard a car screech to a stop in front of the building. Agent Kline had told him he would meet him at Smith and Wesson, but he didn't get out of his car. He pounded on the horn.

The security guard who had left his post leaped out of the way in the nick of time, or Dylan would have plowed over him as he bolted out the door. His brain was on automatic now.

Kline had the window down and was shouting, "Get in! Let's go, let's go." He leaned across the seat and pushed the passenger door open.

Dylan jumped inside. He was pulling the door closed when Kline hit the gas pedal. The car rocketed forward.

"Kate's gone," Dylan roared.

"I know," Kline answered. "I heard it from dispatch. I know where she is," Kline said, hoping to God he was right. "A call was patched through from Savannah PD. Vanessa left the hospital, said it was an emergency. She was meeting Ewan at Compton's house. She's been staying there, and I'm guessing Kate's with her. Process of elimination," he rushed on.

He ran a red light, turned left, and shot down the street.

"Vanessa told people where she was going? It could be a setup," Kline said.

"Yeah, that's what I'm thinking," Dylan said, trying to make sense of it all.

They both knew Kate could already be dead, but neither voiced the fear.

"Kate **has** to be there with Vanessa," Dylan said. "And if she isn't, I don't know where they could have taken her. I never should have left her. I should have stayed."

"We're close," Kline said. "And every available unit is on the way. We'll get to her in time." He took another corner on two wheels, straightened, and, tires squealing, sped on.

Dylan pulled his gun out of the holster, popped the magazine out, checked it, and then snapped it back in with the heel of his hand. "If anyone hurts Kate, I'll kill them. And it's not going to be quick or clean."

Dylan's tirade made Kline nervous. "Try to remember I'm a federal agent, okay? Don't tell me you're going to kill someone. That's called premeditated murder. You're a detective. You know that."

Dylan shoved the gun back in the holster. "Can't you drive faster?"

The radio in the police car Kline had commandeered crackled to life as dispatch relayed the 911 call from Vanessa.

Dylan heard the word "bomb." It felt like a crushing blow hit him in the gut.

The dispatcher was routing police cars, ambulances, and fire trucks to the neighborhood. Kline got on the radio and gave the operator his approximate ETA.

They turned onto a four-lane, heavily congested street flying past other vehicles. Most drivers pulled over when they heard the siren, but there were a few who either hadn't heard the noise or had heard it and didn't care. Kline swung the car in and out with the efficiency of a NASCAR driver.

Dylan still thought he could do better, go faster.

"Vanessa's saying Ewan's got a bomb, right?" Kline asked.

"It's not Ewan," Dylan shouted.

"I know, I know," Kline said. "You convinced me, but what I'm trying to say is that I don't think it's been detonated yet. If it's anything like the other two bombs, we'd have heard about it by now."

"Yeah, that's right." Dylan actually felt a kernel of hope. "I never told her . . ."

"Told her what?"

He didn't answer. "You're slowing down."

"The hell I am. We're closing in. Bomb squad should be right behind us. Damn, another bomb. Third time's the charm? We've got to get this prick."

Kline spotted an ambulance in his rearview mirror weaving in and out of traffic. "One more turn up ahead and straight about a mile," he said. "In this ritzy neighborhood, the estates are spread out—that's good because I hate to think—" He stopped, but not in time.

Dylan finished the thought. "If the houses are crammed together and a bomb goes off, the number of casualties escalates. You think I don't know the problems?" he snapped.

Kline shouted back. "I don't want **you** to become my problem, got that? You're involved with Kate, aren't you? I can hear it in your voice and see it in your face. Emotional involvement makes you a risk. You've got to keep it together, or you'll be no help at all."

Kline didn't slow down enough when he turned the corner, nearly putting the car into a spin. Quickly compensating, he regained control.

"When this is over, Kline, you need to take driver's ed. You drive like an old lady."

"I'm going sixty down a residential street."

Ahead there was a four-way stop. Two police cars raced toward the intersection from opposite directions. Kline fishtailed around the stop signs, narrowly missing both cars.

Cars rushed at the MacKenna mansion from every direction. Two police cars blocked the street, and the uniforms were cordoning off the area. One signaled Kline to stop, but he ignored the directive, driving over the curb toward the iron gates. Through the trees, Dylan glimpsed the house. An ambulance was parked next to another car which obstructed his view of the people clustered together.

Kline had a better vantage point. "Hallinger's here. That's his car, isn't it?"

"I don't see Kate. Do you see Kate?" Dylan asked, reaching for the door handle.

"Hold on! Let me get inside the gate. Keep looking," Kline urged. "Ah, there's Vanessa. Over on the right. You let me handle her, you hear me?"

"I don't see Kate. I don't see her."

"Bomb squad's here. They're getting ready now. Dylan, what the hell are you—"

Kline slammed on the brakes, but Dylan was already out of the car and running flat out toward the gates. Cursing, Kline put the car in park, jumped out, and chased him.

"Dylan, hold on, hold on," Kline shouted.

Dylan wasn't listening. He was frantically seaching for Kate while Kline was frantically trying to get to him before he did anything crazy.

Dylan veered around the bomb squad van. Two policemen stood with Vanessa, who was sobbing and pointing to the house. One of them spotted Dylan coming toward them and ran to intercept him.

"Have you seen Kate MacKenna?" Dylan demanded.

"We just got here, and were the first on the scene. An ambulance followed us in, and a Detective Nate Hallinger pulled in behind us."

Kline caught up, panting for breath.

The policeman continued, "Vanessa Mac-Kenna told us there are people inside. Detective Hallinger just took off, the crazy idiot. He's going to try to get them out before the bomb goes off. I couldn't stop him."

Dylan was already gone. He crossed the drive, vaulting over the hood of a car that was in his way, and sprinted up the hill.

Kate was still inside . . . if the bomb exploded . . . something must have gone wrong because the house was still standing. Maybe Vanessa hadn't timed it right . . . maybe she called it in too soon. What the hell was the plan? His thoughts raced. There had to be a backup plan.

He'd just reached the mansion's entryway when he heard a gunshot.

He pulled his gun, flipped off the safety, and stealthily moved inside the house. There was no one in sight.

Nate stood at the library door at the back of the house. He had jammed the lock in his hurry to get inside and had been forced to shoot it and kick the door to get in. He took the entire room in at once. Ewan was on the floor, face up, eyes closed. Nate searched for Kate, but couldn't find her. He saw the basket of flowers on the desk and rocked back on his heels, knowing that it could go off any second. He opened his mouth to call for Kate, but only a strangled sound escaped. He felt the barrel of a gun against the back of his head.

"Drop the gun or you're dead."

Dylan stood behind him.

Nate flinched. "What are you doing? Are you crazy? Get your gun away from me! I'm trying to get Kate and Ewan out before—"

"Drop the gun, you son of a bitch."

"What the hell's wrong with you?" Nate roared.

"Where's Kate?"

"I don't know. I'm trying to save her," he said.

"Don't you mean 'kill her'? Were you going to use Ewan's gun or your own? Nice and tidy, right? Make it look like Ewan shot her. Then you're the hero if you take him down."

"That's nuts. Why would I—"

Dylan cut him off. "You made a big mistake. You knew about the money, and you hadn't even talked to the attorney yet." Dylan pushed the barrel harder against Nate's skull and shouted, "Where is she?"

"I'm telling you, you've got this all—"

"I'm here." The library door behind them edged forward, and Kate stepped around it, a pair of scissors raised in her right hand. She lowered her arm and in a stunned voice, she said, "I thought Vanessa was coming back, I—"

Nate's gun had been pointed at Ewan, but he inched the barrel up toward the basket on the desk. "I'm not going down for this, Dylan. I pull this trigger, and we all die. Hand over your gun and nobody gets hurt. Kate's gonna be my insurance. She'll walk out with me, and everyone stays alive. I've got nothing to lose. Now hurry up and decide. This bomb could go at any second."

Dylan didn't lower his gun. "Kate, get out of here. Run."

"But Dylan—"

"Go! Now!"

Kate didn't budge. "Dylan—"

The door in the front of the house burst open. Nate's head turned for a split second. Like lightning, Dylan's free hand chopped Nate's arm and sent his gun flying. In one motion, Dylan kicked his feet out and threw him to the floor, holding him with his foot, his gun still pointed at Nate's head.

The bomb squad rushed toward the library in their full protective gear, and Dylan shouted to them as he pulled Nate to his knees. "Get Kate out first. And take Ewan. Hurry!"

Kate was finally able to speak. As the team stepped toward her, she put her hand up. "It's not necessary, I—"

Dylan had Nate on his feet now and gave him a shove toward the door.

"Now, Kate!" Dylan ordered.

"You don't understand—" Kate went to the desk and put the scissors down, then she opened her other hand. A blue wire just a few inches long lay in her palm. "The bomb isn't going to explode."

"But how do you know . . . ?" Dylan began.

She gave a relieved smile and said. "You'll never guess who called me."

Chapter Forty-two

Leaning against the side of a squad car, too weary to move, Kate quietly watched all the commotion.

Dylan was talking to a lieutenant with Savannah PD, but he kept glancing over at her—probably making sure she didn't disappear again.

The paramedics carried Ewan out of the house on a stretcher. He was still unconscious, but she heard one of the policemen say that Ewan was expected to recover. Whenever he did open his eyes, he'd find himself handcuffed to a hospital bed. There were several charges pending against him. Supplying his brother with a stolen gun that had been used in a crime was going to top the list of offenses.

By now, reporters and cameramen from all the television stations that had been monitoring the 911 calls had arrived, but they were being kept outside the gates.

Most of the cameramen focused on the house, expectantly waiting for the suspect to step outside, but Vanessa was getting some attention, too. She was hysterical, and this time it wasn't an act.

"You're making a terrible mistake," she sobbed. "I'm a **victim** here! I was trying to save lives when I called nine-one-one. I haven't done anything wrong. I'm a victim!" she screamed.

She had just been handcuffed by an agent who was telling her she had the right to remain silent. When he was finished reading her her rights, he asked her if she understood. She pulled herself together long enough to say yes, she understood, but then she started screaming again. Her shrieks were grating and terribly annoying.

"Really, lady, you have the right to remain silent. I strongly urge you to exercise that right."

A detective who had loaned Kate his cell phone came back to retrieve it. Handing it to him, she was thanking him when Dylan joined her.

"Did you get hold of Isabel?" he asked.

She smiled. "Yes, and she's just fine. I knew she would be, but I needed to hear her voice. I also called Kiera, and she's okay, too," she said. "When Nate came running into Smith and Wesson's conference room and told me Reece had taken Isabel and that she'd been hurt, I panicked. I didn't think twice about following him out the back door. The only thing I remember is getting in his car . . . and then I woke up on the library floor."

"It's good to know they're okay, but what about you? Are you okay?" He put his arm around her and squeezed her.

"Yes," she assured him. She looked up at the house and asked, "Why are they taking so long to bring Nate out?"

"They're doing everything by the book," he said. "And it hasn't been long. You're just anxious to get out of here, aren't you?"

"Could we leave now?"

"No."

Two paramedics hurried across the driveway to Kate. Dylan saw them coming. "They're going to want to check you out," he said.

"I'm fine, really."

One of the paramedics, hearing her protest, said, "We should look you over, take your vitals and all." He flashed a penlight in her eyes. "Not dilated."

"Kate, go with them, make sure. I'll wait here," Dylan said.

Though Kate insisted none of this was necessary, she walked to the ambulance with them and let them take her blood pressure and pulse. She admitted to herself that she wasn't feeling all that great. She was sure that her nausea wasn't caused by the drug she'd been given. Finding out the truth about Nate Hallinger had made her sick. She didn't mention her queasy stomach to the paramedics.

Once she'd been declared no worse for the wear, a paramedic offered his hand and was assisting her out of the ambulance when he glanced up the hill and saw several men exit the house.

"Hey, they're bringing the suspect down the hill now. Uh-oh. It looks like the detective you were with is waiting for him, and look at his face." He turned to his partner. "We may not be done here, after all."

Dylan had turned away, and Kate couldn't see his face. She ran to him, praying Dylan wouldn't do anything crazy. No, of course he wouldn't. His hand wasn't on his gun. That was a good sign, wasn't it? And his arms were folded across his chest. His stance suggested he was relaxed.

That wasn't a good sign. She wished she could see Dylan's expression. She'd know then.

"Dylan," she called out.

"Stay back, Kate."

She reached him. He didn't look at her when he said, "I told you to stay back."

She put her hand on his arm. "Since when have I ever done anything you've told me to do?"

"Kate . . ." The warning was in his voice.

The ambulance was about ten feet behind her. Dylan grabbed her hand and practically dragged her there. "Get inside."

She stood her ground. "You aren't going to do anything stupid, are you?"

"No."

She wasn't sure she could believe him. "Don't even talk to him."

"He was going to kill you," he reminded her.

Agent Kline shouted something to Dylan.

"Stay here, Kate," Dylan said. "Please."

"All right," she relented.

He looked as if he didn't believe her. "I mean it."

Dylan turned and walked toward Nate, stopping when he was just a few feet away. Kline had a grip on Nate's arm as he led him down the hill. He'd taken great pleasure in putting the handcuffs on the detective. Police officers and detectives were moving in, forming a circle around them as they headed toward a squad car.

Nate glared at Dylan. "This is never going to stick. You've got nothing."

"We have enough," Kline said cheerfully.

"If you have anything, it's circumstantial."

Dylan's smile didn't quite reach his eyes. "You sure have had your troubles, haven't you? And I'll bet you thought it was all gonna be so easy. One bomb, and **boom**, problem solved. Kate's dead before she ever finds out about the will."

"No, you're wrong."

"How long were you with Savannah PD?" Kline asked Nate.

Dylan answered for him. "Long enough to meet Vanessa and start shacking up with her. It was common knowledge that she was sleeping

around. Come to find out—and I did find out—
you were the one."

"You hatched your plan and transferred to the
Charleston police force," Kline said. "You had to
distance yourself from Vanessa, and you also
wanted to find out everything you could about
Kate."

"I transferred because there was an opening,
and I wanted a change," Nate argued.

"What you wanted was eighty million dollars,
you prick," Dylan said. "Vanessa was behind the
camera filming the old man. Compton trusted
her, and he asked her to film his video. She must
have been real pissed off when Compton looked
into the camera and said he was giving it all to
Kate. He'd already changed the will so it wouldn't
do her any good to kill him after the fact."

"She told you all about it, didn't she?"
Kline said.

"You can't prove—" Nate objected.

"You're the one who checked her alibi the day
the video was made. You said it was airtight. Why
would I think you were lying?" Dylan said.

Nate didn't respond, but then, Dylan didn't expect him to. "Did you have the connections to get
to the Florist, or did you go to Jackman and offer
him a deal he couldn't refuse?"

"You can't prove a damn thing. This is all spec-
ulation."

"It got complicated, didn't it?" Kline said, ignoring his protests. "Kate wouldn't cooperate. Two explosions, and she's stayed alive. Her good luck, and your bad. Did you buy all three bombs at the same time, or did you have to keep going back for more?"

"You knew Kate would be at Carl's party," Dylan said. "You knew before it was in the paper. Carl was your source, even though he didn't know it. He likes to promote Kate's company, and he does a lot of charity events in Savannah. Compton mentioned Vanessa's good works had helped uphold the MacKenna name. Vanessa was smart enough not to meet Carl, but she was always there, listening, wasn't she? You knew way in advance and had time to plan it just right."

"You just happened to be in the area when the bomb went off," Kline added. "First on the scene and first to find Kate. Must have disappointed you to see she was still breathing."

"This is ridiculous," Nate shouted.

Once again Kline and Dylan ignored his outrage.

"Putting Reece Crowell's name on the paper in Roger's apartment was overkill, don't you think? Were you trying to confuse us, or was it supposed to be a little clue?" Dylan said.

"You kept having to change the plan, didn't you?" Dylan continued. "You killed Roger and planted the evidence to frame Ewan. This last bomb was meant to kill Kate and Ewan, of course, but the sucker didn't go off. So you had to get in there and take care of it yourself."

"Ewan's gun and his cell phone were in your pocket," Kline said.

"I can explain that," Nate said.

"Can you explain telling Kate that Reece had her sister?"

"I thought he did . . . Ewan called me . . ."

Kline looked at Dylan. "Whew. He's dancing so fast, I can hardly see his feet. Can you?"

"You're a greedy son of a bitch, Nate," Dylan said. "But you made a big mistake. Remember what you said to me? 'I heard she turned it down.' Got me thinking. How could you have known that? Vanessa left before Kate changed her mind and accepted the inheritance. You heard it from Vanessa."

"Anderson told me."

"Yeah, that's what I assumed for a while anyway. Turns out Anderson has a great memory. He hadn't even talked to you yet. You see, Nate, my watch keeps real good time, and I know it wasn't more than ten minutes after we left the office that I talked to you. Anderson remembers your call, all right, but he swears it took at least fifteen minutes to wrap up his business with the police when they came to confiscate Roger's gun, and then he was summoned back to his office to accept your call. You know what? Anderson has the phone logs to prove it."

"Nice guesswork, Dylan, but none of it will hold up."

"I think it will," Dylan said. "Vanessa will give you up." He nodded in her direction. "Look at her. She's watching you, and if looks could kill . . . Well, let's just say she doesn't look like she's your biggest fan right now. When she realizes what she's facing, she'll deal."

Talk about timing.

As Vanessa was being forced into the backseat of a police car, she erupted, "I didn't do anything! It was all his idea. I'm innocent!"

Everyone heard her.

Dylan's smile was genuine now. "There you go."

Chapter Forty-three

KATE SAT IN THE CAPTAIN'S OFFICE. KLINE WAS on one side of her, Dylan was on the other, and she was being questioned by everyone but the mayor.

How had she known which wire to cut? He'd told her. **Who?** The Florist. **How had she known a bullet to the basket wouldn't force the explosion?** Simple. She'd dismantled it. She'd cut the blue wire, then carefully removed the bottom panel and placed it in the drawer of the desk. **Why had she done that?** He had said it needed to be taken out. She didn't know why.

They wanted her to remember every word The Florist had said to her. First one law officer and then another asked her to start from the beginning. She repeated the phone conversation at least five times, but she still never lost her patience.

Dylan was amazed by how calm she was. She seemed to be taking it all in stride.

Had she tried to get out of the library? Of

course she had, but she couldn't get the door unlocked. She'd tried kicking it in, but the wood was
solid and wouldn't give. She thought about going
out the window and getting away before the
bomb detonated, but she knew she would be unable to lift Ewan up and over the windowsill. He
weighed at least one hundred and eighty pounds.
She couldn't have carried him to safety, and trying
to drag him would have been impossible.

Time was critical. Kate felt she had no choice.
She had to take the basket apart.

They all knew she'd had a choice. She could
have run, saved herself, and the fact that she
didn't consider leaving Ewan behind spoke vol-
umes about her character.

Dylan was with her the entire time, trying to
keep the questions to a minimum. Once he felt
the police and the FBI had all the information
they would need, he called an end to the interrogation and got her out of there.

Kate was grateful for the rescue. Her day thus
far had been horrendous . . . and it wasn't over yet.

At exactly seven o'clock, Kate and Dylan
walked into the law offices of Smith and Wesson.
For the next two hours, Kate politely listened to
Compton's smug and condescending advisors and
accountants give their reports. Dylan sat next to
her with his arms folded, remaining silent while
taking it all in.

The attitude of the men, dressed in their dark

suits, white shirts, and conservative ties, was puzzling. They behaved as though the money belonged to them collectively, and they were simply humoring Kate by telling her what they had done in the past and what they would be doing—with her inheritance—in the future. There were forms they wanted her to sign, giving them permission to continue their financial guardianship, but all of them assured her she would receive annual reports that would keep her apprised.

After they had finished boasting, they witnessed as she signed the papers Anderson had prepared, formally accepting the inheritance. Once the transaction was complete, the attorney announced that there were no more stipulations, and all of Compton's wishes had been fulfilled.

The men began to gather their things in preparation to leave, but Kate motioned for them to stay seated as she rose to address them. First, she graciously thanked them for their work and their dedication, and then she told them that their services were no longer needed.

Nearly every chin in the room dropped.

Anderson maintained his composure, although he looked like he wanted to cheer.

One of the advisors jumped to his feet. "What will you do with all that money?"

Another stood and protested, "Compton doesn't want you to squander his life's accumulation, and I'm—rather, we—are concerned with your lack of experience in the financial arena—won't you be doing exactly that? Squandering it?"

Anderson put his hand up when the advisors all began to talk at once. "What Miss MacKenna chooses to do with her inheritance is no longer your concern. You may send your final bills to this office, and I will review them."

In desperation, one of the men turned to Dylan. "Surely you know what a mistake this is. Talk to her," he demanded.

His arms still crossed, Dylan leaned back in his chair and, with an amused smile, he simply shrugged.

The angry man's face turned the color of the red stripes on his tie. "But does she have any idea what she will do with—?"

"Yes," Kate interrupted. "I do know." She gathered up the papers spread out on the table as she explained. "I'm giving it away."

"All of it?" he asked incredulously.

"But . . . but . . ." another man sputtered.

"Who are you giving it to?" a third man asked. He looked positively ill.

"I have several ideas," she answered. "And I will discuss them with my sisters before a final decision is made, but I'm leaning toward a research facility. My mother died of a terrible disease," she said. "I'm also considering a new cancer wing for the hospital in Silver Springs. However," she added, "I do know this. Whatever the money is used for will have my mother's name on it. Leah MacKenna."

They looked horrified.

"Compton will roll over in his grave," sniffed the man with the red-striped tie. "He didn't even consider her a part of his family."

Kate headed for the door, but she turned at the last comment. She thought for a second before answering. "Thank you. What a lovely thing to say."

Chapter Forty-four

HOME NEVER LOOKED SO GOOD TO KATE. THE house was old and run-down, desperately in need of a new coat of paint and new shutters, but she still thought it was beautiful.

By one o'clock in the morning she was pulling back the sheets and slipping into her bed next to Dylan. He was already sound asleep. She'd taken a long, soothing shower. Exhausted now, she was certain she'd be out the second her head hit the pillow.

She had to tug her pillow out from under him first. She'd just gotten comfortable when the trembling started. Within seconds she was violently shaking. She couldn't figure out what was wrong. The bed shuddered. If it had been on rollers, they would have been scooting all over the bedroom.

He came awake with a start. Lifting up, he squinted at her and dragged her toward him.

Kate curled up against him, her head tucked under his chin. His body was warm and comforting.

"Sorry I woke you," she said. "I can't stop shaking. I'm not cold."

He rubbed her back. "The day is finally catching up with you," he said. "You've been operating on adrenaline and fear."

A minute passed, and then she whispered, "Are you ever afraid?"

"Yes, I am." Dylan thought about Kate inside the house with a bomb and a cold-blooded killer. He'd been damned scared then.

"Dylan?"

"Yes, Pickle."

She heard him yawn. "I was thinking . . ."

"That can't be good."

"I trusted him." Her voice quivered. "I had to trust him. I had to believe what he told me . . ."

He tried to ease her mind. "Why wouldn't you trust Nate? The son of a bitch was a cop. You should have been able to trust him."

"No, not Nate," she said. "The Florist. I had to trust him."

Dylan propped himself up on one elbow and leaned over her, waiting for her to continue.

"I followed the instructions of a man who admitted to me that he likes to blow things up . . . oh, dear heaven . . ."

She put her hand over her eyes. The enormity

of what she had been through was finally sinking in.

"You didn't have a choice. Isn't that what you told me? You had to trust him."

She wasn't quite ready to be reasonable. "Yes, I remember telling everyone I didn't have a choice. You know what I didn't tell them about The Florist?"

He pulled her hand away from her face. "What's that?"

"I felt a little sorry for him," she said. "Am I crazy?"

He kissed her forehead. "Yeah, maybe a little."

She thought about the basket of flowers and how terrified she'd been when she'd cut the blue wire. That thought jumped to another, and she suddenly was furious with Dylan.

He was trying to kiss her. She pushed him away. "You ran into that house knowing there was a bomb that could explode any second. You could have been killed! Why did you do such a stupid thing?"

"You were inside. That's why."

Her eyes welled up. "The bomb squad was there. You should have—"

"You were inside," he repeated firmly.

She shook her head. "You take stupid chances."

"I've heard that criticism before—from you, as a matter of fact."

He tried once again to capture her mouth with

his own, but she evaded him. "When did I ever . . ."

He sighed. "In the hospital in Boston after my surgery . . . maybe the day after. I woke up and saw you. It felt good, knowing you were there, but I couldn't figure out why. You were always such a pain in the—"

"I was not."

"Every time you came to Nathan's Bay, you did something to annoy me."

She could hear the smile in his voice. "Give me an example."

"If you got to the phone, and it was for me, you came up with the most outrageous stories."

"No, I didn't," she said defensively.

"You told Janey Callahan I'd enlisted in the French Foreign Legion."

"Well, maybe one time, but if she was stupid enough to believe that, then you shouldn't have been dating her in the first place."

"I lost a lot of girlfriends because of you." He kissed her earlobe. "But the worst thing you did . . ."

"Yes?"

"You ignored me. Drove me crazy." He let out an exaggerated yawn. "Think you'll be able to sleep after?"

"After what?"

He didn't need to explain. His body was already covering hers.

• • •

Dylan walked into Chief Drummond's office at ten o'clock the following morning. The chief was eager to talk to him.

"Shut the door and take a seat," Drummond said. "I want to hear all about it. Did Hallinger have any inkling you knew?"

Dylan placed the gun and badge on the desk. "No, he didn't," he said. Then he sat down and told him how it had all gone down. When he was finished, he said, "I never would have figured it out in time if you hadn't helped. I didn't want to go to Savannah PD on little more than a gut feeling, especially since he'd worked for them."

Drummond nodded. "When you asked me if you could run something by me, and you told me about that peculiar remark Hallinger made . . ."

"That he heard Kate turned the money down," Dylan finished.

"That's right. You were already suspicious. You just resisted the notion. All I did was help out a little. After forty years in law enforcement, I've learned a thing or two, and one of those things is how to get information fast. It didn't take too many calls for me to get a buddy to check phone records and credit card receipts that put Nate Hallinger and Vanessa MacKenna in the same place at the same time. Looks like they had a nice little rendezvous in Cancún about six months ago."

Dylan continued. "Finding out Vanessa was sleeping with Nate. That pretty much put the nail in the coffin."

"What about Jackman?" Drummond asked.

"They had to let him go."

"Lack of evidence, huh?"

Dylan nodded.

"Crying shame," Drummond said.

They talked about the case a few more minutes, and then Drummond changed the subject.

"I'm going to be retiring soon," he said as he stretched his arms up and clasped his hands behind his head.

"Yes, I heard."

"I'll stay in the area, of course. It's too pretty here to leave."

Dylan agreed. "You don't have to worry about traffic," he said. "That's something I appreciate. Boston's another story."

"You like to fish?"

"Yes," he said.

"Great fishing around here. Do you ever think about leaving law enforcement?"

"No."

"Good. We need men like you. What about a change of pace? We don't have many homicides or bombs going off here. Kate's going to be the talk of the town for years to come. She's quite a pistol, isn't she?"

"Yes, she is."

"Like I was saying, I'm going to retire. I could probably hold on another six months. What do you think? Will that give you enough time?"

Dylan was gone.

Kate was just waking up when she heard the front door shut. She bolted upright in bed. She heard a car start and was instantly furious. How could he leave without so much as a "see you later"?

"Oh, I don't think so," she muttered.

She kicked off the sheet and jumped out of bed ready to run after him and give him a piece of her mind because he hadn't bothered to say good-bye. Fortunately, she came to her senses before she left the bedroom. Good Lord, she was stark naked. Wouldn't that be a memory to cherish? A crazed, shrieking, and naked ex-lover chasing him down the street.

He probably left her a note, she decided, but she wasn't in any hurry to read it. It would just break her heart. She took her time getting dressed and finally went downstairs. She walked past his garment bag, stopped, and turned back. Now she felt like an idiot. He hadn't left for Boston after all.

But he would leave today. He was all packed and ready to go, wasn't he? A note in the kitchen confirmed it. He'd written the flight number and time on a piece of paper. The airline's phone number was written above it.

"You knew this was coming," she told herself.

She sighed. Yes, she'd known, but that didn't make it any easier. How was she going to say good-bye to him? She was a wreck just thinking about it. It would be mortifying if she cried. **Don't let me cry**, she prayed. **Plenty of time for that after he's gone.**

It was ridiculous to worry about this a moment longer. He was leaving, and that was that. Breakfast. Yes, she'd fix breakfast because that was what a normal, rational person would do. And when she was finished, she would start her day, and the rest of her life . . . her lonely, pathetic, stupid, I-don't-need-anyone life.

She grabbed a box of Cheerios out of the pantry and opened it. She didn't bother pouring some into a bowl. She stood at the sink looking out at the overgrown garden while she ate dry cereal.

How would Dylan handle their good bye? With style, she supposed. Yes, style. He was a pro, after all. With all of his experience, he had to have the routine down pat. There had been so many women over the years he'd kissed good-bye.

And now Kate was one of them.

How could she have been so stupid? This broken heart was her own fault. Dylan hadn't tricked her into falling in love with him. She knew what he was.

She'd spent all those weekends on Nathan's Bay with Jordan and the Buchanans, and every weekend that Dylan and his brothers joined them, the phone never stopped ringing. The callers were invariably female, and they were always looking for Dylan.

It drove her nuts. And he was still driving her nuts.

Kate would concentrate on keeping her emotions under control until he left. Surely she could come up with something clever to say . . . and she hoped to be inspired any minute now. She heard the front door open.

"Kate?" he called.

And there he was, standing in the doorway, looking almost too good to be out in public. No wonder women flocked to him. He was irresistible.

"You're leaving," she blurted. Oh, boy, that was inspired.

"In a little while, but—"

She interrupted. "Please, no explanations are needed. I appreciate your help with . . . you know, the craziness, but now it's time for you to go home. Your life is in Boston."

His eyes sparkled. What was he thinking? And why was he so obviously amused? Good-byes weren't funny.

"And my life is here," she continued. "I'm not

going to move my company to Boston. This is where I belong. I watched that video, and I know I'm nothing like Compton, but listening to him made me realize I don't want to be on the fast track, and I don't want to become obsessed with building my company. I'll expand, but at my own pace. However," she added, "there will be times when I'm in Boston visiting Jordan, and we're bound to run into each other. It's inevitable. I don't want what happened between us . . . why are you smiling?"

"You're not going to give me the 'that was then, this is now' speech again, are you?"

Well, she wouldn't now. "Good-bye," she blurted out. "That's all I wanted to say."

She considered kissing him on the cheek and telling him she'd miss him, but she decided not to. If she got too close, she'd probably throw herself into his arms and start crying.

"Is it my turn yet?" he asked.

Here it comes, she thought. **The smooth good-bye.**

"Of course," she said, bracing herself.

He was casually leaning against the door, acting as though he had all the time in the world to dump her. "I used to hate pickles when I was a kid. It's an acquired taste," he explained. "I love them now."

Now that, she had to admit, was a unique beginning.

"And I call you pickle."

She gave him a quizzical frown.

He pulled away from the door. "Jeez, Kate, put it together."

"I get it," she said. "But you love lots of foods. You love black olives and pretzels and sweet corn and pizza and hot peppers and—"

"No, I don't. Those are all really swell foods. But . . . I only love pickles."

"This is the strangest good-bye . . ."

"I'm not saying good-bye. I'm saying I love you."

"You love . . . you what? No, you don't." She waved the cereal box around as she reacted. "Don't say . . . you can't . . ." Cheerios were flying everywhere.

"Every time I ran into you on Nathan's Bay, you interfered with my love life. You were such a pain. When you weren't screwing things up, you were acting like I wasn't there. I was so damned mad at you all the time, but I kept coming back for more. Then it occurred to me that I always made it a point to find out when you were going to be there for the weekend, and I'd show up, too. Yes, I love you. It just took me awhile to figure it out. And when I did, I started calling you "pickle" just to make you crazy."

"You knew I didn't like it."

"So? I didn't much like being in love with you. For a long time there I thought you were ignoring me and it . . . unnerved me."

She pointed the box at him. "What do you mean, you thought I was ignoring you?"

"You love me, Kate. It took me awhile to figure that out, too. I think you've loved me a long time. You just hadn't realized it yet."

She shook her head. "No."

"Yes." He stepped toward her. "I love you."

She was afraid to believe it. "Do you tell all of your girlfriends you love them before you leave them? Now that's just mean."

"Jill Murdock."

She backed into the dining room. "Who?"

"Jill Murdock," he repeated, coming toward her. "When she called the house, you told her I hadn't made bail yet."

"I don't recall—"

"Heather Conroy." He kept coming; she kept backing away. "You told her you were my wife, but you and I were keeping it quiet because we were first cousins."

Kate smiled. She'd forgotten that one. "Actually, Jordan came up with that."

"Stephanie Davis."

She bit her lower lip. "I don't remember her."

"I couldn't take her out because I had bubonic plague and was quarantined," he reminded.

"Those constant phone calls were irritating people."

"Like who?"

"They irritated your mother."

He looked absolutely incredulous for a couple of seconds and then burst out laughing. "My mother?"

She shrugged. "I suppose they may have irritated me, too," she admitted.

He was looking a little too arrogantly pleased. She wagged the cereal box at him. Cheerios exploded everywhere. A few landed in the chandelier above the dining room table. Two more landed in her hair. She had never behaved like this before, but then she'd never felt like this before. Dylan trapped her in the corner. The only way out was through him. "And why were you so irritated, Kate?" Dylan asked.

She was afraid to believe him. He couldn't love her . . . could he? There was only one way to find out: commitment. If there was anything that would make him disappear, it was the truth.

"Because I love you," she said.

But he didn't vanish. He just smiled. Shaking her head and frowning, she repeated. "I love you. The door's behind you."

He planted his hands on either side of her and leaned down. His mouth was just an inch from hers when he whispered, "Marry me."

Epilogue

On a glorious friday afternoon, kate—with her sisters, Isabel and Kiera—walked into the First National Bank of Silver Springs and happily ruined three lives.

It was a fine day indeed.

Following her instructions, Anderson had had a long chat with the new bank president, Andy Radcliffe, and had set up the meeting. There was quite a group assembled in Radcliffe's office. Leah MacKenna's former accountant, the weasel, Tucker Simmons, and his insipid wife, Randy, were waiting for what they believed was the transfer of Kate's company to them. Edward Wallace was also there. He was the loan officer who had added a few extras to the loan papers after Leah had signed them.

Chief Drummond was waiting for the sisters in the lobby and followed them into the office. Isabel and Kiera refused to sit. They stood with the chief by the door.

Kate didn't bother to introduce herself or say hello. She simply handed the president a file. "Inside you'll find loan papers my mother, Leah MacKenna, signed. You'll note she listed all of her assets. Now please read the copy of the original that's filed here at the bank."

"You broke into bank files," Wallace protested. "That's illegal."

"Illegal? Did you hear that, Chief Drummond?" Kate asked.

Radcliffe stopped Wallace from saying anything further. "I pulled the files for Miss MacKenna." He turned back to Kate. "Now, what can I do for you?"

"Do you see what was added?" she asked. "Whoever changed the document didn't even bother to imitate my mother's handwriting."

" 'And all other assets including the Kate MacKenna Company,' " Radcliffe read. "Yes, there's no question this was added."

Everyone looked at Wallace. He jumped to his feet. "I remember now. I had forgotten to add that little extra. I had done a search . . . yes, a search, and I found that Leah MacKenna was a partner in the Kate MacKenna Company."

"Excuse me for interrupting, but who are you?" Randy Simmons asked Kate.

Kate refused to look at the woman. Chief Drummond answered for her. "She's Kate MacKenna, that's who she is."

Randy grabbed her purse. "I think we should leave now, Tucker. There's no reason for us to stay."

"Sit right back down," Drummond commanded.

"May I have a look at those loan papers?" Tucker asked. He pulled his glasses out of his pocket and put them on. Leaning forward, he read the fine print and Wallace's notations.

He must have seen the incriminating proof because he suddenly stiffened. His head snapped back, and he discreetly but frantically signaled Wallace to stop talking. He was trying not to be obvious as he shook his head a bit, coughed to get his attention, and wide-eyed, shook his head again.

The not-too-subtle hint to keep quiet didn't register. Wallace plunged ahead, cocky now because he was certain no one could prove he'd done anything wrong.

"This is all just a big misunderstanding. I added the Kate MacKenna Company to the list of assets, and I advised Mrs. MacKenna of the addition."

"You notified my mother," Kate said.

Tucker coughed and shook his head again.

"I most certainly did," Wallace said. "I called her and advised her of the change over the phone, and she stopped by the bank to initial it." Turning to Radcliffe, he said, "I like to be thorough, and I try to do everything by the book. You'll see at the bottom of the page I wrote down the date and time I talked to Mrs. MacKenna."

"You spoke to my mother?" Kate asked.

Tucker was doing everything but the wave to get Wallace to stop.

"Yes, I most certainly did speak to her."

"That must have been tricky."

"No, not at all."

"According to the date you wrote, you spoke to my mother three weeks after she died." Kate lost her composure then. "My mother was dying, and you knew it. She came to you for a loan to help her pay her medical bills. You saw an opportunity, and you took it. You hooked her up with Tucker Simmons and his wife, and the three of you had it all worked out."

"Did you think Kate would just roll over and accept it?" Kiera asked.

"Or did you think that by the time she figured it out and realized what you had done, it would be too late?" Isabel added. "Shame on you," she railed. "Our mother would never have jeopardized Kate's company. Never."

"How many others have you fleeced?" Kate asked.

"Don't worry, Kate. I'll find out," Drummond said.

"If I lose my job because of these false accusations—" Wallace began.

Drummond interrupted him. "I doubt you'll be able to do your job from jail."

"Tucker, take me home. Now," Randy pleaded.

"Oh, I don't think you'll be going home just yet," Drummond told her. "The prosecuting attorney has been busy all morning reading the evidence. I think he's going to have a few things to say about conspiracy charges first. Why don't you all come down to the station with me?"

Drummond herded the unhappy suspects out of the bank.

Once the office was quiet, Mr. Radcliffe turned to Kate. "I assure you the bank will give Chief Drummond its full cooperation in the investigation. We are also prepared to accept payment of your mother's loan with another loan—an unsecured loan. If you'll drop by the bank tomorrow, I'll have the papers drawn up."

"Thank you," Kate said.

"No, it is I who should thank you," he answered. "First National Bank is honored that you've chosen us—under Anderson Smith's supervision, of course—to hold the funds for the charitable trust."

Kate and her sisters were smiling when they left the bank. The second they stepped outside, Isabel started laughing. "You just took out a loan and gave away millions of dollars. You wouldn't use any of your inheritance to pay Mom's loan."

"She wouldn't have wanted me to," Kate explained.

"What am I going to do with land in Scotland?" Isabel asked.

"After you graduate, go see it, and then decide."

"What about you, Kiera? What will you do with the bonds you received?"

Kiera shrugged. "I'm not sure yet, but whatever I decide, it will have Mom's name on it."

They stood outside Kiera's car and waited while she dug through her purse for her keys.

"Hey, guess what?" Isabel said. "I heard the funniest news. Reece Crowell is engaged. Some European girl, I think."

"Poor girl," Kiera said.

"Hurry up and find the key," Kate urged. "Dylan is coming this afternoon."

"Have you set the wedding date, and am I in the wedding?" Isabel asked.

"No, we haven't set the date, and yes, you're in the wedding."

"I knew you were destined to marry Dylan."

"Because you're so smart about men," Kiera said. She found the keys, and they were soon on their way home.

"I am smart about men," Isabel insisted.

"You wanted me to go out with Nate Hallinger," Kate reminded. "How smart was that?"

"I offered that man a beverage." Isabel was outraged.

Kate stopped paying attention to her sisters' conversation when they pulled into their driveway. She saw Dylan standing on the porch waiting for her. His flight must have been early. Excitement surged through her.

Giving away millions of dollars and taking out a huge loan seemed inconsequential now.

Dylan waved to her and smiled.

She had it all.

ABOUT THE AUTHOR

JULIE GARWOOD is the author of many **New York Times** bestsellers, including **Killjoy, Mercy, Heartbreaker, Ransom,** and **Come the Spring.** There are more than thirty-two million copies of her books in print.